T0050090

THE PLAYBOY'S *Princess*

JOY FULCHER

OMNIFIC PUBLISHING
LOS ANGELES

The Playboy's Princess, Copyright © Joy Fulcher, 2014
All Rights Reserved. Except as permitted under the U.S. Copyright Act of 1976,
no part of this publication may be reproduced, distributed, or transmitted
in any form or by any means, or stored in a database or retrieval system,
without prior written permission of the publisher.

Omnific Publishing
1901 Avenue of the Stars, 2nd floor
Los Angeles, CA 90067
www.omnificpublishing.com

First Omnific eBook edition, October 2014
First Omnific trade paperback edition, October 2014

The characters and events in this book are fictitious.
Any similarity to real persons, living or dead,
is coincidental and not intended by the author.

Library of Congress Cataloguing-in-Publication Data

Fulcher, Joy.
  The Playboy's Princess / Joy Fulcher – 1st ed.
  ISBN: 978-1-623421-41-0
  1. Contemporary Romance — Fiction. 2. Money — Fiction.
  3. Marriage — Fiction. 4. Disney — Fiction. I. Title

10 9 8 7 6 5 4 3 2 1

Cover Design by Micha Stone and Amy Brokaw
Interior Book Design by Coreen Montagna

Printed in the United States of America

*This book is dedicated to my great-grandparents, Arthur and Lily.
I never met you, but the story of your love
has inspired me from a very young age
to believe that true love really does exist,
and that sometimes, you find it
in the most unexpected places.*

Love is like a friendship caught on fire.
~Bruce Lee

CHAPTER ONE

Black and White

Black. Drew looked around and all he could see was black. Black clothes, black expressions, black moods. Gran would've hated that. Drew knew if there was any part of her still watching over them, she'd be deeply disappointed in her funeral.

"Margaret Finlay was a strong woman who overcame many challenges in her life and rose to become one of the most celebrated artists of her time…" the priest droned on.

Drew looked down at the program in his hands and at the photo of Gran. Her wrinkled, smiling face looked back at him, and he felt a tear prickle behind his eyes. He was going to miss that old bird; she was the only person in the family who understood him. She was the only one who let him be free, who let him be himself.

Drew's parents loved him; he knew they did. But he was a huge disappointment to them. He should have been successful like his father or motivated like his mother. He should have been married by now and have a junior Malik to carry on the family name.

He looked over at his mother and saw her crying quietly against his father's shoulder. She'd lost her mother, but in a way it felt like Drew had lost his too. His parents hadn't been the hands-on type, often leaving him with a nanny while they indulged in their life of parties and functions. So, Drew had often spent time with his Gran when he got lonely.

People started moving and standing up. Drew looked around, confused. He knew he should've been paying more attention to what was going on, but he just couldn't listen to people talk about his Gran when they hadn't really known her. They didn't know anything about her real life, only what they'd read in the papers. When his grandfather had died four years ago, it was Gran who had stood up to give his eulogy. It felt wrong that she didn't have someone to give hers. Drew's mother had said she wasn't strong enough, and they'd said it wasn't proper for Drew to do it. His reputation as a playboy wasn't the image they wanted portrayed to their friends or the media. As if it wasn't already all over the tabloids.

"Are you coming, Drew?"

"Where?" He looked up, staring at the cold eyes of his father.

"For God's sake, weren't you even listening? Don't you have any respect for anyone?" Sounding frustrated, his father repeated the words Drew had heard him say more times than he could count.

"Please calm down, Aaron." Drew's mother, Laura, put a hand on her husband's shoulder and whispered into his ear.

Aaron Malik sighed and gave his son an irritated look. "We're going to hear the reading of the will."

Of course. The will. It made sense that his father was more concerned about the financial aspect of his mother-in-law's passing than the emotional effects his wife and son were obviously feeling.

Drew walked slowly behind his parents as they made their way to one of the back rooms. It seemed morbid to read the will in the church, but Drew wasn't going to provoke his father further by questioning it.

They entered a small room and sat down on some uncomfortable, rigid wooden chairs with Mr. Goldsmith, the family's lawyer.

"I'm sorry for your loss, Laura."

She gave a weak smile and folded her hands tightly in her lap. He fumbled around in his suitcase and pulled out a thick stack of papers.

"I, Paul Goldsmith, in the presence of the deceased's family, am reading the official will and testament of Mrs. Margaret Rosemary Finlay." He cleared his throat. "The Hollywood Hills property and London property, as well as Mrs. Finlay's entire share portfolio and bank account contents, are left to her daughter, Laura Louise Malik."

Drew's mother and father both nodded. It was expected; his mother was an only child and would of course be the main beneficiary.

"Andrew Aaron Malik, grandson of the deceased, is to receive the property in Los Feliz," Paul read on.

Despite his low mood, Drew couldn't help but smile at the news. That house had been Gran's hideaway. His grandfather had bought it for her as a getaway/art studio ten years before, and she'd spent much of her time there. Drew had often visited, and it was a special place for him. He was glad Gran had known how much it meant to him. It also meant he could finally move out of his parents' house.

"Are you sure that is a good idea? Maybe we should wait until he's a bit older," Aaron asked.

"I'm twenty-six years old. Most people my age have long since moved out of home, Dad," Drew protested.

"Yes, but most twenty-six-year-olds have worked hard at college and made something of themselves. You, on the other hand, have done nothing in the past few years but drink and *hang out* with your friends." He said the words "hang out" with disgust, as if his son had committed some horrible crime.

"We can discuss Drew's living arrangements later," Laura scolded. "Let's just listen to the rest of the will."

Paul nodded and looked down at the papers again.

"Drew is also to receive full payment of his trust fund, in the amount of eighteen million dollars, on his thirtieth birthday, or the day of his marriage, whichever occurs first."

Drew stared blankly at Paul to see if he was joking. He wouldn't get his inheritance until he turned thirty or got married? Well, there went the idea of moving out of his parents' house. There was no way he could afford to live on his own without the trust fund. Acid burned all the way up his throat and left a bitter taste in his mouth.

Drew's friends had all received their funds when they'd turned eighteen or, at the latest, twenty-one.

"We agree with those terms," Aaron said.

Drew sighed. "Of course you do."

"Mrs. Finlay also states she would like ten percent of her liquid assets to be donated to the California Arts Council," Paul added. "With any of her unsold works to be auctioned for charity."

"We can facilitate that," Laura agreed.

"Okay. Well, that's everything. If I can just get each of you to sign this, to state you agree to the terms of the will, then I will arrange the transfer of funds to you," Paul said, holding up a pen and pointing to a piece of paper on the desk.

Laura signed, and Drew stood up, slowly walking over to the table. He knew there wasn't anything he could do, besides contesting the will, and that would take time and money to pay for a lawyer. Money he didn't have. Sure, people would look at him and laugh if he told them he couldn't afford something. Drew was the only child of one of Hollywood's biggest action movie stars, and the only grandchild of the very successful painter Marg Finlay. But the money wasn't *his*. He had no access to it, and his father made sure he knew about every dollar Drew spent from the family account.

Grudgingly, he picked up the pen and signed his name.

"Thank you, Paul." Aaron reached out to shake the lawyer's hand.

"If there's anything else I can do, please let me know. I'll be in touch when the transfer documents are ready." Paul packed up his briefcase.

Aaron looked over at his son with a smug smile. Drew rolled his eyes and walked out of the room. As he passed Gran's coffin, he stopped and laid his hand on the smooth polished wood.

"Good-bye, Gran," he sighed.

"Over here!" Sam called loudly as he held his arms up in the air.

Drew threw the ball around Simon's waving hands and then ran past him to the hoop. Sam took a shot. He and Drew cheered as it swished through the net.

"Damn!" Chris said loudly.

"Can't help that we're awesome!" Sam laughed back.

"Whatever. This is boring, anyway. Let's go get a beer," Simon said, walking off the basketball court.

Drew shrugged and followed his friends. It was a hot day, and a cold beer sounded great. He grabbed his shirt up off the asphalt and pulled the hot material down over his chest.

"What's up with you?" Sam asked as he came over and clapped Drew on the back.

"My parents are really pushing me to get a job." Drew let out a loud sigh and scratched at his scruffy face. He really needed a shave.

Aaron had spent half an hour over breakfast that morning lecturing his son on how important it was to contribute to the family, and to society, and to stop being lazy.

"What about all the money your grandmother left you in her will?" Chris asked when they were seated in one of the back booths of their favorite bar.

Drew laughed sarcastically. "I won't get my hands on that until I turn thirty or get married."

"Well, it's only four years away. Just suck it up and wait," Simon said with a shrug. He took a cigarette from the pack in his pocket and lit it, blowing a long stream of smoke directly up into the air.

"That's easy for you to say," Drew said to his smug friend. "Your trust fund kicked in years ago."

"I could give you a loan," Chris offered.

"Or..." Sam started to laugh.

"Or?" Drew asked curiously.

"Or...you could get married," he said with a smile. Sam took a drink of his beer and looked at Drew over the rim of the glass.

Chris and Simon both burst out laughing.

"Drew? Get married?" Simon coughed and almost choked on his beer.

"Fuck you. I don't have any problem getting women," Drew shot back.

"No, you certainly don't, which is why you'll never get married." Simon laughed.

Drew knew they were right. He didn't *want* to get married. He wasn't the settling down type of guy. He had a new girl every few weeks, and that was the way that he liked it. He was free.

"How would someone go about finding a wife on short notice?" Sam asked. "Hypothetically."

"One of those Russian bride web sites?" Chris asked, looking up at the smoke-stained ceiling in contemplation.

"Or an ad in the newspaper?" Simon added.

"I'm guessing it would have to be a real marriage, though, not a fake one," Sam said.

"Well, it wouldn't be that hard, really," Simon explained. "I mean, think about it. You put a discreet ad in the newspaper for a girl, you both sign a secret contract to state it's a fake marriage, and you tell everyone you are dating her. Then marry her, get your money, and you can divorce her. I think it would work."

"That is the most ridiculous thing I've ever heard!" Drew told him.

"Ridiculous or genius?" he asked with a smile.

Drew rolled his eyes. While his friends joked around, continuing their fantasy about the fake marriage, Drew excused himself and headed to the bar. He needed a shot of tequila — now — to calm himself down.

As he downed his drink, he looked over and saw the guys whispering together…something bad was being planned.

White. Everything around her was white. White chairs, white flowers, white dress. What was so romantic about the color white, anyway? Why was white the traditional color for weddings? Wouldn't red be more appropriate? Red was passionate. White was stark and cold and…perfect.

Jade drank a whole glass of champagne in one gulp — she needed it. All around her were happy faces. Her best friend, Clare, had just married the love of her life, Stuart, and Jade was happy for them. Really, she was.

Jade loved Clare like a sister and was thrilled beyond measure that she'd found love. Jade was happy for Clare. But she wasn't happy for herself.

"Bridesmaid again, Jade? You must be getting used to that role."

Jade gritted her teeth and tried her best to smile. "I'm so glad to be able to support Clare today." She turned and walked from Martha, her supervisor at work, and headed for the bar. She whispered to herself over and over, "Punching your boss isn't a good idea," as she made her way through the crowd.

Two shots of tequila and another glass of champagne later, Jade was happily dancing with a groomsman. Clare and Stuart twirled past them, and Clare winked, their secret code that she thought the groomsman was hot.

Jade looked at his face with blurry vision. He was tall, obviously younger than her, and his green eyes were mesmerizing. He smiled, apparently having noticed that she was staring.

"You wanna get out of here?" he asked, his voice gravelly.

"Yes."

The word was out of her mouth before she'd really thought it through, but the fact that someone wanted her was too good to pass up. If there was a sure-fire cure for feeling rotten about yourself, it was a hot guy finding you attractive. At least it was a short-term cure, and that was all she needed.

Jade woke up naked with a pounding head on a mattress on the floor of some apartment she didn't recognize. She could hear snoring next to her but didn't want to face the nameless groomsman who had momentarily boosted her self-confidence. Instead she decided to creep out of bed, put on her bridesmaid dress, and run outside to find a taxi.

"I love Sunday morning shifts," the driver said with a laugh when she climbed inside his car.

"Excuse me?" she asked.

"I get to see all the girls doing their walks of shame," he explained and then laughed again.

"Just shut up and drive." She slumped back into the seat and closed her eyes.

She didn't need guilt and shame laid on her by a taxi driver. She felt it enough already. She must have looked a sight, wearing a large pink tulle dress with makeup smeared all over her face and her hair sticking out in various directions from the massive amounts of hairspray she'd had to use yesterday for the wedding.

When she got home, Jade threw her bag and heels down on the floor and went straight to the bathroom, stripping the dress and corset off on the way and leaving them on the floor in the hallway. She turned on the shower but had to wait a few minutes for the ancient system to heat the water before she could get in. She shampooed her hair three times to get all the product out before she scrubbed her face with exfoliant and finally started to feel like herself again.

Once she was dry and dressed in an old pair of sweats, she picked up the dress from the floor and hung it in the closet alongside the bridesmaid dresses she'd worn for other weddings. Slamming the closet door a little harder than was necessary, she stomped into the kitchen and pulled a large tub of ice cream out of the freezer. Accidently banging her wrist on the broken drawer next to the sink, she took a spoon off the drying rack and sat down in front of the TV. A spring in the couch cushion was sticking into her thigh, and she sighed loudly. She wished she could afford to buy new furniture and not have to put up with flea market or yard sale cast-offs.

A part of her felt guilty for eating ice cream at eight in the morning, but a bigger part of her didn't care—and, besides, she didn't have much other food in the house. After she'd eaten about a quarter of the tub, her restraint came back. She forced herself to put it back in the freezer before she finished the whole thing. It had happened before.

She picked up yesterday's newspaper, which was still sitting on the coffee table, unread. The headline caught her eye.

MARG FINLAY DIES AT AGE 72.

She scanned the article. It seemed the famous artist had died of lung cancer. Her seven-figure estate was left to her daughter and grandson, who was the son of Aaron Malik, the actor. As if that family needed more money.

She began to flick through the pages and decided to have a look at the classifieds, just for a laugh. She often enjoyed reading the messages people wrote and thought it might cheer her up to know she wasn't the most lonely, desperate person in Los Angeles.

She chuckled her way down the columns of singles ads but stopped when one caught her attention.

WIFE WANTED. WRITE TO DREW.

There was a post office box address supplied. Was this guy for real? She stared at the ad, wondering if it was meant to be a joke. Was that what our society had come to…advertising for a wife? What about courting and romance and falling in love over long walks under the moonlight? Who did this *Drew* think he was, anyway? He was probably in his fifties, balding and overweight, with too much money for his own good. He probably wanted a trophy wife who cooked, cleaned, and sucked his cock like a Hoover. What an ass.

Jade felt heat rise in her cheeks as her blood boiled. He was making light of something she was desperate for, something she dreamed every night of finding. Her fury continued to build until she decided to write him a letter and give him a piece of her mind.

She pulled out her notepad, found a pen under one of the cushions of the couch, and started to write. Onto the paper poured every thought, every injustice from her past every idea about what love and marriage meant to her, and when it was done, she read through it to make sure she hadn't missed anything important.

Satisfied, she sealed it in an envelope and dug around in her purse for a stamp. She wanted to make sure she sent it before losing her nerve.

She ran out of her apartment to the mailbox down the street and dropped it in, relishing the clanking sound the slot made when it closed. She wondered if the mysterious Drew would contact her back. Probably not. He'd read her letter, throw it in the trash, and look for a bimbo with fake tits and a bubblegum name ending in an I. (What was so wrong with ending names with Y or IE—like they were meant to, anyway?) At least it made her feel better to have written it.

CHAPTER TWO

You've Got Mail

Monday morning was no different than any other. Drew didn't get the Monday morning blues that the rest of the population lived with; he didn't have to get up and do anything. There was no difference between Monday and Thursday, or even Saturday. Day after day of the same thing.

He wondered if that was why people went to work: to entertain themselves with something, to have something to break up the week. Was work a way to gain more enjoyment from their time off—a "value what you don't have" kind of thing? Drew had nothing but spare time. Day after day of hours to fill.

He was lying in bed, staring at his bedroom ceiling and pondering his life, or lack thereof, when his phone beeped. He reached onto his nightstand for the phone and read a text message from Sam.

You might wanna check your mail! Ha!

Drew wondered what that could mean, but he decided that he probably should get out of bed regardless. It *was* almost noon.

He went downstairs and saw a large stack of envelopes and boxes piled on the kitchen bench. The family housekeeper, Caroline, must have already been to the post office to collect it all. If not for the text from Sam, he wouldn't have looked twice at the postage haul. His father was always getting fan mail and packages from sponsors wanting him to promote their products.

He grabbed a muffin out of the fridge and made his way over to the pile of mail. Every single envelope and box was addressed to him. It wasn't his birthday, and he couldn't think of any other reason to receive so many packages, but he figured the only way to find out what this was all about was to open them.

He picked up a box, ripped it open, and tipped the contents onto the counter. Horrified, he stared at the folded piece of paper and the pile of lace. Was that a *thong?* He left it and opened another box, allowing several photos to fall onto the bench, all of a very naked woman.

What was going on? He quickly scanned the letter that accompanied the thong and found that the sender had some kind of idea that they would be getting married. He picked up the letter that went with the nude photographs and found the same theme.

"The world has gone crazy!" he muttered to himself, taking a bite of his muffin.

He knew Sam was behind it, so he picked up the wall phone in the kitchen and dialed his number.

"Yo," Sam answered.

"What the hell?" Drew yelled.

Sam burst into hysterics and kept trying to get words out. Eventually he calmed down.

"What did you do?" Drew asked, staring at the thong still sitting on the counter.

"I got you a wife," Sam said, still chuckling.

"You got me a hundred stalkers—who all appear to be strippers or porn stars."

"Huh?"

"Well, I've only opened two of the dozens of packages, and I've already got a thong and a handful of naked pictures," Drew explained.

"I'll be there in ten minutes." The line went dead, and Drew could practically see Sam running to his car.

Drew sighed and stared at the pile of unopened mail that he would still have to go through. He thought about just throwing it all in the trash, but he couldn't deny he was a bit curious to see what else people had sent. He piled his arms high with the boxes and letters and carried them up to his bedroom, dumping them on the bed and then heading back downstairs for a second load. As he carried the last of the mail upstairs, he heard the doorbell ring.

Knowing Caroline would let Sam in, he sat on the floor of his bedroom and started opening the packages. Sam, Simon, and Chris all filed into the room and burst out laughing when they saw Drew sitting cross-legged, surrounded by mail.

"Let's see these titty pics," Simon said with a laugh. He sat down on the end of Drew's bed and started rifling through the envelopes.

"Ha! Listen to this one…" Sam started to read from a letter. "Dear Drew, I would make the perfect wife. I can cook, clean, and I always swallow. I have the ability to deep-throat the biggest dick without gagging—"

"What did you guys do?" Drew asked, cutting his friend off.

"We put the plan into action. Out of all these girls, there has to be *one* you might like. So, you marry her and get your inheritance. Easy," Chris said with a shrug of his shoulder.

Simon whistled and held up a picture. "This girl is hot!"

"I'm not going to marry some random girl," Drew said. "And especially not any of *these* girls!"

"Let's just open them all and put them into 'yes,' 'no,' and 'maybe' piles," Sam reasoned.

"Fine," Drew said with a long sigh. "But I need a drink to get through this."

He pulled some vodka from his desk drawer and drank straight from the bottle. They spent the next hour opening letters and deciding if they were suitable or not. Drew wanted to put them all in the "no" pile, but the boys added some they thought were interesting to the "maybe" pile.

A lot of the letters smelled of perfume and most of them included photos. Some of the photos were nude, but a lot of them were just pictures of smiling girls. In a way, Drew felt bad for them; they'd put themselves out there, and he wasn't even going to let them know he wasn't interested. There was no way he could contact every one of them.

"This girl just wrote out her whole life story," Chris said as he threw her letter into the "no" pile.

"I think this one is after a green card," Sam scoffed as he scrunched up the letter.

"This one is promising four blowjobs every single day." Simon laughed, but then he put the envelope in his pocket when he thought no one was looking.

"Whoa! We have a hater." Chris waved the letter he was currently holding in the air. "Check this out, Drew," he said as he handed Drew several sheets of paper.

> Dear Asshole,
>
> Your ad for a wife disgusted me. How could you treat something as sacred as marriage with such disrespect? I have been searching for love for years, and time after time I have been left with a broken heart and a little less self-esteem.
>
> You might think of marriage as a joke, but trust me...I am a single girl who has all married friends. I would do anything to find that right guy and commit our lives to each other.

Drew stopped reading and looked up to see Sam sling-shotting one of the many thongs at his face. He was only just able to duck out of the way in time.

"Gross, Sam. I think that one had been worn!" Drew yelled.

"So, what does the hater say?" Simon asked.

"I don't know. I didn't get to finish reading it. But from what I can gather she's disgusted with the idea that someone would be so disrespectful as to advertise for a wife, and I have to agree with her. I can't believe you guys would do that to me."

"We were seriously just trying to help. There has to be *one* girl here who's caught your eye. What about that blowjob girl? Simon... which letter was it?" Chris asked.

"Uhhh...I'm not sure," Simon said, his face turning red. His hand automatically touched his pocket.

"Look, so far the only girl who has any sense is this—" he looked at the bottom of the letter to see the hater's name "—Jade."

"Well, I hate to tell you this, Drew, but I don't think the hater is going to marry you," Sam said, standing and clapping his friend on the back.

"This was a stupid idea!" Drew said angrily. He stood too and gathered all the envelopes so he could throw them in the trash.

"Wanna go see a movie?" Simon asked.

"No, you guys go. I'm just gonna clean up this mess," Drew said dismissively.

He didn't feel like being around them anymore. He couldn't believe they had been such idiots as to think he would find a wife through an ad in the newspaper. After the three of them left, he collected all the envelopes and boxes and took them down to the garbage.

"Is everything okay, Drew?" Aaron asked over breakfast the following day.

"Yeah." Drew spooned in another mouthful of Count Chocula.

"You've seemed down for the past few weeks…Are you still upset about Gran?" his father pressed.

Drew shrugged. He and his father had never been very close, and talking with him about emotions was extremely uncomfortable. Drew hoped he would just drop the subject.

"I know you were disappointed with the terms of the settlement, but your mother and I have been talking. We think it might be good for you to move into your grandmother's house."

Drew's head shot up, and he looked at his father carefully. "Really?"

"Yes. You're an adult, and having to take some responsibility for yourself might help you to mature. Now, you would have to pay all your own bills and clean up after yourself. I'm not going to pay for a maid, and I don't want to hear about you calling Caroline over to work for you. She has enough to do here."

"I can't afford to live there," Drew said. "I know I should have a job by now, but there isn't anything that I want to do, and I don't see the point of starting a career when in a few years I won't need to work anyway. It's a waste of time."

His father's face went cold. Drew knew his father didn't like his attitude about work. Aaron certainly had enough money that he didn't need to work, and yet he had a new movie coming out every summer. Drew and his father just didn't have the same work ethic.

"Your mother agrees with you," Aaron said through gritted teeth. "So, we have a suggestion. I will pay you a generous allowance until your trust fund is released…"

"Deal!" Drew said with a smile, cutting him off.

His dad leaned back in his chair and pressed his hands carefully onto the table top. "I have a condition"

"I knew you would."

"You have to do volunteer work. I don't care what kind of volunteer work it is, as long as you do it."

"How much would the allowance be?" Drew asked, trying not to show how interested he was.

"Three thousand a month." Aaron took a bite of toast.

"That's not enough," Drew said simply, shaking his head. He knew there was no way he could live on that. He could go through that in just one weekend out with his friends.

"Drew, many people support whole families on that amount of money, and you won't have rent to pay because you own the house. If you budget properly, it will be more than enough."

"Why are you doing this?" Drew asked.

"Your mother and I love you, Drew, and it makes us miserable to see you so down. And you're right when you say that most people your age are looking after themselves. I would've liked it if you had gotten a job and worked to support yourself, but your mother agrees with you that starting a career isn't a priority for you. We want to help you to learn how to budget and look after yourself so that when your trust fund is paid, you can be independent. The monthly allowance is *all* you will get. Don't come and ask for anything else, because I'll say no."

It made sense, even if it was uncharacteristic for him to see things from Drew's point of view. Drew thought about it for another second, but there really wasn't much else to consider. It was the only option he had if he wanted to get out of the house. All he'd have to do was find some volunteer work, and that shouldn't be too hard. His mom had been doing it for years. He was sure she could help him pick something.

"Deal!" Drew said, holding his hand out for his dad to shake.

"Good," Aaron said. He shook his son's hand, and for the first time in a very long time, he looked proud.

After breakfast, Drew raced up to his bedroom and started to pack his belongings. He couldn't believe he was actually getting out to live on his own. Caroline would've happily done the packing for him, but he was so excited he *wanted* to do it himself.

Drew got down on his knees and started pulling storage boxes out from under the bed when he saw a folded piece of paper on the floor. He opened it up and laughed when he realized it was the letter from the hater girl. It must have been dropped when he threw the rest out into the garbage. He put it in the trash pile and kept working.

After he'd packed the majority of the things he wanted to move, he went to have a look at the house. Paul, the lawyer, had brought the keys two weeks ago, but Drew hadn't been there yet as it was too depressing to know it was his and not be able to live there.

He pulled his car into the drive and looked up at the house. It was imposing and looked vacant. Newspapers were piled up on the stoop, and several of the windows to the front room were smashed. The homey feeling he associated with it was gone.

When he got inside, he coughed from all the dust lying around. It looked like Gran hadn't used this place in a while before she died. He made his way around and got more and more disheartened the more he explored.

The electricity was disconnected, and there was some kind of insect infestation that would need to be taken care of. The floor of the front room, which Gran had used as her studio, was coated in paint splatters, and one of the steps to the top floor was broken. When he walked into the formal lounge, there was shattered glass all over the floor and a rock on the rug. Someone had thrown it through the original stained glass windows. There must be thousands of dollars' worth of repairs needed before he could move in.

There was no way his father would give him that much money, and the allowance he was offering wouldn't cover it. Drew was back to square one. He'd have to sit in his parents' house for the next four years or find a way to get some money.

He drove home feeling extremely depressed and went straight to his bedroom, avoiding his parents. Drew hated feeling bad, so he found the almost empty bottle of vodka in his desk drawer and drained it. Hopefully it would kick in soon and lift his mood. He lay down on the bed and rolled onto his side. He just had to find a way to get some money. It was so frustrating to have such a huge amount sitting and waiting for him and not be able to get his hands on it. If only there was a way to get...

He glanced over and saw the hater's letter sitting on top of the pile of trash he hadn't taken out yet. He snatched it up and read it again. The girl was actually quite funny. She was angry, that was obvious, but she had a dry sarcasm that he liked. Maybe his friends hadn't been so stupid after all.

Drew got up and went over to his desk to write her a reply.

The days went on as they usually did, and Jade forgot about the jerk, Drew, who thought he could advertise for a wife. She went to work every day and hung out with her friends most evenings before returning to the tiny, grungy apartment. It was the same routine she'd had since moving from Florida.

Jade enjoyed her job working as a character in the world's happiest theme park. She got to dress up as a princess every day. It was like fulfilling a childhood dream. That was how she'd met Clare; they worked there together. They spent their days wearing gorgeous gowns, smiling, waving, and having their photos taken. There were worse jobs in the world. The illusion of being a princess was short-lived, however, when she went home to her shoebox of an apartment with a hot water system that kept breaking down and a refrigerator that only worked some of the time.

She waved good-bye to the smiling children who were calling out to her — "Ariel! Ariel!" — and went to the break room.

"You're so lucky you don't have to wear a wig!" Clare groaned as she pulled the mass of brunette curls from her head. Her own blond hair was smashed under a hair net.

"One advantage to being a natural redhead," Jade laughed.

She fluffed the thick red hair that fell down her back in soft waves. The starfish clip that held her bangs back was pinching her scalp, so she repositioned it and then grabbed her lunch out of her locker.

"So, you've been back at work for three days now. Are you settled back in?" she asked Clare.

Clare and Stuart had just spent two weeks in Mexico, lazing on the beach for their honeymoon, and Clare had come back with the most delightful tan.

"I guess," she sighed. "I miss the beach. Maybe we could go over to Malibu one weekend? Or a weekend in Hawaii would be amazing!"

"Yeah, maybe," Jade said. She knew she wouldn't have the cash for that. She was saving up for a new fridge so her food wouldn't go bad. She didn't feel like dying of food poisoning anytime soon. Although if she did get food poisoning, she'd probably have a killer bikini body after all the vomiting.

That afternoon she collected the mail on her way home. It was something she did weekly, so she only got that depressing I've-got-more-bills-than-money feeling once instead of every day. There were several bills and some advertising catalogues as well as one hand-addressed letter.

She threw the rest of the mail down on the counter to look at later and ripped open the envelope. A quick scan of the handwriting told her she didn't recognize it, and the signature at the end, *Drew Malik*, was also unfamiliar. She wracked her brain but couldn't think of anyone she knew by that name. Of course there was Aaron Malik's son…Jade thought his name was Drew. She'd seen him stumbling drunk on TMZ a few nights before. But what would *he* be writing to her for? With her curiosity piqued, she started to read the letter.

Dear Jade,

Thank you for taking the time to share all of your concerns with me. I agree that advertising for a bride is a horrendous thing to do. I assure you I had nothing to do with it. My friends placed the ad in the newspaper as a semi-joke.

I find myself in a situation where having a wife would be greatly beneficial to me, and my idiot friends were trying to help me out. I assure you I don't take the idea of getting married lightly.

Since we seem to have a similar view on this, I was thinking maybe we could get together and see if an arrangement could be made to benefit us both.

If you're curious, or interested to hear my proposal, please meet me at the Griddle Café on Sunset at 7 p.m. on Friday night. I'll wait for you, in hopes that you'll come.

Drew Malik
aka "The Asshole"

She stared at the letter and re-read it three times before she gave up trying to understand it. The letter didn't confirm if he was Aaron Malik's son, but one thing was for sure — this was the same Drew she'd written that letter to two weeks ago. Jade didn't know whether to believe he'd had nothing to do with the ad. And she certainly couldn't think of a reason why it would be advantageous for him to have a wife.

But he was right about one thing: she *was* curious.

CHAPTER THREE

The Proposal

Tonight was the night. Jade still hadn't decided if she was going to meet Drew or not. He'd said he'd be waiting for her, which in a way made her feel like she *should* go. She knew how bad it felt to be stood up. But did she really want to face a guy who thought of marriage as a joke? On the plus side, if he pissed her off, she could throw her coffee in his face — she'd always wanted to try that.

Would she or wouldn't she? Should she or shouldn't she?

Her mind was made up when she got home and stood naked in her bathroom for nearly ten minutes, waiting for the shower to get hot. Eventually she gave up and settled for a freezing cold shower. She couldn't live like this anymore.

As she toweled herself dry, her stomach rumbled loudly, and she sighed, knowing she didn't have any food in the cupboard. She worked full time, but the majority of her wages paid her rent and tuition loans. There wasn't a lot left over for luxuries like food. In his letter, Drew had said his proposition would benefit them *both*. Could she interpret that to mean that she would get some kind of payment for helping him?

She changed into a pair of jeans and a sweater that didn't have any holes and ran out the door before she changed her mind. She wasn't sure if it made her a prostitute for offering a service for payment. It felt wrong. But she shook her head to clear the thoughts; she didn't even know what he wanted from her. Surely it wasn't sex. And she knew she wouldn't do that anyway. She would rather starve.

Her car door creaked as she opened it, and her heart clenched in the daily routine of would or wouldn't the car start? She buckled her seat belt and rubbed her hands on the steering wheel.

"Come on, Gertrude, you can do it," she said as she turned the key.

The car sputtered but came to life. Jade quickly put it into gear and pulled onto the street before the engine stalled.

"Good girl!" She found it helped to encourage the car.

Her mind raced the whole way to the Griddle Café. She'd heard of the place but never actually eaten there. There was a long line of people standing outside in small groups, chatting as they waited for a table. She checked in, giving her name, and followed the balding man as he led her into the tiny, crowded space, ignoring the grumbles of the other people in line. Her stomach rumbled at the smell of pancakes and coffee as she squeezed her way through the tables.

She realized she didn't even know who she was looking for. She scanned the room and saw several teenagers, some couples, an older man reading a book, and one guy sitting on his own who was about her own age. He looked familiar, the way a radio personality did... You'd seen their faces on billboards, but you didn't know them personally. It was Drew Malik...the actor's son. Shit!

Slowly, she started to walk toward his booth while trying to casually smooth her hair. As she got closer, he smiled and stood up.

"Are you Jade?" he asked.

She nodded and sat down, in shock. She hadn't actually expected the Drew Malik from the letter to be *Drew Malik*. What was she going to say to him?

"I'm Drew," he said, smiling, and held his hand out for her to shake.

Jade moved her hand forward, almost hesitant to touch him. Drew was handsome, and not just normal guy-in-the-street-that-you-look-at-as-he-walks-by handsome. He was movie star handsome. His blue eyes sparkled as he smiled at her, and his perfect white teeth shone in the dim lights of the diner. He looked almost exactly like his father.

"I'm glad you came," he said when he released her hand and ran his fingers through his messy brown hair.

Jade tried to open her mouth to speak, but no words came out. All kinds of dirty thoughts ran through her mind, and she was frightened that if she did say something it would be about how much she wanted to suck on his luscious bottom lip. Suddenly the idea of prostitution wasn't as repulsive as it had been.

"Would you like anything? Coffee?" he asked politely.

She nodded, and he waved over the server, asking her to bring two coffees.

"So, what do you do?" he asked.

"Excuse me?" Jade forced herself to concentrate and to stop staring at him.

"I feel at a bit of a disadvantage. I'm sure you know about my life already from the media, and I know nothing about you. What do you do?"

"I'm a princess," she replied.

Drew laughed and waited, but when she held her neutral expression, he frowned. "What?"

"At Disneyland. I'm one of the princesses."

Drew's eyebrows raised. "Seriously? You wear the dresses and the crown?"

She nodded.

"Which princess are you?"

"Can't you guess?" she asked, her voice a little flirty, flipping her long hair over her shoulder. *That's it, girl. Just be cute and casual.*

"You're the sexy mermaid one!" he cheered.

"Well, I'm not *sexy* at Disneyland. But, yes, I'm Ariel."

The waitress put two cups of coffee down on the table, and they each drank, allowing their conversation to fall away.

"You must think I'm very strange." Drew chuckled, sounding just as nervous as Jade felt.

"What? Oh…no, not at all," she said meekly.

"You seemed to think so in your letter," he countered.

That snapped Jade out of her trance. She smiled shyly, keeping her eyes locked on the Formica table top. "Yeah, sorry about that."

He laughed again. "It was actually quite refreshing, and I want to assure you again that I didn't place that ad. I swear it was my friends."

"If you don't mind me asking, why would they do that?" she asked and immediately felt nosy.

"It has to do with what I wanted to talk to you about tonight. Maybe I should start at the beginning?"

Jade nodded and reached for the coffee cup that had just been refilled. She brought it up to her lips, blowing on it gently before taking a sip.

"My grandmother died recently…"

"Oh, I'm sorry," she blurted, cutting him off. "I did read about that in the paper."

"She lived a good life," he said with a shrug of his shoulders. "In her will, she left me a house and a trust fund."

Jade nodded to show her understanding, although why the son of Hollywood's biggest action hero needed a trust fund was beyond her.

"There were certain stipulations laid down in the will about when I could access the money. I was willing to wait until I turned thirty and it came to me by default, but the house she left me is in shambles and needs a lot of money spent on it before I can move in."

Jade was utterly confused. She couldn't understand what his grandmother's will, his trust fund, or a run-down house had to do with her. She couldn't see how she could possibly help him with his situation.

"So, that's where you come in, Ariel," he said with a smile.

"I'm sorry. I don't understand."

He laughed. "Well, not *you* specifically; any woman could help me. But I'm hoping it will be you who agrees to do it."

"Go on," she said, her curiosity piqued.

"If we were to…get married," he said cautiously, looking at her with a guarded expression, "I would get my trust fund and be financially independent. I would, of course, offer you compensation."

"You want me to marry you for money?" Jade asked, trying to make sure she understood.

"Well…yeah." He gave her a sheepish grin.

"How much money are we talking about?" she asked.

"Eighteen million dollars."

Unfortunately, Jade had taken a mouthful of coffee right at that moment, and she spat it all over him and the table. "I'm so sorry," she said, mortified.

He mopped the coffee off his shirt while she dabbed the spots off the table.

"Don't worry about it. My offer to you is a payment of half a million dollars when I receive the fund, which would be our wedding day, and another half million dollars as a settlement on the day our divorce is finalized. In total, you would receive one million dollars."

She stared at him dumbfounded, and then she blinked her eyes a few times to make sure she wasn't dreaming.

"You want to give me a *million* dollars for being married to you?" She couldn't believe what she was hearing. She began to wonder if Clare had set her up on some new reality television show and her face was currently being broadcast to millions of people all over the nation…maybe even the world. Was that guy at the next table wearing a hidden camera in his glasses?

"For a year," he added. "After that, we go our separate ways and never have to see each other again."

Jade's instinct was to stand up, throw her coffee in his face, and walk out, but the empty feeling in her stomach and the knowledge that she would be going home to another cold shower made her stay in her seat.

"We'd have to date for a little while so my family believes we really are a couple," he continued when she didn't say anything.

She continued to just stare at him, unsure what to say. There was a part of her that thought this whole idea was crazy, but there was another part, the hungry part, that thought it might be nice to have money to buy groceries and move into a nicer house. And she couldn't deny how much she would enjoy seeing people's faces when she said she was getting married.

"What are you thinking?" Drew asked nervously.

"I'm considering what you said."

They both sat in silence as Jade spun the coffee cup slowly in her hands. After a while, Drew cleared his throat.

"Why don't I give you some time to think about it? Here is my cell phone number. Give me a call once you've made up your mind. The offer is there if you want it." He grabbed a napkin and wrote a string of numbers on it.

She folded it slowly and placed it in her pocket before standing up and giving him a weak smile.

"Thanks for meeting with me, Ariel," he said.

"I'll call you soon," she replied, half in a daze, and walked back out onto the street.

Drew pressed the button in the keyless entry for his convertible, and the lights flashed once. He settled into the soft leather seats and pulled out into the Hollywood traffic. Jade had not been what he'd expected *at all*. He'd hoped she would be about his age and attractive, that would make the sell to his parents that the marriage was real, but he hadn't expected to actually like her.

She was beautiful in a unique way. Most of the girls he spent time with wore stylish labels and full makeup. Jade had worn clothes she looked comfortable in, and her hair fell in loose waves down her back. He'd never dated a redhead, but he'd found himself mesmerized by her hair, the way it shone with gold and chocolate streaks, depending on how the light hit it. She'd smelled like raspberries, not French perfume.

He thought back over their conversation as he drove down Santa Monica Boulevard toward Beverly Hills, trying to gauge her reaction. She'd said she would call, but what would she say?

"She'll say yes," he said aloud to himself. "She has to. No one would turn down a million dollars."

A year of her life wasn't that much to give up, was it? She'd certainly be well compensated for the time. Although she didn't appear to be someone who was motivated by money. Her clothes had been simple, and he'd never seen her out at the clubs. He knew he would have remembered her.

His cell phone rang just as he pulled up into the driveway.

"What do you want, Tully?" he answered, seeing the name flash on the screen.

"Drew! Come out with us tonight." She already sounded drunk. Her voice slurred when she said his name.

"Where are you going?"

"Does it matter? I'll be wearing a very short skirt, just for you."

Drew groaned. There was nothing worse than when your hook-up wouldn't take a hint.

"I think I have plans tonight," he lied.

"What are you? Some old married guy? Man up and come out with us."

Drew felt the hairs on the back of his neck bristle. He wasn't a married man, but he might be soon. This might be one of his last opportunities to go and have fun before he started playing the role of husband, if everything went according to plan.

"All right."

"Yes!" she hissed, dragging the word out. "We're at SkyBar."

"I'll be there soon."

He ran up the stairs, waving off his parents' questions about where he was going in such a rush. After a quick shower and begging Caroline to iron his blue shirt before she went home, he was back in the car, driving to Sunset Boulevard.

Drew knew he looked good. He got his looks from his father and his knowledge of how to dress from his mother. He knew the shirt he wore made his eyes look intensely blue. He knew that rolling the sleeves halfway up his arms made his biceps look more defined under the material. He knew that slicking his hair back made him look more sophisticated. He used all the cards in his deck. Drew was going to have a wild night before it was time for him to settle down.

He knew Jade would say yes to his proposition. She had to.

CHAPTER FOUR

The Beginning of Deception

Jade was so consumed by her thoughts that she drove past her apartment block and had to double back. She didn't know what she should do. The idea of getting a million dollars for not doing much was appealing, and she was seriously tempted. But there was a part of her that was holding back. Getting married for money just seemed so underhanded and deceitful, and she wasn't sure if she could do it. Especially after the letter she'd written condemning Drew for his casual approach to finding a bride. It would make her a hypocrite.

As Jade climbed the stairs to her apartment, she tried to put her thoughts into some kind of logical order. She had a good job, and if she kept working hard, she'd be next in line for the promotion from Princess Ariel to Minnie Mouse. Everyone wanted to be the mouse. They were the most trusted character actors and always the most popular with the kids.

Her mind raced as she put in a load of laundry, washed her face, and got into her PJs. She would just convince herself she wasn't going to accept Drew's offer, and then her stomach would rumble, she'd remember she'd be having two-minute noodles for dinner again, and she'd reconsider. Then, just when she was satisfied that she could marry Drew and take the money with no regrets, her conscience would kick in, and she'd be back to square one.

She was surviving without that million dollars, and she would continue to be fine. Even if she had to move further out of the city to find a place with cheaper rent. The longer commute would give her time to think about and plan for her future. There was always a silver lining.

With her mind made up, she plopped down onto the couch with a sigh. The spring that'd been threatening to break for the past few weeks used that exact moment to burst out of the thin material lining. With a loud *boing* it flew out of the couch, cutting her thigh with a stinging slice as it went flying across the room.

Jade watched the spring slide across the floor toward the front door and sighed again. The pain from the new cut on her thigh throbbed, her stomach rumbled, and now her couch was broken too. Everything overwhelmed her, and before she could stop herself, she burst into tears. She didn't know why her life had to be so hard. She worked, she paid her taxes, and all she wanted was a hot shower, a couch that wasn't poking her with broken springs, and a decent dinner every night. She didn't think that was too much to ask, but maybe it was.

Drew's beautiful blue eyes and crooked smile danced before her own watery eyes, and she took a deep breath. She had an easy way out. Suddenly the choice didn't seem so hard anymore; it was a matter of survival. The survival of her sanity.

She rifled through her bag until her hand clasped her cell phone and the napkin Drew had written his number on. Her fingers fumbled as she tried to dial too quickly, and she had to actually stop herself and take a deep breath before she was able to dial successfully.

The phone rang, and then rang again. After six rings, she was starting to think that he wasn't going to answer. She was about to hang up when his voice came on the line.

"Hello?"

"Hi…Drew, this is Jade." Her voice was nervous, but the decision was made.

"That was fast," he said, sounding shocked.

"Yeah…I was just thinking about it and—" she started before he cut her off.

"Before you turn me down, if it's a matter of the amount of money, I'm willing to negotiate a higher fee," he stated.

"No, no…it's not that. I was actually calling to accept." She closed her eyes and cringed internally.

"Oh, well, I feel stupid now. You just called so quickly after we'd met, and I assumed that you weren't interested. So…you accept?"

"I accept."

"Tim, who's that guy that fixed our refrigerator?" Pam asked across the dinner table.

"The fridge repairman," Tim replied as he stuffed more mashed potatoes into his mouth.

"His *name*, jackass," Pam said, rolling her eyes.

"How am I supposed to know? I looked him up in the phone book and called the number, that's all," Tim protested.

"You talked to him the whole time he was working and then had a beer with him afterward," Pam said, exasperated.

"I don't remember," he replied, shaking his head. "I can't even picture who you're talking about."

Clare, Stuart, and Jade all gave each other subtle smiles; they knew what would be coming next. Pam took a deep breath and put her fork down gently.

"Tim Harrison, you are just trying to be difficult. You know exactly who I'm talking about. He was overweight, kind of balding. His name was Billy or Bobby or something."

A huge grin spread over Tim's face. "Bobby McBaldandfat?" he asked.

Stuart laughed and spat beer across the table, causing Clare and Jade to burst into laughter as well.

"Oh, that's mature!" Pam sneered as she started stacking the plates. "I'm trying to help Jade out by suggesting someone to fix her fridge, and you have to go and be your typical moron self."

"Oh, come on, Pammy. I was only joking. I honestly don't remember the guy's name," Tim said, trying to calm his wife down.

For the two years that Tim and Pam had been together, their friends had witnessed many arguments exactly like this one. However, they knew after a few sweet words from Tim, Pam would turn into a big messy pile of goo. It made Jade sick...with jealousy.

Jade thought of Drew and how they would be getting married soon. It seemed so surreal. Jade...getting *married*. Of course, it wasn't a real marriage. They wouldn't be in love or get to make up from little domestic spats, but it was still oddly comforting to know that soon she would be paired. This could be the last time she'd be a fifth wheel at dinner, at least for the next year.

"Why don't you boys go and watch whatever game involving a ball is currently on TV, like I know you've been dying to do all night, and leave us girls to chat?" Clare said, rubbing Stuart's arm.

Both boys shot out of their chairs and disappeared into the living room so fast that if they were in a cartoon, they would have been blurry lines surrounded by clouds of dust.

"Coffee?" Pam asked.

"Yes, please," Clare and Jade said at the same time.

Pam disappeared into the kitchen for a few minutes and came back out with three cups of the best-tasting coffee in the whole world. Jade wasn't sure how Pam always made such delicious coffee, but she wouldn't be surprised if she turned on the news one day and saw that Pam had been arrested for drug cooking.

"The remote control is broken!" Tim yelled loudly.

"No, it's not. You just don't know how to use it," Stuart said with a laugh.

Pam rolled her eyes and got up to close the door that led to the living room so they could have some privacy.

"Can I ask you a hypothetical question?" Jade asked tentatively.

"Always," Clare said with a smile before taking a sip of her coffee.

"Well...how soon do you think is too soon to get married?"

Both Clare's and Pam's mouths dropped open.

Pam gasped. "Have you met someone?"

"Who is he?" Clare demanded. "Why don't we know anything about him?"

"Calm down!" Jade hushed them. "I've just met a guy this week, but it might lead somewhere."

"This week?" Pam clarified.

"And you are already thinking marriage?" Clare squealed excitedly.

"I don't know. We just have a connection…and it's gotten serious really fast…and…" Jade stuttered, trying to think how to make the story believable.

"You're pregnant," Pam said matter-of-factly.

"No!" Jade yelled, almost knocking over her coffee cup. "I'm not pregnant. But if I were to get married soon, do you think that would be…I don't know…What would you think?"

"Does he treat you well?" Pam asked.

Honestly, Jade had no idea how Drew would treat her. They'd met in a diner for a fifteen-minute meeting and then talked on the phone for five minutes. She was going to have to lie.

"He treats me great," she said.

"Does he feel this connection? Is he thinking marriage too?" Clare asked eagerly.

Seeing as Drew was the one who had thought up this whole marriage thing, Jade was confident she could say he was thinking about it too. And that wouldn't even be a lie.

"He was the one who brought it up," she said.

"He proposed?" Clare squealed.

"Not exactly, but we have talked about marriage," Jade clarified. "I just wanted to know if you thought it was crazy."

They were both silent for a moment, and she prepared herself for the backlash that she assumed was about to hit. Pam and Tim had been together for four years before they got married, and Clare and Stuart were high school sweethearts.

"I think if you love him and he treats you well, then there is nothing wrong with getting married quickly…but what's the rush? Why not get to know each other a bit?" Pam questioned.

"No, don't wait! I love the spontaneity of it. It's so romantic," Clare said wistfully.

"But you wouldn't think I was crazy?" Jade asked, wanting to make sure that if she told them within the next few weeks that she was getting married, they wouldn't freak out on her.

"We'd have to meet him before we could say for sure," Pam answered, with Clare nodding her head in agreement.

"I think that can be arranged," Jade said.

"Just as long as he's not like Subway Guy," Pam said thoughtfully.

"Or Chipmunk Guy," Clare added, giving Jade a meaningful look. "But Pretty Boy was hot."

"Ooh, what if he's like Construction Guy? Didn't you say he was awesome in the sack?" Pam asked.

Jade shifted in her seat. Having her previous bed-buddies listed off wasn't her idea of a fun night. "Yes, Construction Guy was a great lay," she said, sighing.

"This new guy needs a name too," Clare said.

"What's something defining about him?" Pam asked, her eyes lighting up.

Jade found it funny how her friends never used guys' real names. They all had nicknames.

"I've got it!" Clare jumped out of her chair. "Commitment Guy."

"Commitment Guy?" Jade asked, scrunching up her face in disapproval.

"Well, you've only known him a week, and he's already talking marriage," Clare said, defending herself.

Pam smiled with an air of having the perfect suggestion and knew she couldn't be wrong. "How about The Groom?"

"Don't you dare," Jade warned. The last thing she needed was the girls calling Drew "The Groom" to his face.

"Okay, well, give us something to go with, then," Pam insisted.

"He has really dreamy eyes," Jade said.

Clare clapped her hands and squealed. "That's so it. Dream Guy."

After another cup of coffee and Tim doing a victory lap around the house cheering "Dodgers! Dodgers! Dodgers!" Jade headed home.

Drew Malik. *Andrew Malik*, son of Aaron Malik. Jade felt like she'd just had some crazy dream. And yet, the voice message on her phone asking if they could meet up again proved it was real. When she talked to him, he seemed so normal, but he wasn't.

"He's famous," she reminded herself.

Jade found it fascinating to see who became famous and who didn't. There were some extremely talented actors and musicians who were completely ignored by the media, and then there were people like Drew Malik, who showed very little interest in having a career of their own and were only famous by association. As far as Jade knew, Drew had never acted in a movie or TV show. The only reason he was famous was because he was the son of someone famous.

All Jade really knew about him was that he was a party boy, a suspected man-whore, and very rich…except that part wasn't true.

Drew wasn't rich. He was desperate for her help to get his hands on money. If she'd turned him down, would he just find some other girl to fill her role? Probably. If the impression of wealth wasn't true, then perhaps the rest of it wasn't true either.

She didn't have Internet at home—she couldn't afford it—but she had her cell phone. Her fingers tapped quickly on the screen as she typed his name into the search box. Was it wrong to do an Internet search on him? Would she learn anything she couldn't just ask him about in person at their next meeting?

"Anyone else can look him up, so why can't I?" she mumbled under her breath and hit the search button.

A list of web sites came up, along with a link to a photo gallery. She clicked the link first and scrolled through the pictures. Drew's shining blue eyes stared back at her through the screen as if he was disappointed in her for looking him up.

She shook that feeling away and kept scrolling. Most of the pictures were of him stumbling out of nightclubs. It looked like he spent a lot of his time partying, which lived up to his reputation. The photos of him when he was younger were mostly of a grumpy-looking teenager. He was usually with his parents, and he glared at the cameras.

She clicked the back button on the browser and went to the first fan web site.

A bright pink page covered in hearts and a collage of Drew's face loaded. Jade scrolled down the page reading about sightings in Hollywood, clubs he frequented, and even some fanfiction written by a girl who fantasized about Drew dragging her into a toilet stall in a club bathroom. Jade bit her lip. Was that Drew's style?

A picture of Drew being wheeled into a hospital caught her eye, and she read the article below.

Drew Malik, son of Academy Award Winner
Aaron Malik, was admitted to Cedars-Sinai
Hospital late last night. It is believed
the actor's son fell down a staircase in a
Sunset Boulevard night club and was found
unconscious. Friends called 9-1-1 and he
was rushed to the hospital in West Hollywood
with a suspected concussion. Aaron and Laura
Malik were spotted arriving at the hospital
shortly after their son. A witness in the
club tells us exclusively that Malik Jr.
was extremely intoxicated. This is another
embarrassing event for the Maliks after Drew
was arrested for DUI just three weeks ago.
He is due to face court at the end of the
month. This drunken fall won't aid his case.

Jade put the phone down and walked to the kitchen. As the kettle boiled, she thought about Drew's life. What was she getting herself into?

Jade's stomach churned.

Drew had called several times over the past few days, and she was surprised to discover they actually got along really well. He had a dry sense of humor that amused her, and she kept picturing his crooked smile when they spoke. They had agreed it was time, now that they knew they could get along, to meet up again and work out some of the details of their arrangement.

She was standing outside the same café they'd met in last week, taking deep breaths. Butterflies were churning in her stomach, and her palms were sweating.

Taking one last deep breath, she walked into the diner and saw Drew smiling at her from a booth at the far end of the counter. He gave a small wave as she walked toward him, and she instantly knew why she was so nervous; he was gorgeous. Drew was even better looking than she remembered, and she had to remind herself they had a business agreement, not an actual relationship.

"Hi," Drew said with a smile. His voice was familiar to her now because of their phone conversations, and when she heard it she felt much more relaxed. "Can I get you something, Ariel?"

"Iced tea would be great," she said softly. "And you know that's not really my name, right?"

Drew winked at her as he stood up and walked over to the counter to place the order. Jade watched him walk away and sighed a little louder than she would have liked when she saw how good his ass looked in those jeans.

"She'll be right over with it," he said, sliding back into his seat. "So…how have you been?"

"Pretty good. You?"

"All right," he replied with a shrug.

Jade cringed. Small talk had never been her strong suit. She hated feeling awkward and was more comfortable just sitting in silence than trying to fill the space with pointless words.

"I thought we should talk about some of the details," Drew stated.

Jade nodded, not sure what to say. The waitress brought over her iced tea, and she gulped down half the glass quickly.

"I actually had a contract made up. I hope that doesn't offend you, but it's just a general thing that says that I will pay you for services rendered. Services being that you become my wife."

"I don't mind signing a contract. What are the details?" When she thought about it, it seemed like a really good idea.

"What do you mean?" he asked.

"Well, what will we tell our family and friends? Where will we live? Can we still see other people romantically?" Jade listed off from the top of her head.

Drew shifted in his seat and leaned forward. "What do you think would be appropriate?"

"Well, I think if people are going to believe it's a real wedding, we'll need to appear to be dating."

"I agree," he said with a nod.

"So, will we have official dates or just tell people that we're dating?" she clarified.

Drew thought for a moment. "I think it would be good if we could go on two or three dates a week. I know my parents will expect to meet you soon, so I think we would need to do anything that a normal couple would do. We'll need to know each other well to be able to convince people that we're in love."

"That's what I was thinking too," she agreed. Suddenly a thought popped into her head—*anything a normal couple should do.* Was he expecting her to kiss him in public? "How…affectionate should we be?"

A slight blush rose up Drew's neck, and he gave her the crooked smile that she remembered from their first meeting. It was something that she'd missed during their phone conversations.

"What would you be comfortable with?" he asked.

"I don't know."

"Are you comfortable with this?" he asked, reaching his hand across the table and trailing his fingertips lightly over the back of her hand.

She stared at their hands and nodded. Her heart thudded in her chest, and she wondered if he could hear it.

"How about this?" His hand clasped hers, and their fingers intertwined.

She nodded again, admiring how the milky colors of their skin almost matched. His skin was smooth and slightly warmer than hers, and she shivered slightly as she imagined what it would be like to have more of his skin touching her. All too soon, his hand broke free and disappeared back under the table.

"Well, I think that's all we'll need for now. As we start to see each other longer, we'll negotiate more affection as it becomes necessary," he said.

The cold, businesslike words and tone of his voice snapped her back to reality, and she looked down at her hand sadly. She would just have to keep reminding herself that this was *not* a real relationship.

"I've also been thinking about your last question," he said.

"Huh?" Jade asked, shaking her head to bring her back from her thought process.

"About us being able to see other people. Obviously, a year is a long time for either of us to be celibate. We could always help each other out with that, but I think that could become very messy, and I would like to try and keep this relationship as professional as possible." He kept his eyes glued on the table and tapped the wooden surface with his fingertips as he spoke.

Jade nodded. She knew he was right, and she wanted to keep it professional too, but it was hard not to think romantic thoughts while staring into his eyes.

"So, I think that as long as we can be discreet and not get caught, then we should be free to live our lives. Obviously, none of our family or friends can know if we're seeing other people, but a one-night stand in secret every now and then would be acceptable," he posed.

Again, she nodded. She actually didn't think that being sex-free for a year was that big of a deal, but Drew had a very different lifestyle. She looked at him and wondered if he'd recently had sex...Probably.

"You mentioned being celibate for a year. What kind of time frames are we looking at for this arrangement?" Jade said, sitting up straighter and trying to make sure she kept her words as formal and businesslike as his.

"I've actually put a lot of thought into this. I was thinking that we could date for a month before getting engaged. It's a short period of time, but it's not unheard of to commit quickly. People do it all the time. Then I would give my mother two months to plan the wedding. She'll say it's impossible and beg for more time, but I'll be adamant that we want to be married sooner rather than later. If she can see that I'm happy, then she'll agree. We would marry and appear to be in love for a few months, fulfilling the fine print of my grandmother's will. Then, over a six-month period, our relationship could appear to be breaking down before we finally separate. California divorce law states that both parties have to agree that the relationship has been broken for a period of six months to allow a divorce. Are you willing to put a year into this?" he asked. "I think that's the quickest we can pull it off."

Jade thought about the timeline he was proposing. One year of her life would be wasted on this. One year of celibacy or one-night stands. One year she would never get back. What if she met the man of her dreams during that time? Could she say to him, "Sorry, I'm married to a guy I don't love, but I'm going to divorce him in a few months. Will you wait for me?" He would think she was crazy.

On the other hand, the million dollars Drew was promising was very enticing. So enticing that twelve months didn't seem like such a long time. What was one year, really? Twelve months, fifty-two weeks, three hundred and sixty-five days. A million dollars over one year; that worked out to be over eighty thousand dollars a month. Surely she could give up just one tiny year of her life for that kind of money. And it wasn't as if she had a guy— or even the prospect of a guy— that would be put out by the arrangement. She might not even meet anyone in the next year that she was interested in.

"A year is doable," she said.

Drew gave her a toothy grin. "Great!"

"Where would I live?" she asked, wondering if he was going to ask her to move in with him.

"Well, when we're married, we'll have to live together. After the wedding, when I get my inheritance and the house can be fixed up, we can live there until we separate. Until then, you can stay in your apartment. Is that okay?" He chewed his lip as he waited for her response.

"That sounds fine," she replied. A part of her had hoped he would ask her to move in sooner than the wedding; it was still three months away. Her apartment was barely habitable, but she would just have to make do.

"I really think this is going to work," Drew said with a smile.

"What do we do if someone suspects us?"

"Nothing. We deny it. No one can prove that we're not in love. It'll be our word against theirs. Don't worry. We're going to pull this off," he assured her. He handed her an envelope. "Here, why don't you read this over? Give it back to me once you've signed it. If there's anything in there you think we should change, we can talk about it."

She opened it and peeked inside; it was the contract.

"What are you going to tell people about me?" he asked curiously.

"I've already told my two best friends that I met someone. I thought it would be better to tell them as soon as possible so it appeared we had been dating longer," she said. "Was that okay?"

Drew stood up and dropped some money on the table to pay for their drinks.

"You don't have to do that," Jade said, putting her hand out to give the money back to him.

"That's what boyfriends do," he replied, giving a wink.

They walked out of the café together and down toward her car. Jade would be heading south, and Drew was going to Beverly Hills, so it was time to say good-bye. She felt her chest tighten slightly as they both came to a stop next to her car.

She felt the urge to kiss him as he stared into her eyes.

"You have really pretty eyes," he said.

"Thanks."

"I've never seen eyes that green."

Jade blushed. "That's how I got my name. Mom was going to call me Emma, but when she held me in the hospital, she said my eyes were so green she had to call me Jade."

"It suits you."

Jade blushed even further, looking down at the ground.

"I'll be in touch," Drew said before reaching up and brushing a loose strand of hair behind her ear.

She shied away, and he chuckled softly.

"You might want to work on that flinch, Ariel," he told her. "You should look like you enjoy me touching you."

"Sorry. I wasn't expecting it," she lied.

He leaned forward, pressed his cheek against hers and whispered, "We need to appear comfortable around each other, so I might touch you even when we're alone, just to help us get used to it. Is that okay?"

Jade's chest started thudding again, and she gulped before nodding her head. Surely he could hear the pounding in her chest and see how nervous he made her. Her eyes closed involuntarily as a spicy scent wafted around them and she breathed him deeply; damn, he smelled good. His warm cheek pressed against hers for a second longer before he pulled back slightly and pressed his lips to where his cheek had just rested.

"I'll see you soon," he said softly after he kissed her cheek, and then he was gone.

The wind whipped her hair around her face as she stood on the street and continued to breathe in the delicious scent that lingered after he walked away. She raised her hand up and lightly touched her cheek in the spot where his lips had been just a moment ago, smiling.

"Shit!" she said loudly, annoyed with herself for allowing Drew to affect her so much.

Just in that moment, an old man walked past and mumbled something about the youth of today being riffraff and using foul language. Jade didn't pay any attention to him, though, because she'd just realized she was starting to get a crush on her future husband. That was *not* good.

CHAPTER FIVE

Slam Dunk

Jade was pretty. Drew wasn't blind. He was well aware of how attractive she was. From their first meeting, he remembered her moss-green eyes and her strawberry curls, but what he hadn't remembered was the way her whole face lit up when she smiled, or how fucking amazing she smelled.

As he walked away from her on the street and headed home, he thought about the fact he would get to kiss her and touch her whenever he wanted with no strings attached. Well, he supposed being married was the biggest string of all; it was a fucking steel cable. But they weren't tied to each other; they had a clear plan that would allow them to part easily.

There was no doubt he was attracted to her, but that was a good thing. His parents and friends would never believe he was attracted to an ugly girl. As shallow as that sounded, it was the truth. He hoped his attraction would make things easier for them. He was drawn to her, which he prayed would make it easier for people to believe they were falling in love. He already wanted to touch her, so hopefully their affection would look natural—if she could hold back her flinching. Drew smiled; it really was adorable how nervous she was around him.

Jade never left Drew's thoughts as he walked, even as he entered the large foyer of his parents' house. He must have had a huge smile on his face, because his mom gave him a strange look.

"What's made you so happy?" she asked.

"I met a girl."

His mom's face lit up, and she leaned forward in her seat. She patted the cushion next to her on the couch, inviting him to sit down.

"Tell me," she said quietly.

Drew's mother had never really been the hands-on type, but they had a good relationship and talked about the things that mattered. Unlike his father, who he barely had anything to talk about with.

"Her name is Jade," Drew said, sitting down next to her.

He wasn't sure how much he should play it up. He wanted her to think that he was dating Jade, but he didn't want to be a gushing, sissy fool.

"Do we know her family?" Laura asked.

Typical. Of course his mother's first question would be about her social standing. To be honest, Drew had no idea about Jade's background. He made a mental note to ask her some questions next time they spoke.

"No, I don't think so. I met her last week, and I just saw her again. I gave her my number, and we'll probably meet up again soon."

There, that sounded realistic…he hoped.

"Is she in the business?"

"In a way." She wasn't a film actor, but she was a character actor. Drew thought he could stretch it to say she was.

"Where did she go to school?"

Shit. He didn't know *anything* about Jade or her life. He had her cell phone number and an address in the valley, but apart from that, he knew nothing about her. He couldn't believe he hadn't thought to get more information. The conversations they'd had on the phone hadn't really gone into much personal detail, concentrating more on setting up the plan than getting to know each other.

"Ahhh…we've only just met, so I don't know much about her yet," he said honestly.

"Oh, well, I'd love to meet her," Laura pushed.

"When the time is right. Just let me get to know her and see if it's something that might turn into a relationship. There's no point in you meeting her if we only have one date and don't like each other." He knew he couldn't seem too eager. He'd never brought a girl home before because there had never been anyone he'd been interested in longer than a few dates. He needed to make sure he wasn't acting out of character, or his parents would be suspicious.

"I suppose you're right." Laura sighed. "I just want to see you happy, Andrew. I want you to know love."

"Well, maybe this girl is the one," he said, smiling.

His mother patted his knee and nodded her head. "I hope so. May I tell your father?"

"Sure," he said with a shrug of his shoulders. "But there's not much to tell yet."

His father was going to have to find out about Jade some time, so it didn't matter if it was sooner rather than later. And, to be honest, Drew would rather not have to tell him himself, because he knew the mocking look he would get. His dad would assume Jade was just another girl that Drew was only semi-interested in and wouldn't take it seriously.

Well, Drew would show him. In a few months, they would be married, and Drew would have access to his own money. But, up until that point, he still had to support himself, and that meant charity work. He'd tried his best to think of something he could do, but working in a soup kitchen or volunteering at a church weren't really things that would hold his interest. He knew his mom would have some advice as she'd been doing charity work for years, and he'd been waiting for some time to bring it up.

"Mom, can I talk to you about something?"

"Of course, honey," she replied, her hand still on his knee.

"Dad suggested I do some charity work, and I wanted your opinion on what I should do."

"Well," she said, titling her head. "There are lots of different things you could do. I do charity work for homeless youths mostly, but I've also done fundraisers for AIDS research and animal shelters. The key is to find something you enjoy doing and see if you can find a way to help someone by doing it. You know, I believe many of the high schools take on volunteer sports coaches. Would that interest you?"

"That sounds perfect," Drew said, liking the idea. It wouldn't even feel like working. Sports was something he could definitely help kids with.

"I think I actually heard of a school in south LA that's looking for a basketball coach. I could put in a call for you if you'd like."

"That would be great, Mom!" He kissed her cheek and stood up. "I think I'm going to have an early night."

"Good night, dear. Oh, and Drew?" Laura called as he walked down the hallway toward the large mahogany staircase that lead up to the wing of the house where his bedroom was.

He stopped and turned back to look at her, cocking an eyebrow in question.

"I have a good feeling about this Jade." She smiled.

"Me too." He laughed as he made his way upstairs.

After a quick shower, Drew pulled on a pair of old sweat pants and lay down on his bed. He hadn't been able to get Jade out of his head. It was a conflicting feeling. Part of him was happy about that; it would make their ruse all the more realistic, but at the same time, he didn't want to *actually* develop feelings for her. Yes, they would be married, but they had to keep it professional. The last thing they needed was for either of them to develop feelings and ruin the whole plan.

No, he would make sure this stayed a business arrangement. It shouldn't be too hard; all they had to do was stay focused.

He wiggled down into a more comfortable position on the bed and closed his eyes. His mother would probably have arranged for him to start *work* by tomorrow, so he wanted to get in as much sleep as he could.

Hours later, he rolled over, and his arm slipped around something warm and soft. He half-opened his eyes and saw a large mess of red curls. Breathing in deeply, he recognized Jade's sweet scent and smiled.

"Jade," he breathed softly as he snuggled in closer to her back.

His fingers traced figure eights on the silky skin of her stomach as he lightly peppered kisses on the back of her neck. She hummed in contentment, reaching her hand back to run her fingers through his hair. Arousal swept through his body, and his hands traveled up her torso to lightly stroke the underside of her bare breasts.

Jade pushed her hips back against his hardening length, causing him to hiss at the contact. Drew had no idea how she'd gotten into his bedroom, but he wasn't going to fight it. She seemed to be as into this as he was, and they could just put it down as a bonding exercise.

"You like that?" She laughed as she wiggled her hips over his cock, causing more friction than he was ready for, and he let out a soft grunt.

"Shhh, don't wake the baby," she whispered as she rolled over to face him, her eyes seeing right into his soul as she sleepily smiled back at him.

"Baby?" Drew questioned, confused.

"Margaret...our daughter," Jade said slowly. "What's up with you?" Her hands gently cupped his face.

Drew froze. They had a daughter...named Margaret, after his grandmother? He didn't remember that, and come to think of it, he didn't remember Jade coming into bed either, let alone her being naked.

Drew looked around the room as the soft dawn light filtered through the windows. They weren't in his parents' house. From the look of it, they were lying in Gran's bedroom in the house she'd left him. How had they gotten there?

He broke out of Jade's grasp and sat up. Suddenly everything went dark. He blinked a few times and looked around the room again. He was back in his own room at his parents' house. He turned to look down at the bed, but Jade was nowhere to be seen. The only remnant of her being in the bed was the throbbing erection in his lap.

He groaned loudly and fell back onto the pillow, swinging his arm over his eyes. The dream was so intense and realistic that he could still slightly smell her in the air. He had to put a stop to dreams like that right away.

A shrill whistle blew from across the court, and Drew jumped. He was usually comfortable in basketball courts, but that was when he was playing with his friends and the only pressure was to win. Now he had a group of young boys staring him down.

"Okay, guys, this is Drew. He's going to be coaching you for the rest of the season. Let's all give him a huge Tigers welcome!" the teacher called with more enthusiasm than should be legal.

The boys all stared at their new coach. None of them looked impressed.

"Uh...hi?" Drew said, feeling like an idiot. He had no idea how to talk to kids.

"What a dick!" a young blond boy scoffed, and the rest of the group started to laugh.

Drew noticed one boy in particular who stood back from the others a little. He was tall and looked to be about sixteen years old. His shiny black hair was tied back in a loose ponytail, and his clothes were ratty and slightly too big for him — like hand-me-downs. In fact, when Drew looked around, all the boys appeared to be wearing second-hand clothes.

"Let's get started," he said, trying to put as much authority in his voice as he could, and pointed at them. "You, you, and you are on one team, and you, you, and you are on the other. Go!"

They all stood around for a minute, looking at each other as if deciding whether or not they were going to accept Drew as their coach. He knew he would have to take some action if he was going to lead these boys, so he grabbed the ball, dribbled it up to the hoop and did a slam dunk.

"Are you ladies coming or what?" he yelled.

All the boys smiled at each other and raced out onto the court. The teacher nodded and clapped Drew on the back before handing him the whistle and heading back into one of the classrooms.

The game began, and Drew had to admit those boys could play. He was sure if he was up against them, he would have to play at his best to win. He had to break up two almost-fights, and he blew his whistle more times than he could count for traveling and contact. Those boys played rough, but they were good.

As the sun started to set, Drew began to get tired. His shirt was soaked with sweat, and he could feel it clinging to his back. All he wanted to do was go home and take a shower. He looked at his watch and saw it was almost six. They'd started playing straight after school at three, so that was three hours of coaching — not too bad for his first day.

He blew the whistle loudly to get everyone's attention.

"Okay, next hoop wins!" he said loudly. Luckily the game was tied, so it made the boys play even harder, trying to get that final basket.

Drew ran up and down the court as the ball was thrown from one end to the other and back again. The blond boy who had called him a dick threw the ball hard, trying to get it to one of his teammates at the other end of the court. The ball flew over the hoop, past the fence and out onto the street.

"Ouch!" a woman yelled, and everyone on the court froze.

"Shit. You hit someone, Dave," one of the boys said.

The tall boy with the black ponytail raced out to collect the ball, and Drew followed him, ready to apologize to the poor woman. When he got outside the fence, he was stunned to see Jade standing there, rubbing her head and talking to the boy.

"Jade?" he asked.

"Drew?" she replied, sounding just as shocked as he felt.

"Are you okay?" he asked. He reached out to her, but pulled his hand back.

"Yeah. I'm fine. I'll probably have a headache, but I'm not injured," she explained as she continued to rub her head.

"We're really sorry," the kid said as he took the ball and ran back onto the court.

"What are you doing here?" Drew asked her, wondering if she was there to see him.

"I live just down there." She pointed down the street.

"Oh. I'm coaching basketball here now. Hey, what are you doing tonight?"

"Apart from holding an icepack to my head?" she said with a warm smile. "I'm meeting some friends for a late dinner, but I have some time before that."

"If you don't mind waiting for a few minutes, I'd love to walk you home so we can get to know each other a bit more."

"Yeah, that sounds good," she said and followed him into the school grounds.

Drew pointed to the bleachers around the court and asked her to take a seat while he packed up. When he got back over to the group of boys, they were all laughing and staring at Jade. One of them whistled as Drew got closer.

"Is that your woman?" the whistler asked.

Drew looked over his shoulder at Jade and then turned back to the boys.

"Yes, that's my girl," he said, smiling. It was surprising how nice it was to say out loud.

"She's a slam dunk, coach!" Dave said loudly.

All the boys started wolf-whistling and making obscene gestures in Jade's direction. Drew was surprised by how much it bothered him.

"Okay, that's enough. Dave, you just scored yourself pack-up duty. Gather up the balls and make sure they get put away in the sports shed. I'll see you all at three tomorrow."

The boys all nodded and cheered—all except Dave, who grumbled as he collected the scattered basketballs lying around the court.

Drew turned to walk over to Jade but noticed one boy not joining in on the horseplay with the other kids. The tall boy with the black ponytail that Drew thought held a lot of promise kept his distance from the others. He walked slowly toward the gate and paused to let a group of the boys pass him. Drew wondered why he wasn't fitting in.

"Hey, kid," he called out.

The boy turned around to look at Drew with a curious expression. Drew jogged over to him and held out his hand.

"I'm Drew. I didn't get your name."

"Alex," he said softly, looking at the ground and not accepting the outstretched hand.

Drew pulled his hand back and ducked his head, trying to catch the boy's eye.

"You played great today, Alex. I think you might be the best player on the team," Drew told him honestly.

Alex looked up skeptically. "Mario plays better than me, and so does Ben."

Drew shook his head. "The others have their technical skills down really well, but you have a natural talent they don't have. The way you move with the ball is very fluid, and that's something that can't be taught. As for the practical skills, well, I'd be happy to give you some private training sessions if you'd like."

Alex beamed at Drew as a huge grin spread over his face. "Really?" he asked, sounding as if he couldn't believe the offer.

A part of Drew couldn't believe he'd offered, either. It wasn't like him to do something for someone other than himself. He didn't think he was a selfish person per se, but at the same time, he didn't really go out of his way to help other people.

"How about after the group practice tomorrow?" he suggested.

Alex nodded, and his whole face lit up. "Thanks, coach!"

"No problem. I'll see you tomorrow. And call me Drew," he said as he clapped Alex on the shoulder and turned back to see Jade smiling at them. He walked over to her and sat down in the hard plastic seat on her right.

"Hey, you," he said with a smile.

"Hey," she chuckled.

Drew was shocked by how happy he was to see her. It had been a completely unexpected surprise, but it felt nice to be around her.

"Shall we get going?" she asked.

"Lead the way," he said, holding his hand out to allow her to go first.

They walked down the road and turned the corner. The streets were loud and busy; there were people everywhere. It was a nice atmosphere. Not like the street his parents lived on, where he felt like if he stepped on the wrong piece of grass someone would call the police. Jade led them to a Spanish-inspired complex of villas that looked like they were caked in dirt. She let them inside, and he looked around the room.

Her apartment was small, unless there was a huge area down the hallway that he couldn't see, but he doubted it. The paint on the walls was peeling, and the furniture was old and ratty. In fact, where he sat on the couch, it felt like it was missing a spring.

Jade stood nervously in the doorway, and Drew wondered if she was embarrassed about where she lived. It honestly didn't bother him at all. "Are you okay?" she asked.

"Just tired," he said.

"Oh!" she exclaimed, running out of the room and down the hallway. She reappeared a moment later and handed him a stack of papers. "I signed your contract," she explained before sitting down in the faded armchair with ripped material on the backrest.

"Thanks. Were you happy with all the conditions?" He flipped through the pages. Her elegant signature was at the bottom of each one.

"Yes, it's all very generous," she said, nodding. "I would get you a drink, but I'm sorry, I don't really have anything to offer you." Her cheeks turned a light pink.

"Just water would be great. I'm exhausted from the game."

Her blush got even darker as she looked him up and down and then went into the kitchen. Drew wondered what that was about.

He must have been a horrible sight. He could still feel the dampness of his shirt, and he knew his face was probably flushed.

He started to feel embarrassed, wondering if he should go home, but then he realized if they were going to be living together eventually, she would see him much worse than this. The thought of his hair first thing in the morning made him chuckle. She was in for a treat.

Jade came back holding a glass of water that had little condensation beads on the outside of the glass. He took it from her gratefully and swallowed the whole glass in a few large gulps.

"So, I told my parents about us," he said.

"Oh? How'd they take it?"

"Well, my mother wants to meet you, but I told her to give me some time to get to know you better first."

That reminded him that he wanted to ask her some questions about her life. "Speaking of which, shall we play a round of twenty questions? I thought it might be a nice way to break the ice. You know...to get to know each other?"

"Sure," she said with a casual shrug. She went and sat on the faded chair again, curling her legs up underneath her. "You go first."

Drew thought for a moment. "So, you're a character actor at Disneyland. Can I see you in your costume?"

"You don't find it weird?"

Drew shook his head. "My dad's an actor. I grew up on movie sets. Trust me; I've seen way weirder costumes."

"Well, I'm not allowed to take the costumes out of the Park. But if you come one day to go on the rides, stop by the princess photo house, and I'll come see you when I have a break."

"Do you wear a mermaid tail and seashells?"

"No. I wear a gown."

"Could you wear a tail and seashells at home? Just for me?"

She choked. "Um...well, I thought we weren't going to be intimate like that."

Drew smacked himself in the side of the head. "Sorry. That was stupid."

He couldn't believe he'd said that. He'd already acknowledged he was attracted to her, but after his dream the night before, he'd promised himself that he'd keep it professional. Here he was asking her to dress up for him? He needed to change the subject.

"You said when we first met that you'd moved from Florida."

"Yeah, a couple of years ago for college."

"What did you study?"

"Marine biology at Fullerton. I grew up in Sarasota. I was at the beach all the time and had a summer job at an aquarium while I was in high school. I love the ocean."

"So, why do you work at a theme park if you're a marine biologist?" He sat forward with his elbows resting on his knees.

She chewed her lip, and her eyes fell to the floor. "I never finished. I wasn't expecting LA to be so expensive, and I couldn't support myself. I started working at the Park over the summer to save up for the following semester, but I just never went back. I'm another college drop-out statistic."

Drew frowned. "That sucks." A thought occurred to him, and his face brightened. He might be able to help her make her life better. "After we're married, you'll have enough money to finish your degree."

Jade smiled, her eyes lighting up, and she leaned back in her chair. "I'd thought about that."

They smiled at each other, and Drew felt reassured they were doing the right thing. He'd been curious why Jade would be willing to marry a man she didn't know. Sure, money was a strong motivator, but the potential for the life she wanted made a lot more sense.

The room had become dark as the sun set, and Jade reached over to turn on a lamp.

"I'd better get going," he said, standing up.

"It's okay. You don't have to leave."

"Are you sure?"

"I'm sure. I haven't asked you any questions yet."

"Okay, hit me." Drew relaxed back into the sofa and crossed his legs.

"How is your mom is going to feel about you dating someone who's dead broke? Won't she think I'm just after your money?"

"Don't worry. My mother may be a snob, but she's also a romantic. If she believes we're in love, she won't say anything about where you work."

Jade looked slightly appeased and gave Drew a shy smile.

"Any more questions?"

"What were you doing this afternoon with those kids?" she asked.

"Oh! Well, I've decided to do some charity work, and I love playing basketball, so coaching seemed like a fun way to give something back to the community."

"And what where you talking about with that boy after the game?"

"Hang on. You already asked your question," Drew said, narrowing his eyes at her playfully, reminding her of their twenty questions game and causing her to blush again. "But I'll let you off...just this once. That's Alex. He's got a lot of natural talent, so I offered him some private lessons to help develop his skills. I think he could really be a great player."

She smiled. "That's nice of you."

Drew wouldn't have been surprised if there was some red rising up his neck. He wasn't sure what it was about Jade, but all his emotions were heightened around her. Instead of just feeling happy, he felt content. It was strange; no one had ever done that for him before.

Suddenly Jade jumped out of her chair. "What's the time?" she asked hurriedly.

"Um, almost seven," he said, looking at his watch.

"Oh, shoot! I'm supposed to be at my friend's house at seven thirty." She sighed as she ran off down the hallway. He could hear drawers and closet doors opening and closing.

"Oh, okay. Well, I guess I should go," he called out.

She didn't respond, but after a few minutes, she reappeared in a pair of casual jeans and an off-the-shoulder sweatshirt that was slightly too big for her. Her hair was out and cascading down her back in loose curls. She'd removed the makeup she'd worn to work, and her skin was glowing. She looked beautiful and sexy all at the same time. Drew suddenly hoped that the friend she was going to visit wasn't a guy. But he'd told her it was okay for them to see other people. He suddenly felt very confused.

He wanted to leave her thinking about him just as he knew he'd be thinking about her, so he walked over and put one hand on her waist, the other cupping her neck as he looked into her eyes.

"Jade, will you go on a date with me tomorrow night?" he asked in a soft, gravelly voice.

She opened her mouth, but no words came out. He smiled and leaned in, dragging his nose up her jaw. The fingers resting on her waist were rubbing small circles, and he slipped them under the hem of her shirt so he was touching her bare skin. He had a brief flashback to doing something similar in his dream the night before, but he pushed that thought aside.

"Umm…" She tried to speak, but couldn't seem to get anything out.

"I'd really love to continue learning all your secrets," he whispered in her ear. He could feel her rapid pulse as he caressed her neck, and he breathed out, intentionally blowing air over the soft skin of her throat.

He took a tiny step closer to her so his chest was pressed flush against her, the heat of her body radiating all around him.

"That would be nice," she whispered back.

He moved the hand from her waist up to the small of her back and pulled her into a tight hug.

"I'll call you in the morning to make the arrangements. Have fun tonight." He chuckled as he pulled away from her.

She gulped loudly and nodded. He noticed her eyes were slightly glazed over, and he felt a smug feeling come over him; if she *was* going to meet a guy, he knew that he would still be on her mind… not that it mattered to him.

He released her and walked quickly to the door. His hand rested on the doorknob, but before he let himself out, he turned back to her.

"Oh, and Jade? You might want to work on the stunned deer look before tomorrow night. Our first official date will be a test to see if we can pull this off, and we wouldn't want people to think that you're afraid of me or something." He winked and gave her a broad smile.

"I…I will," she said with a nod.

"See you tomorrow," he reminded her as he walked out the door.

Quickly, he walked down the stairs and found himself back on the street. All the way home he thought about Jade's obvious reactions to him. She always seemed so nervous around him, and anytime he tested the physical boundaries, she clammed up. That could be a problem.

He knew being touched by someone you didn't know was slightly uncomfortable, but she'd agreed to be a part of this situation, so she'd just have to man up and get over her nerves. Drew decided that on their date the following night he would dial up the physical touching to try to desensitize her as quickly as possible.

Bring on the first official date, he thought to himself as he walked back to the school to get his car.

CHAPTER SIX

The Importance of Night Butt

"Oh, shit!" Jade swore as her phone started to ring. She rummaged through her handbag and dropped her keys. Bending down, she grabbed them off her welcome mat and held the phone to her ear with her shoulder as she shoved the key in the lock and swung the heavy door open.

"Are you home yet?" Clare asked impatiently, forgoing a greeting.

"I'm just walking through the door now," Jade said as she tossed her keys and handbag onto the kitchen counter and walked over to the couch.

"Well, don't even think about sitting down. Tell me what you're planning on wearing tonight," Clare demanded.

With a loud sigh, Jade bypassed the couch and headed down the hallway to her bedroom. Lying on the bed were the clothes she'd picked out before she went to work that morning.

"I'm going to wear my dark denim jeans and that black halter top you insisted I buy," she said, hoping her selection would please Clare.

"Hmm. Are those the jeans that hug your butt?"

"Yes, the ones that you said my ass looked sexy in when we met for brunch last weekend." Jade nodded, even though she knew that Clare couldn't see the action.

"Nope! They won't do *at all!*" her friend replied firmly.

"What?" Jade gasped. "You specifically told me that those jeans made my ass look hot."

"They make your *morning* ass look hot," Clare corrected. "You need a whole other look for night butt."

Jade froze with her mouth open, not quite sure how to respond to Clare's logic.

"Huh?" was all she managed.

Clare sighed and began to talk slowly, as if Jade was stupid. "Your butt is perkier in the morning, so those jeans emphasize that. At night, gravity has had a whole day to pull your cheeks down, so you need a different style of pants to get the same sexy look." She spoke as if it were the simplest concept in the world to grasp.

"I see. And what kind of style do I need for night butt?" Jade asked, playing along.

"Well, something firm, to hold your butt in place, but something softer than denim so it's sexy."

Again, Jade was silent. Clare wanted something to hold her butt in place? Where did she think her butt was going to run off to?

"I've got it!" Clare shrieked. "Wear those three-quarter black capri pants that make your legs look longer."

Jade pulled open her closet and grabbed the black pants off the hanger before smirking. "My legs longer? I thought these were supposed to give me nice night butt."

"Oh, well, *those* pants will do both! They're tailored, so your ass will look phenomenal, plus your legs will look amazing," Clare said proudly.

"Problem." Jade stared at the pants she had just laid down on the bed next to the black halter top. "I look like I'm going to a funeral."

"You're right. You can't wear black pants and a black top on your first official date with this mystery hottie…What about the red wrap-around shirt I bought you for your birthday?"

Jade groaned. The red shirt Clare had bought her showed way too much cleavage and was so tight it looked painted on.

"I, um, don't know where it is," she said while staring at it hanging in the closet with its tags still attached.

"Liar." Clare laughed. "Just try it on."

Grumbling to herself, Jade pulled it out of the closet and held it up, pulling on the material to see if she could stretch it out at all.

"Stop messing around and just put it on," Clare encouraged through the phone.

With an exaggerated sigh so Clare would know she wasn't happy, Jade took her T-shirt off and dropped it on the floor before wrapping the red fabric around herself and tying the straps at the front under her bust. She looked into the mirror and rolled her eyes. Her breasts looked like they would fall out of the flimsy fabric if she sneezed too hard.

"I'm not wearing it, Clare," Jade insisted.

"Take a photo and send it to me," her friend insisted.

Jade flicked through her cell phone's menu until she found the camera, took a quick photo of herself in the mirror, and sent it in a text message.

"Oh, God! What have you done to that shirt?" Clare shrieked when she saw the photo. "You *cannot* wear it like that!"

"That's what I'm saying," Jade agreed.

"You've tied it up all wrong. Untie it and wrap the straps the other way so that they tie at the back, in the small of your back."

Jade undid the straps and wrapped them around herself, awkwardly reaching around to tie them at the back instead of the front. When she turned around and saw her refection in the mirror, she was shocked to see the difference it had made. The top now looked classy and elegant. Even though there was still cleavage showing, it was sensual, not slutty.

"Photo," Clare chirped. Jade gladly took another photo and sent it to her.

She stood admiring herself in the mirror while she waited for Clare to open the text message and cursed herself for not wearing the shirt before. What a waste it had been sitting in her closet for the past few months.

"Oh! It's perfect! Now…shoes," Clare cooed.

An hour later, Jade climbed into a taxi to go and meet Drew. The nerves and excitement that she'd felt before the "dress up Jade" session came flooding back. She and Drew were actually going on a real date, and if his moves during the dinner invitation were anything to go by, she'd be melting in her seat.

As she thought of Drew, images of him on the basketball court flooded her mind. The tight T-shirt that clung to his upper arms and showed the definition in his chest, making her want to growl and bite his shoulder. The sweat that glistened on his skin as he ran around the court. The crooked smile he gave without even realizing it when he'd seen her unexpectedly…And those shorts, the baggy shorts that hugged his ass and only hinted at what lay beneath them…Jade hadn't been able to stop thinking about those shorts.

"Where should I let you out?" the taxi driver asked, breaking her out of her shorts-induced haze.

"Umm, just on the corner here is fine," she replied as she looked out the window.

"Twenty-seven bucks," the driver replied and held his hand out expectedly.

She passed him three ten-dollar bills and climbed out of the car. He took off just as she slammed the door closed, and she felt lucky not to have been knocked over.

"Jade!" Drew's voice called, and she spun around to see him running across the street and waving, with a huge smile on his face.

She couldn't help but smile back at him and scolded herself for being so transparent. She was supposed to *act* like she was falling in love with him, not actually *do* it.

"You look gorgeous!" Drew exclaimed as he slowed to a walk and stopped in front of her, his eyes traveling over her body.

"Thanks. I wasn't sure how formal I should dress," she said with a shrug. The truth was she knew she looked great.

She allowed herself to take him in. His hair was standing in all directions but still looked perfectly styled. His sleeves were rolled halfway up his forearms, and the top button of his slate gray button-up shirt was open, showing just a hint of chest hair. His dress pants hit low on his hips.

"You look perfect," he said with a smile, mirroring her thought of him. "Shall we?" He reached out and laced his fingers through hers gently, squeezing and pulling her close to walk beside him.

"Are you hungry?" he asked, leaning down and whispering in her ear.

"I could eat."

"Great. There's somewhere I'd like to show you. Come on."

He led her back to his car, and they drove through a residential area. Drew pulled up outside a house in Los Feliz.

Jade looked around curiously but still couldn't see any reason why Drew would have stopped them in this spot. There was no restaurant or café anywhere in sight.

"Come on," he said, smiling as he took her hand and pulled her up the driveway. "What do you think?" He stood in front of the porch and threw his arms out wide.

She looked around, still confused. "Umm, it's great. What is it?"

Drew chuckled and pulled a set of keys out of his pocket.

"This is the house I inherited from my Gran. Once we get married, this is where we'll live." He turned and jogged up the few stairs to the doorway.

Jade's mouth fell open as she stared up at the tall, historical, and probably extremely expensive house in front of her. This was where she would be living? Drew unlocked the door and held it open for her with an excited grin.

When Drew had called this place a house, she'd pictured something similar to where her parents lived, but nicer. She had *not* been expecting to step foot into a two-story villa with a pool and tennis court in the back yard. She looked around the large entryway and marveled at the stained-glass windows that lit up one side of the room. One of the windows had been smashed in, but the others hinted that they had once looked majestic.

"Would you like a tour?" Drew asked after he had closed the door and switched on the lights.

She nodded, unable to speak.

Drew moved through the rooms, pointing out the parlor, the formal lounge, kitchen, butler's pantry, and living room before they moved upstairs to see the three large bedrooms, a study, and two more bathrooms.

"There is also an attic. It was used as the butler's quarters," he explained with a shrug.

Jade wondered if having a butler was something Drew was used to. She would have to ask him about that one day. At the moment, though, she was in too much shock to think of questioning him.

"This will be your bedroom and en suite," Drew said as he indicated a door opposite the master bedroom suite.

"May I?" she asked timidly.

"Of course," Drew replied with a smile.

Jade opened the door and gasped when she saw the huge four-poster bed and double glass doors that opened out onto a small private balcony. The furniture was all antique and looked to be very expensive. She could just see herself tripping over the rug and crashing into the full-length mirror standing by the dresser.

"Sorry about all the dust. I'll have some cleaners come through here before we actually move in," he explained.

"It's beautiful," she said in awe as she took in the smaller details around the room. She stuck her head into the en suite and saw that the counters, bathtub, and shower were all made of a white marble with gray flecks through it.

"The balcony overlooks a park. It's a bit too dark to see it now, but I'm sure you'll enjoy the view," Drew said as he came up behind her.

"I'm sure I will," she agreed, nodding.

She wasn't sure why, but she felt both extremely calm and completely on edge all at the same time, and it was very overwhelming.

"I'm going to be fixing it up little by little as I can afford it, and hopefully it'll be livable by the time we're ready to move in," Drew told her.

Jade cocked an eyebrow at him curiously. This place was in much better shape than where she was currently living. She couldn't see anything that would make it unlivable except the broken window in the front room.

"Come on, let's go downstairs and get comfortable," Drew said, reaching his hand out and grasping hers tightly.

He pulled her down the grand staircase, and she let her free hand gently slide along the polished wood of the banister. Everything was so elegant; she wondered if she would ever feel comfortable living there.

"Shall we eat?" Drew asked, turning to face her as he pulled his cell phone out of his pocket.

"Uh, sure," she said, wondering if he was going to cook for her or if he had a chef stashed away somewhere in one of the ornate cupboards.

Drew pulled out his cell phone, and wanting to give him some privacy, she wandered into the informal living room. That was a room she could almost feel comfortable in. The couches were nice but not antique, and the walls were painted a light blue that made the room feel open and breezy. There was an old-fashioned turn-knob television in the corner and doilies on the small tables scattered around the room. It was obvious that an older lady had lived there.

Jade sat cautiously on the couch and pulled the small decorative cushion from behind her back to hold against her chest.

"Change of plans. Can you bring it to the Los Feliz property instead?" Drew's phone conversation floated from he stood at the foot of the staircase to where she was sitting. "Great, see you soon."

"There you are," he exclaimed as his head popped around the doorway.

"Here I am," she agreed with a small smile.

"I had originally planned for us to have a picnic in the park, but I wondered if maybe we could have it here instead?" he asked coyly as he ran his left hand up through his hair.

"That sounds nice."

Drew frowned and walked over to her slowly, taking the seat beside her on the couch.

"You don't seem very comfortable, Ariel. Is everything okay?" Concern laced his words.

"Yes...I think I'm just a bit overwhelmed. This house is just so...so...huge, and I'm not used to being around such nice things," she tried to explain. "Plus, you make me nervous."

She slapped her hand over her mouth in horror when she realized what she'd said. If she could have given herself a face-palm without him seeing it, she would have.

He gave her a smug smile and leaned in a bit closer, brushing his cheek against hers. "Does this make you nervous too?" he asked in a deep whisper.

"No," she said with as much confidence in her voice as she could, but he seemed to know better and cocked an eyebrow at her. She gulped and then slowly nodded her head.

One side of his mouth twitched upward, but he kept a stern look on his face. "I thought we talked about this. Do we need to do some desensitization exercises?" he whispered, leaning closer to her so that she could feel his warm breath cascading over her cheek.

She couldn't speak, she couldn't move, she couldn't even breathe steadily. All she could do was stare into his deep blue eyes and feel her heart thundering in her chest. A part of her registered that his fingers were gently stroking her cheek as his other hand reached up and tucked a loose strand of hair behind her ear.

Jade's own hand moved, without her consent, and snaked up his chest and around his neck. Her fingers grasped the soft hair at the base of his neck. He smiled and brushed his lips against her cheek before stopping by her ear, whispering so softly that she barely heard him, "Good girl."

Jade was shocked with herself. Two minutes ago, she'd been so nervous she could barely move, and now touching Drew seemed like the most natural thing in the world. She didn't just want to touch him; she needed to touch him.

"Ahem." A throat cleared from behind them, and Drew jumped back from her quickly, shock on his face.

"Oh, Caroline! I wasn't expecting you so quickly," Drew said as he stood and took the large picnic basket the woman was holding. "Caroline, this is Jade. Jade, this is my family's housekeeper, Caroline."

"Hello," Jade said politely, but she knew her face must have been as red as a tomato. She let the word *housekeeper* sink into her brain and then rolled her eyes. So Drew *was* used to having a staff to serve his every whim. That was one less question she would have to ask.

"Will there be anything else, Drew?" Caroline asked.

"No, thank you," he said with a smile, and Caroline winked at him.

It looked like they had a friendly relationship, and that comforted Jade a little. They said you could always tell the character of a person by how they treated the people in their employ.

"Have a good night," Caroline said before turning and letting herself out.

"So…you have a maid?" Jade asked with a half smile.

"Well, my parents do," he replied with a shrug. He placed the large basket down on the coffee table and then started pushing the armchairs against the walls.

"What are you doing?" she asked as he came over and pushed the couch back, with her still sitting on it.

"Making room for our picnic." He laughed.

She watched curiously as he pulled a blanket out of the basket and laid it on the floor before kicking his shoes off and kneeling down.

"Join me?" he asked, holding his hand out.

She slid off the couch and crawled across to the blanket, where she kicked off her own shoes and curled her legs under herself.

Drew gave her a smile and started to unpack the basket. Jade wasn't sure what she was expecting him to have brought for them to eat, but she was pleasantly surprised to see salad, sandwiches, and fruit. There was a part of her that had half-expected him to pull out seafood and caviar.

"I hope this is okay. I didn't want to do anything too fancy and set your standards too high. I'd have nowhere to build to," he said with a wink.

"It's perfect," she assured him as she reached out and took one of the turkey sandwiches off the plate.

"Drink?" he asked as he pulled a bottle of white wine from the basket and expertly removed the cork.

"Thanks," she said through a mouthful of food, and Drew smiled at her again before handing her a glass.

"You know, it's kind of funny that you've trained to be a marine biologist and you got cast as Ariel." He laughed and took another drink from his wine glass.

Jade rolled her eyes. "That was a complete coincidence. I think I was cast purely for my hair."

"Nah, you must be good at what you do. Disney only has the best actors in their parks. They have a reputation to uphold."

"I'm really lucky. I actually love the job. The auditions were brutal but worth it."

"What was it like growing up in Florida?" he asked, changing the subject.

She shrugged. "It was normal, I guess. My parents were one of the few who weren't divorced, so I guess I was different from my friends in that way, but my life was pretty boring. I did well in school, only had one boyfriend..."

Drew choked on his wine and spat it over the plate of sandwiches.

"Sorry," he said, looking mortified. He grabbed the plate of soggy bread and put it back in the basket, obviously thinking of the "out of sight, out of mind" philosophy.

"It's okay," she said, but she couldn't help but giggle a little. It was so nice to not be the clumsy fool in the room. It was a relief to know that Drew was just human, even if he was an extremely attractive human.

"What happened with your boyfriend?" he asked, and she noticed that his voice was a little harder than it had been before.

"Oh, nothing really. I left for LA, and he went to college in Boston. I haven't seen him since."

Drew nodded, but Jade could see he was thinking deeply about something.

"What about you? Any ex-girlfriends hiding in your closet?"

Drew laughed. "I'm not the type of guy who has girlfriends. There have been many girls, but no one I care to remember."

That troubled Jade. He sounded so cold and unfeeling in his disregard for the women in his past. Even though her ex-boyfriend hadn't been the love of her life, she still thought fondly of him. If Drew was that cold toward the other women he'd dated, how could she ever expect him to be a husband? She stopped her train of thought and had to remind herself *again* that he wasn't *really* going to be her husband. She felt her mood sink instantly.

Jade looked at the half-eaten sandwich in her hand and suddenly didn't feel very hungry anymore. She was angry at herself for forgetting so easily that this was all just a financial arrangement. Drew didn't actually care about her, and she shouldn't be allowing herself to care about him, either. It was so easy to forget that when they were sitting so close having a good time, when they'd just shared such an intimate moment on the couch.

Drew was oblivious to Jade's change in mood, and he kept eating. He poured her another glass of wine. "So, what about your future? What plans do you have besides finishing school?"

She stared at him for a moment, seriously thinking about telling him that she wanted out of their agreement. She suddenly didn't know how she could have ever thought of getting herself involved with a fake marriage with a man who cared nothing for the women in his life. How would he think of *her* once he'd gotten what he'd needed and they'd parted ways? Would he laugh and think of her as pathetic? Would he try to forget her, the same way he'd said he didn't want to remember the other women from his past?

But she couldn't stay mad at him. He was looking at her with his soulful blue eyes and that contented, crooked smile, and she couldn't help but want to be around him. And it wasn't like she wasn't going to benefit from this arrangement; a million dollars was a lot of money—and he was just handing it to her. Would it really matter if he didn't want to remember her? She was starting to feel dizzy from the whiplash of her thoughts.

"Sorry...what?" she asked.

"What do you have in mind for your future?" he repeated.

She thought for a moment. The only thing she really wanted was to have someone, to be in love, to be loved in return. But she couldn't exactly tell *him* that, so she gave her standard answer when someone asked her what she wanted from her life and she didn't want to seem like a pathetic love-sick fool.

"I'd love to travel," she said. It was true; traveling had always been something she was interested in.

"Oh, me too. My parents took me to Europe as a kid, but I'd like to see it again as an adult," he explained.

"I just want to see absolutely everything. Go everywhere and see *every single thing* the world has to offer. I want to walk along the Great Wall of China and swim the Great Barrier Reef in Australia. I want to crawl through the Vietcong tunnels and see the pyramids," she said.

"That's a pretty extensive list," Drew commented, looking impressed. "The one place in Europe I want to see again is Italy."

Drew slid across the blanket so he was sitting right next to her. He reached up, moving her hair over her shoulder so that the side of her neck was bare to him.

"*Bella Ariel, prometto di fare il vostro sogno si avvera,*" he whispered into her ear, causing shivers to run down her spine.

"Wh-What does that mean?" she asked, her voice huskier than she intended.

Drew leaned back, smiled, and shrugged before grabbing a shiny red apple out of the basket and taking a bite. She knew he wasn't going to tell her what he'd said, and in a way, that made it more romantic. It was almost as if knowing the words took some of their power away.

"What are *your* dreams?" she asked, trying to take the focus off of herself.

Drew took another bite of his apple and pondered the question. After swallowing, he shrugged again. "I don't really have any," he said.

"You don't have any dreams? There's nothing you want for your life?" she asked, shocked.

"Well sure, I want *things*. I want a nice house, comfortable finances—but those are just material things. I don't really have a goal or a purpose," he explained.

They sat in silence for a minute while Jade thought about what he'd said. "You know, I think there are a lot of people like that out there. People confuse things that they want with life goals."

"All I know is that I *want* a dream. I want something to want. I just don't have it yet," he said seriously.

"Well, that's a start," she replied, and stretched her hand out to hold his.

He smiled back at her and squeezed her hand. Jade couldn't help the way her heart swelled at the thought of spending the next year of her life with this man.

CHAPTER SEVEN

Getting Hers

Jade tossed and turned, flinging the sheets off her body.

"Go to sleep, damn it!" she mumbled to herself.

Inside, she felt restless, uneasy. No matter how many lullabies she sang in her mind, or how many sheep she pictured jumping behind her closed eyes, her body wouldn't relax. She felt like she needed a good, hard fuck.

It had been over a month since her last hook-up, and that hadn't even been very satisfying. She'd been placating herself with Mr. Right, the name she'd given her vibrating friend, but the thought of pulling him out and then having to clean him afterward was all too much. What she needed was a *man!*

Briefly, her mind turned to Drew. His blue eyes swam into her thoughts. Ideally he would be her choice, but she just couldn't bring herself to muddy that water. She had to keep her head on tight around him now. Imagine how hard that would be after they slept together. No, she had to find someone else.

Jade had never been a friends-with-benefits kind of girl. She'd had one-night stands when she was drunk, but never a repeat with the same guy. And she hadn't had a proper boyfriend since she'd moved away from home. Suddenly the idea of having someone, not a romantic someone, who she could call up for sex when it suited her, was very enticing. No strings, just orgasms. What a concept!

She wondered if one of the guys at work would be up for it. She knew they would be. Dancers tended to have higher libidos than other people, in Jade's experience. She thought it was from the connection they had with moving their body to a rhythm. Whatever it was, it translated into great sex.

Rick, one of the live stage performers, flirted with her constantly, and she knew he was single. Nerves built inside her, as well as something else, something good. Excitement. She promised herself that she'd talk to him about it at work the next day.

But, in the meantime, she'd make do with Mr. Right.

"Hey, princess," Rick said, handing her a cup of coffee.

"Rick…" She tried to give him what she hoped was a sexy smile. The nerves from the night before returned, and coffee slopped over the side of the cup as her hand shook.

"Oh, watch out! Man overboard," Rick said, chuckling and taking the cup from her.

"Sorry. Did I get it on you?"

"Just my shoe. No harm done. You okay?"

"Yeah, thanks." She took the cup back from him, making sure to stroke his hand.

His eyebrow arose just a touch, and she smiled at him, glad that he'd picked up on the energy she was putting out.

"So," he said, his cheeks going red. "What are you up to tonight?"

"Oh, nothing."

"Is that so?"

"Yep. What are you doing tonight?" She tried to keep her tone playful. All she kept thinking was *I might be having sex tonight!* The idea sent a thrill through her whole body.

"Taking you out."

She wanted to groan at the corny line but held it in.

"Yeah, that could work…Oh, damn it! I'm sorry. I just remembered I have plans for dinner. But maybe afterward?" She'd completely forgotten she'd agreed to have dinner with Drew.

"Afterward?" His voice cracked as he picked up her meaning. "Yeah. Yeah, okay."

"Here's my number. Give me a call at about ten. I should be home by then."

She scribbled her number on his hand and then walked away. She couldn't believe she'd just done it. A mixture of excitement and terror washed over her as she fled the staff room and went to get into her costume.

"Come on, Gertrude! Don't do this to me," Jade begged as she turned the key in her car's ignition. The engine sputtered and died.

"Shit." She kicked the door closed and ran the three blocks to the metro station. The train would take twice as long, so she texted Drew to let him know she'd be late.

She calculated her budget as the train took her to Hollywood. If she skimped on groceries and canceled her cable, she *should* be able to afford to get her car fixed.

"You look beautiful," Drew said when she walked up to him.

He leaned over and kissed her cheek, resting a hand on her hip, which he didn't remove after he pulled back. The smile on his face was radiant.

"Thanks." She'd taken a little extra care with her looks tonight, in case she had to go straight from dinner to meet Rick. Thankfully, the train ride hadn't wreaked havoc on her hair.

"So, I was thinking for dinner we could take a trek out to Long Beach and do the ghost-tour on the Queen Mary. What do you think?" He gave her an expectant look.

"Umm, actually, I was hoping we could have a quiet one. I wouldn't mind an early night."

His eyebrows shot up, and she chewed her lip. It was obviously not the answer he'd been expecting.

"What…Do you have plans later?" He chuckled.

Jade sucked in a breath. Here was her chance to just tell him the truth. They'd both agreed they could see other people on the side, so she wasn't doing anything wrong. But the way he looked at her, with affection and expectation, made her only want to be with him. All thoughts of Rick flew from her mind.

"No, nothing like that," she lied. "I'm just tired. It was a long day at work."

He smiled. "I really should come see you in action. When are you working next?"

"Tomorrow."

He grinned. "I'll be there."

Drew agreed to a quick dinner in Hollywood, and then he walked her to the train station at Hollywood and Highland.

"Aren't you worried people will notice you?" she asked as they walked over the stars in the pavement.

Tourists swarmed around, taking photos of the people in costumes and of the names on the ground. It seemed like a risk to come to such a public place. Every single person around them was camera-ready and dying to see a celebrity.

"Nah, people don't expect to see me walking down the street. Especially in such an obvious place. They're all distracted by the glitz anyway." Despite his calm words, he pulled a baseball cap from his back pocket and fitted it to his head, giving a quick scan around them.

He walked her down to the platform and pulled her to him. His hands rested loosely around her hips, and he cocked his head to the side as he looked down at her.

"I'm really enjoying the time we spend together, Ariel. I didn't expect that. I'd thought it would be work…a chore to spend time with you. But I find myself feeling sad to say good night."

"Me too," Jade said, meaning the words. "I didn't expect that either."

They looked at each other for so long that Jade was sure he was going to kiss her, and something about the look in his eyes made her think it wouldn't be a fake kiss.

"So…tomorrow," he said finally.

"Tomorrow?"

"I'm coming to see you work."

"Oh, you don't have to do that. Really, I'll just be posing for photos all day."

"That's something I can relate to." He squeezed her and gave a playful smile.

She giggled. "That's true. But really, it won't be any fun for you."

"Are you kidding? It's *Disneyland!* How could I *not* have fun there? Look, I know you'll be working, and I don't expect you to slack off for me. I haven't been to the Magic Kingdom for years. I'll go on the rides, relive my childhood, and watch you from afar if that's all that's possible. I'd just like to see you in action."

Jade smirked. "Okay. The park opens at ten, and other than parade time, I'll be around Cinderella's Castle most of the day."

"Great. See you then."

Drew kissed her. It wasn't the intense, emotional kiss she'd expected earlier, but it was warm and tender nonetheless.

On the train home, she thought about the change she'd seen in Drew during dinner. He'd been sweet and familiar, as if they really were dating. A trust had grown between them without her even realizing it. She felt comfortable with him. She could trust him.

Her phone beeped, startling her and waking the elderly man who was drooling on a very colorful sweater.

"Sorry," she said as she rummaged through her bag for her phone.

The man shot her a grumpy look and then closed his eyes again, his mouth hanging open.

There was a text from Rick on her phone.

Are we still on for tonight?

Jade chewed her lip. Were they still on? Had anything happened with Drew to make her think she *couldn't* see Rick? No. Sure, he'd been sweet, but it was more like a friendship. There was nothing about their interactions that was more than that. Except the fact they were technically dating.

She quickly typed a reply that she was almost home, gave him her address, and said to come by in about an hour. She held her breath until he replied with an *Okay!*

Twenty minutes later she ran upstairs, let herself inside, and became a cleaning tornado. With clean sheets on her bed, the toilet scrubbed, and scented candles burning, she felt better. Then it was a waiting game. She almost texted him three times to cancel. One time she typed out the whole message and then erased it. She wasn't committed to Drew. Hell, he was probably with another girl at that moment.

She paced the living room, convincing herself that she could do this. She'd had one-night stands before. What was the big deal anyway? Rick was a nice guy.

She stared at herself in the bathroom mirror, convincing herself that she should just go to bed. Was she that desperate for sex that she'd just sleep with a guy from work? Was she that weak? Was a vibrator not good enough for her? Did she want to be *that* girl?

She rearranged the pillows on the bed, fluffing them and building a pyramid. She was a strong, confident woman. There was nothing wrong with having sexual needs and taking action to satisfy them.

She opened and closed random cupboards in the kitchen, looking for something to offer Rick so it seemed less like a booty call. Surely if they had coffee and some cookies, it was kind of like a date.

Her breathing quickened when she saw the time on the wall clock. He was late. A mixture of annoyance and relief surged inside her. She watched the seconds tick by, and when he was fifteen minutes late, she resigned herself to the fact he wasn't coming.

She switched off the kitchen light and decided she'd have a bath and then use her vibrator. It was better than nothing. A soft knock on the door startled her.

"Shit," she said under her breath.

As disappointed as she'd been when Rick hadn't come, it had been a comfort too. Now she couldn't back out. She opened the door, and Rick smiled.

"Hey, sorry I'm late. I don't know this neighborhood, and it took me longer than I thought to find your place."

"Oh, no problem. Come in."

He stepped inside and gave a quick look around. His eyes fell on her, and he didn't even try to hide the lust in the stare. He knew exactly what she'd invited him over for. Shit again. She suddenly felt like a slut.

Her mind raced as his eyes drank in her curves. It was one thing to go home with a groomsman at a wedding after she'd drunk two bottles of champagne. It was a complete other thing to just invite a guy over for sex. Her palms felt sweaty. Since when did her palms sweat?

"Your place is nice."

She knew it was a lie. Her place was a crap-hole. But she didn't call him on it.

"Thanks. Would you like something to drink?" She went to turn back to the kitchen, but his arms threaded around her waist, and he held her in place.

"I'd rather just get to know you better," he said, his warm breath flowing over her throat as he leaned in to kiss her.

"Anything in particular you'd like to know?"

He chuckled and kissed her neck, his hands sliding down to cup her ass. "I'd like to know what you look like without this shirt."

Right. So, he was getting straight down to business then. It was time for her to woman up. What was her final decision going to be? She could kick him out and apologize for his wasted trip, or she could go with it. He'd only be there an hour, and what was an hour of her life if he made her toes curl?

With his lips on her skin, it was hard to say no…but she did.

"Look, Rick…" She pushed on his chest, wiggling out of his grasp.

He gave her a confused look.

"I'm really sorry."

"I don't understand." He cocked his head to the side and stared right at her as if he was trying to read her mind. "I thought this was what you invited me over for?"

"It was. I mean, I thought I wanted this."

His eyes darkened, and he stepped toward her, closing the distance she'd made when she broke their embrace. "Just give it a chance. It's normal to be nervous the first time with a new person."

Jade closed her eyes, her head swimming with hormones and the smell of Rick's cologne. A war raged inside her. Her head told her to be logical. She barely knew this man. Her lady parts were begging her to rip his clothes off and do the horizontal tango. But it wasn't her head or her ovaries she wanted to listen to. She listened hard to the beating of her heart.

Each thud sounded like Drew's name. *An-drew. An-drew. An-drew.* She sighed. "I'm sorry, Rick. You haven't done anything wrong. I'm sure you're a really nice guy. I'm just kind of involved with someone else. I'm really sorry to screw you around."

He ran a hand through his hair. "I don't mind being a revenge fuck. Did he cheat on you? You wanna get back at him? I can help."

He reached his arms out to her again, but she took a definite step back. Rick got the message and moved toward the door.

"Looks like my work here is done," he said, smiling, trying to sound like a superhero that'd just saved the day.

She smiled, grateful he wasn't being difficult.

"Sorry," she said again.

When he'd left, she felt the tightness in her chest relax. She grabbed her vibrator and headed for the bathroom.

"I love you, Ariel. When I grow up, I want to be a mermaid just like you."

Jade smiled down at the little red-haired girl. She had a smattering of freckles over her cheeks and bright blue eyes. She kind of reminded Jade of herself when she was younger.

"The ocean would be lucky to have you," Jade said.

The flash went off, and she smiled for what felt like her thousandth photo of the day. The girl ran back to her mother, and the next child stepped up.

"Look at you!" Jade gushed.

The girl had obviously had a princess makeover at the gift shop. She wore a Snow White outfit, complete with wig. The girl curtseyed. Jade mirrored the gesture. They took their photo and then another because the girl had blinked the first time.

Jade stretched her back, hoping it looked like she was just standing taller. She wouldn't want anyone to think she wasn't enjoying the job. She loved her work. But standing for hours on end did leave her achy. She could use a break.

"Hello, Ariel."

Jade glanced up. She knew that voice. Drew smirked at her.

"Are you having a photo, sir?" Kristy, her photographer, asked.

"Yes, please," Drew said, walking up to Jade and giving her a wink.

"Hello, sir," she said, bowing slightly. It wasn't often she had photos with grown men, and when she did, they were usually leering and trying to peek down her dress.

"Can we do a special photo?" Drew asked the photographer.

Kristy looked to Jade for confirmation, and she nodded.

"All right, but we have to keep the line moving," she said, balancing the large camera on her other hand. Kristy needed a break too.

Without warning, Drew dropped to his knee and looked up at her, holding onto her hand. He obviously thought it was funny to do a fake proposal. Several women in the line whispered to each other, and Jade was pretty sure he'd been made.

Kristy clicked away, enjoying having a different photo to take than the standard pose. The women pushed forward, trying to get a better look at Drew. Yep, they'd definitely identified him.

"All right, let's move along," Kristy said, holding the photo card out for Drew to take to the gift shop.

He stood up, grinned, and whispered, "Can I see you tonight?"

Jade felt a blush rise on her cheeks and nodded. Drew took the photo card, winked at his "princess," and then moved on to the next room where Cinderella was waiting.

"Was that really Drew Malik?" a woman asked.

"It sure looked like him. When we get outside, we should try to find him."

Jade wished she had her phone on her so she could text him to be careful. But she would get a break soon, and she could warn him then. Not to mention, he seemed to take the whole *son of a celebrity* thing in his stride. It never seemed to bother him.

DREW MALIK PROPOSES AT DISNEYLAND.

Jade stared at the headline and shook her head. A fuzzy photo of Drew on his knees and Jade in her princess dress was on the cover of *Fame* magazine. If anyone believed that was real, then they were so stupid they deserved to be misinformed. Seriously, it was obvious that she was a character actor.

People got dressed up to go to Disneyland, sure, but not in full princess costumes. Hats, ears, and T-shirts were the common costumes in the park. One of the ladies she'd heard whispering must have gotten phone-camera happy when Jade wasn't looking.

The date with Drew the night before, although impromptu, had been fun. He'd hung around the park until she'd knocked off her shift, and then they did the rides together. Splash Mountain was especially funny because Drew nearly vomited.

He didn't find it funny, of course, but Jade was thoroughly entertained. He'd been all man on the Tower of Terror, though. Didn't even scream when the elevator dropped. Jade had been on all the rides so many times she couldn't count them, but it was always fun to go with someone new. Drew's reactions were especially entertaining.

The most annoying part of the evening had been when he'd insisted on taking her through The Little Mermaid ride over at the Adventure Park and asking her the whole time if it made her homesick.

"Look, it's *you!*" he'd proclaimed when they passed the Ariel statue. "Is that my competition?" he asked when they passed Ariel and Eric almost kissing in the boat.

Jade just rolled her eyes and went along with it. She was having too good of a time to start a petty fight. He was trying to be cute and funny and she just rolled with it.

Jade's least favorite part of the night, though, had been when he'd walked her to her apartment. She hadn't had to catch public transportation because Drew had his car. He dropped her home and walked her upstairs.

"I had fun," she said, feeling as if she'd been on a real date.

"Me too. You're fun!"

"You sound surprised."

"No, just happy." He gave her a goofy grin.

"Do you…?" Jade bit her lip. She'd been about to ask him if he wanted to come inside.

Was that allowed? Did she even want to take their relationship to that place? It was all so confusing. She was saved having to sort her head out by Drew's statement.

"I should be getting home. Thanks for a really fun night. I mean it — that might be the best fake date I've ever had. Hell, maybe the best date period."

And there it was. He'd called it a fake date. Jade was glad she hadn't finished her question and made a fool of herself.

"I had a great time. I don't tend to hang out at the Park much anymore. Working there has taken some of the magic of it away, but I'm really glad we stayed tonight. Thanks."

He kissed her on the cheek and then disappeared. He didn't look back over his shoulder to see if she was safely inside. After she showered and climbed into bed, she placed her phone on the nightstand in case it rang. But he didn't text or call that night.

CHAPTER EIGHT

Intervention

Sweat coated every inch of Drew's body. When he'd agreed to be a basketball coach, he hadn't realized how much running around he would do. His vision of coaching was to just stand on the sidelines, yelling orders and blowing his whistle. The reality was that he worked just as hard, if not harder, than the players. But as tired as he was, he actually loved the work. His individual sessions with Alex were going great, and he could see real potential in that boy.

Once he got home, all he wanted to do was have a long, hot shower.

"Did you have a good day at training?" Caroline asked when Drew walked through the foyer to head upstairs.

"It was great. What time are my parents expecting me for dinner?"

"The reservation is for eight."

"I'll be ready," Drew promised.

Caroline laughed. "I'll take that bet."

Drew gave Caroline the finger and then took the stairs two at a time, Caroline's laughter echoing after him.

He showered, washing the sweat from his body and thinking about maybe calling Tully after dinner. She would be up for going out for a drink. As annoying as she could be, she knew how to have fun.

When he was dressed, Drew pulled the bottle of vodka out from under his bed and downed two shots, getting himself ready for the night. He stowed the bottle again, rolling it into the shadows so Caroline wouldn't find it.

"Told you I'd be on time," he called, but there was no response.

He went through into the dining room and paused. His mother and father were seated together, with Caroline next to his mother. They all wore stern expressions.

"I'm not late," Drew said, checking his watch to be sure.

"Drew, have a seat," his father said.

"O…kay," he said, elongating the word.

Laura leaned forward and grasped his hand tightly across the table.

"You know we love you," she said.

"Oh God, what's going on?" Drew really wanted to run upstairs and have another shot. He eyed his father's well-stocked bar on the buffet behind the table.

Caroline whimpered and dabbed her face with a scrunched-up tissue. Drew did not like the atmosphere in the room, and he pulled his hand free from his mother's.

Aaron cleared his throat. "Drew, son, this is hard for us, but you know it's been coming for a while."

Drew stared at them with a blank face. His father's words didn't make any sense. Now he *really* wanted a drink. The two shots he'd had upstairs hadn't given him nearly as much of a buzz as he'd hoped.

"The way you live your life…what you're doing to your body," his mother said.

"What's this about? I thought we were having a family dinner." Drew shot Caroline a dirty look, and she cowered in her seat. "Are we eating or not?"

Aaron leaned forward. "Drew, we need to talk to you about your drinking."

"Oh, give me a break," Drew yelled, finally understanding what was going on. There was no dinner. He should have known something was up as soon as he came downstairs.

"Drew, please listen. Don't let anger stop you from hearing our concern." Laura reached for her son's hand again, but he'd pulled it out of her reach. "We love you, and we're concerned about your health. The amount you drink isn't healthy."

"Mom, I know you think you know what you're talking about, but you don't. I'm fine. I can handle a few fucking drinks."

"Be respectful when you talk to your mother," Aaron scolded.

"Sorry, Mom," he mumbled as if he were a small child.

Drew's head started to pound. The last thing he felt like doing was sitting at the table, being lectured by his parents about alcohol.

"Doctor, why don't you come in?" Aaron said.

A middle-aged man entered the room from the living room and sat at the table.

"A doctor?" Drew asked.

"Hello, Drew. My name is Peter. I'm a general surgeon. Your parents asked me to come and speak with you about what alcohol does to your body."

Drew rolled his eyes and scrubbed his hands through his hair.

"This is a joke, right? Someone set me up." He started to laugh and looked around the room, expecting his friends to come busting in with drinks for everyone.

"Drew, this isn't funny. We'd like you to listen to the doctor." Laura watched her son with an emotional stare.

Knowing the only way to escape this torture would be to let them get this out of their system, Drew slouched back in his chair, hanging his right arm over the back and stretching his legs out. "Okay, Doc, let's get this over with." He let out a bored sigh.

Peter looked at Aaron, who nodded his head for the doctor to continue. Drew tried his best to pay attention as the doctor explained about the damage alcohol did to the liver, heart, and brain, but it was all so pointless. He didn't have a drinking problem.

Drew held his hand up for the doctor to stop speaking. When he was silent, Drew sat up straight and leaned his elbows on the table.

"So, Doc, you never drink?"

Peter coughed and shifted in his seat. "I'm not going to lie to you, Drew. On occasion I have a drink, but I don't get drunk on a regular basis."

"But did you, when you were younger?" Drew pushed.

Again the doctor looked at Aaron, who shrugged his shoulders.

"I indulged as a young person, yes, but not over a long period of time."

Drew nodded his head, trying to keep a straight face.

"And, Dad," he said, turning to Aaron, "I know you drink."

Laura grabbed her husband's hand and held it tightly.

"This isn't about me, Drew. I don't have a problem."

"And neither do I," Drew said triumphantly.

Caroline started crying again, turning her tissue into a soggy, shredded mess.

Aaron stood up, dropped his wife's hand, and pointed down at his son.

"Now, listen here, boy. We're here because we love you and we want your life to be a long and healthy one. This isn't us ganging up on you, and it's not a tit-for-tat about who drinks the most. Do you know that your mother lays awake at night waiting for you to come home, with her phone clutched in her hand in case the police call?"

Drew's heart dropped into his stomach. Aaron's face had gone as red as a ripe apple, and he forced himself to take a few deep breaths before sitting down.

"Mom, I'm sorry that you worry. I really am. But I'm smart when I go out. I don't drive drunk, and I'm always with friends."

"Friends who are just as drunk as you. Great lot of help they'll be in an emergency," Aaron muttered.

"I'm just having fun!" Drew yelled, making his mother and Caroline jump. "I won't party forever. Just let me have my fun while I can. Please. You've got me doing charity work, and I haven't missed a single session. I'm even doing extra work with one of the kids because he shows promise. Can you really think I'm wasting my life when I'm jumping through your hoops anyway?"

Aaron cracked his knuckles, a sign Drew knew meant he was thinking of a response and stalling for time.

"Your mother and I are very proud of the determination with which you've taken on your charity work. You've impressed me. But one day you'll be living on your own, and to be honest, we're not convinced you can look after yourself. The last thing we want for you is to be drunk all day and night and waste your life in a never-ending hangover."

"And that would be a short life," Peter chimed in. "If you were drinking every day, you'd cut years, maybe decades, off your life."

"I get it, okay? You don't all need to keep up the same story. You think I drink too much. I don't agree. That's the end of it." Drew stood up and went to walk to the garage. He wanted to head into Hollywood and meet up with some friends.

"You're drunk right now," Peter said, sniffing the air as he walked past. "I can smell liquor on you."

"I'm not drunk!"

"Have you been drinking?" Aaron demanded.

"I had a few shots to get my night started. I'm nowhere near drunk." Drew shrugged, showing it wasn't a big deal.

"I didn't see you at the bar, which means you have a bottle stashed in your room," his father said.

"Hiding is one of the symptoms of addiction," Peter said.

Drew'd had just about enough of this conversation. He lunged for Peter, planning on giving the guy a black eye to go with his smug expression.

"Andrew!" his mother gasped as Aaron leapt up and grabbed Drew around the chest, holding him back.

"Caroline, search Drew's room. I want any alcohol you find removed right now," Aaron said, struggling to hold onto his son.

"Stay out of my room!" Drew yelled.

Caroline gave a whimper but ran from the room, her footsteps loud as she went up the stairs.

"What are you going to do, lock me up?"

"If that's what it takes," Aaron seethed between gritted teeth, still holding his son.

"Aaron, maybe we should take a step back. This isn't what we planned," Laura said, standing up. Her eyes were wide, and her hands were shaking.

The worry on his mother's face made Drew stop struggling, but when he saw the fear in her eyes, he sighed in defeat.

"Fine, I'll stay home tonight. It's not a big deal. I can go a night without drinking."

Aaron slowly released his grasp but stayed close to Drew in case he tried to make a run for it.

Laura turned to Peter and walked him out, thanking him for his assistance and promising to invite him for dinner on a more pleasant night.

Drew sat down with a huff, his father moving with him like a shadow. Caroline appeared after about fifteen minutes with three bottles in her arms, including the vodka from under his bed. Drew swore under his breath. He'd hoped she wouldn't find that one.

"Pour it down the sink," Aaron said.

Drew looked up, realizing that his father was speaking to him. "All right."

He followed the older man into the kitchen and twisted the top off the vodka bottle, tipping it into the sink and watching the liquid swirl down the drain. He tried to convince himself it was just water, but the smell made his stomach churn and his mouth water.

"All of them," Aaron said when Drew hesitated at the final bottle.

Laura carried several more bottles in from the dining room, placing them on the counter next to him.

"You're getting rid of your entire bar stock?" Drew asked.

"Unlike some people, I don't need alcohol in my home. If I want a drink, I can have just one. But we don't want to have anything to make this harder for you. It all goes."

"Even this one?" Drew held up a dusty bottle of red wine. He knew it cost a fortune and was a gift from one of Aaron's director friends.

Aaron hesitated but then squared his shoulders. "Yes. It *all* goes."

Drew watched the alcohol disappear down the drain. It was such a waste. When every last drop was gone and Caroline started putting all the bottles into a plastic bag for the garbage, Drew turned to his parents.

"Can I go upstairs now?"

He felt like a stupid child. He hadn't asked his parents' permission for anything in years, least of all to go to his room.

"Be honest with me, Drew. Is there any more that Caroline didn't find?"

"No, Dad. She got it all."

Aaron looked at his wife, and she gave a small nod.

"All right. You're not to leave this house tonight, do you understand?"

"Yes." Drew hung his head, feeling scolded, and shuffled out of the room. He grumbled to himself all the way up the stairs and threw himself down onto his bed. He'd told the truth; Caroline had found his entire stash. He was in for a long night with no entertainment.

A soft knock made him sit up.

"What?" he asked.

"Are you hungry, dear?"

"Not really. Thanks anyway, Mom."

"Come downstairs if you change your mind. Caroline has ordered Indian food for us."

"Okay."

Drew loved Indian food, but there was no way he could go down and eat with his parents. Not tonight. He'd sneak down after they went to bed and help himself to any leftovers.

Drew hadn't been kidding about it being a long night. He did game plans for his coaching for the next two weeks, played wastebasket basketball for over an hour, had another shower, and played all his lives on Candy Crush—twice. When he heard his parents finally go to bed, he sighed in relief and opened his bedroom door. Or he *tried* to open the door. It was locked from the outside.

Drew punched the door and swore under his breath.

He wasn't going to sneak out to drink. He just wanted to get something to eat. He flung himself down on the bed and remembered there was a bag of chips in the backpack that he took to his coaching job.

He ripped the bag open and shoveled the greasy potato slices into his mouth. When he'd shaken out the last of the crumbs, he looked around for a drink, finding nothing. He had no choice but to cup water to his mouth with his hands from the bathroom sink.

He'd make sure to let his parents know that, if they planned to keep him locked up, he needed proper meals. The fact that Laura had offered him dinner and he'd turned it down only made him angrier.

Having exhausted every other form of entertainment, Drew swore he'd buy a TV tomorrow so he had something to do while in his bedroom. Then he remembered he didn't have any money to buy a TV, and he swore again, punching a pillow.

Soon, he reminded himself. He just had to be patient and bide his time until the wedding. Then he'd have all the money he needed. He could buy a thousand TVs, a hundred thousand. It was time to get that ball rolling. He grabbed his cell and dialed Jade's number.

"Hello?" she asked, sounding husky as if she'd been sleeping.

"Oh, shit, sorry. I forgot it was late." He glanced at the clock by his bed and saw it was almost midnight.

"Drew?"

"Yeah. Is it okay that I called?"

"Are you drunk?" she asked.

He huffed. "No, I'm not fucking drunk. What is *with* everybody?"

She was silent for a moment, and then he heard a rustling sound as if she were moving around in bed.

"What are you talking about, Drew?"

He explained about the night he'd had and how ridiculous his parents' accusations were. "Don't you agree they were totally overreacting?"

"Umm…"

"Ariel, come on!"

"I'm sure they were just concerned about you. But if you don't think you have a problem, then I believe you. I don't really know enough about your life to have an opinion. If I believed what the tabloids said, then I might be concerned, though."

"They're liars. You know that."

She let out a long breath. "I'm sorry you've had a bad night. Is there something I can do to help?"

"Just talking is nice. It's good to have someone on my side. Hey, do you want to meet up tomorrow? Maybe lunch?"

"I can't. I'm working."

"Prince Eric foils my plans again."

"If you say so." She giggled.

The sound of her laughter was soothing and he wanted to hear it again.

"Knock, knock," he said before he lost his nerve.

"What?"

"Oh come on, Ariel. Everyone knows the response to a knock-knock joke!"

She sighed. "Who's there?"

"Interrupting cow."

She was silent for a moment before giving her response. She had a wary tone in her voice as she said, "Interrup—"

"Mooooooooooooo!" Drew said, interrupting her. He laughed. He couldn't help it. The joke was stupid, but it was funny. Jade groaned but gave in to a few giggles of her own.

"Hey, you wanna meet up?" he asked when they were both quiet again.

"It's really late, Drew."

"I know. I just want to see you. It's been such a shit night and talking to you has really helped."

He waited, hoping she'd say yes.

"All right. Can you pick me up?"

"Ahh, fuck. Sorry, I just remembered that my parents locked me in."

"That's a bit extreme. You're a grown man."

"Tell me about it!" Drew felt his anger come alive again, being reminded that he was trapped like a baby in a crib.

"Drew," she said, her voice hesitant.

"Hmm?"

"Please don't get mad. As I said earlier, I don't really know you well enough to make a judgment, but I just want to ask something, okay?"

Drew didn't like the sound of that.

Her voice was a whisper as she asked, "*Do* you have a problem?"

"My parents are a fucking problem."

"Drew, please be honest."

He let out a long breath. "It's under control. Everyone has a few drinks."

"I don't drink very often," she said. "Only a glass of champagne for a special occasion or something."

"Well, bully for you. Living up to your Disney image."

"Drew! Don't be an ass. I'm your friend."

"I better go before I say something I regret."

He hung up the phone, feeling worse than he had before he'd called her. Guilt from being rude to her when she was trying to help him boiled in his stomach. He'd woken her up and then teased her. Nice work there, Drew!

He typed a quick text and sent it, hoping that would be enough to smooth things over.

Sorry. Had a bad night. I didn't mean it. Sleep well, Ariel.

Her response came almost instantly and put a smile on his face.

No damage done. I'll still marry you, but remember that I need my beauty sleep. No more late night rants. And Drew, if you decide you want to make some changes in your life, I'm here for you. Friends, right?

CHAPTER NINE

Engaged

"So, we're on for Saturday?" Drew asked into the phone.

"Yeah."

"This is going to be a very important day for us, Jade. My parents aren't stupid, so we have to make sure our act is flawless."

"I know. Don't worry. I might just surprise you with how convincing I can be." She laughed, and the sound made him smile.

"I have a little surprise in store too."

"Oh, really?" Her voice raised an octave with her curiosity.

Drew loved how flirty and playful she'd become since they'd grown more comfortable with each other.

"And what might that be?"

"If I told you, I'd have to kill you," he replied. "Just be prepared for everything."

"You're so dramatic."

"It's a pretty big surprise."

"Interesting. Should I be expecting strippers? Maybe a cake with a person who jumps out of it? Oh! Drew, are you going to wear a dress?"

Drew snorted. "Where do you come up with this stuff?"

"I'm just gifted like that."

"Obviously. I think you might keep me on my toes, Ariel."

"Stop calling me that," she snapped.

"Calling you what…Ariel?"

The dial tone sounded in his ear, and he laughed, shoving his phone in his pocket. He was very much enjoying getting to know Jade. He was sure that, at the very least, they would have a good friendship. That would make the whole marriage situation easier.

He got out of his car, which he'd parked ten minutes ago, and walked into the jewelry store.

"Good afternoon, sir. May I show you something in particular?" an older woman asked from behind the glass counter.

Everything in the store was glistening. The glass counters, the jewelry, even the saleswoman's teeth. Drew wondered if there was special lighting.

"I'm looking for an engagement ring."

"How delightful. May I enquire about your budget?"

"It doesn't matter."

Drew felt a slight niggling of guilt that he was about to use his emergency credit card. He'd never had to use it before, because his parents had been quite generous with his allowance, but since his father's new rules about living on a budget, he had to use drastic measures.

He had a plan, though. Drew would use the card his parents had given him for emergencies and explain to them that they could either give him the money for the ring as an engagement gift, or he would pay it back when he got the money from his inheritance.

"Our selection of diamond rings are in this cabinet."

Drew followed the woman to a particularly well-stocked cabinet and made his selection.

"Are you nervous about meeting his parents?"

"Of course I am, Clare! And I don't need you reminding me of it every thirty seconds." Jade threw her arms up in the air and glared at her friend.

"Whoa! Bitch alert. Take a breath!"

Jade did as her friend asked and took a deep breath. "Sorry. I'm just freaking out."

"I would be too. You're going to meet Aaron Fucking Malik!" Clare's eyes got wider with each word that left her mouth.

"You're going to meet him too, may I remind you. And I don't think that's really his middle name."

Clare poked her tongue out.

"I'm going to meet him, but I'm not the one sleeping with his son. He won't care about me."

"I'm not sleeping with…"

Clare's eyebrows went up as Jade hesitated. "Hold up. You haven't bumped uglies with this guy?"

"Uh, not yet." Jade bit her lip and busied herself with a hangnail.

"Then *why* are you meeting his parents? I know you're not one of those people who abstains until marriage, because you've had more guys than—"

"Careful, Clare."

"You know what I mean."

"We're just taking things slow. God knows I haven't had the best history with guys, and maybe that's because I always rush into sex. I'm just trying something new with this guy. I think he could be special."

"Huh." Clare popped her hip and put her hand there in a dramatic gesture. "I guess that kinda makes sense, in a boring kind of way."

"Thank you. Now, can we please move on from my sex life and decide on my outfit?"

"But your sex life is so much more interesting than mine!" Clare whined.

"I really doubt that, seeing as *you* are a newlywed and I'm not getting any."

Clare rolled her eyes. "All right, all right. Let's pick something that's sexy enough to get this guy's blood flowing and maybe get you some action but that's also appropriate to meet parents."

"Yeah. Because *that* won't be hard."

"Have faith in me, Jade."

Jade had to give it to Clare—she was good. Somehow, from the depths of Jade's closet, she'd put together an outfit that was sexy and yet still conservative. The green dress contrasted with her hair and made her eyes pop. At least that's what Clare said.

"Okay, you look stunning. Use a little green in your eye shadow… not too much…and wear those false eyelashes I bought you. Keep your lips soft, maybe a coral or sand, and leave your hair out," Clare said once she was satisfied with fluffing the skirt of Jade's dress.

"I was going to braid my hair."

"No. Trust me. Leave your hair out. It'll make you look softer and more girl-like. It'll charm his father and make you more likable to his mother."

"If you say so."

"I do. I'm going home to get ready. Stuart and I will see you at the restaurant."

"Thanks, Clare. Love you like pancakes."

"Love you like chocolate," her friend called over her shoulder as she showed herself out of the apartment.

Jade took her time getting ready. She hadn't told Clare how nervous she actually was, but she was dreading their upcoming dinner. *Why* had Drew thought it was a good idea for them to meet each other's friends and family all at the same time? She would have much preferred to have a quiet dinner with his parents without all of Drew's friends staring at them.

The only positive she could convince herself of was that meeting everyone together was like removing a Band-Aid. All at once, quick and painless. Jade washed her hair and then cursed herself for twenty minutes as she tried to get the frizzy, fluffy mess under control. She fought the urge to slick it with hairspray and tie it back and instead decided to hot iron it straight. It took more time than she'd planned, and then she had to rush her makeup.

She looked at herself in the mirror and rolled her eyes. She was a mess. Her hair was too long. It usually curled to halfway down her back, but being straight, it hung well below her waist. She tried to put some green in her smoky eye shadow, but it just looked muddy, not highlighted. She'd done the best job she could with the eyelashes, but the left one was slightly crooked, and the corner of her right eye was glued closed. Every time she blinked it pulled apart slowly, giving the impression that she had a lazy eye. She put the dress on and dug around in the bottom of her closet for shoes.

"No wonder you can't find a *real* husband," Jade said to her reflection when she was dressed.

She couldn't wallow in her self-pity for long, though, as there was a knock on her door.

"I'm coming!" she called as she ran through the apartment.

She pulled the door open, and her breath caught in her throat when she saw Drew standing there. Each time she saw him, she was shocked at how handsome he was—as if her memory dulled him down so she wouldn't try to picture him all the time. She decided it was a coping mechanism.

"You look gorgeous!" he said, smiling.

"Oh, this old thing?" she said, flicking the hem of her skirt.

He laughed and leaned forward, kissing her quickly on the cheek. "You ready to go?"

"Ready as I'll ever be." She swallowed her nerves and grabbed her clutch purse.

Drew's hand felt warm laced with hers as they walked out to the street.

"My parents are very excited to meet you. My mother bought several different dresses for tonight because she couldn't decide what to wear."

"Did you get a new car?" Jade asked, stopping dead in her tracks and staring at the black sports car at the curb. Drew's usual silver sedan was nowhere in sight.

"It's my dad's. He let me borrow it tonight."

Jade's nerves returned in an avalanche. It was abundantly clear how different their lives were. His mother had bought *several* dresses for this dinner, and Jade had worn something out of her closet. Drew's dad drove a car that cost more than her annual salary, and she had a broken Volvo that she couldn't afford to fix. This plan suddenly seemed ridiculous.

"What's wrong?" Drew asked. "Your face has gone the same color as your dress."

"I'm fine. I just realized how different we are."

"I think we're more the same than you think. I couldn't afford that car. Right now, I'm broke."

"That makes two of us."

He reached up and stroked her cheek. "If we pull off tonight, we'll be one step closer to getting my inheritance. You haven't changed your mind, have you?"

"No, I haven't. I'm just nervous."

He wrapped his arms around her shoulders and pulled her into a hug.

"This isn't a cake walk for me either. You don't think your friends are going to give me the third degree?"

Jade thought about that and then laughed. Clare would undoubtedly give him the third degree. "Oh, you're in so much trouble!" she said, giggling.

The car ride went quickly, as each of them gave the other details about their childhoods and hobbies. They felt it was important to know as much about each other as possible to help pull off their ruse.

"How old were you when you lost your virginity?"

"Drew! I really doubt anyone is going to ask you that," Jade said, scolding.

"This is just my curiosity."

She rolled her eyes. "Seventeen."

Drew grinned. "Let me guess. Prom night?"

"Hey! I'm not a cliché."

"I never said you were. It was just a lucky guess."

Drew seemed to be finding their whole conversation quite entertaining.

"Okay, is there anything else I should know about you before the dinner?" she asked as they drove through downtown LA.

"My favorite Disney princess is Ariel."

"Shut up."

"I'm serious. What's not to love about her? She wears a shell bra and lies around on the beach."

"You are utterly ridiculous."

He chuckled and pulled the car into a parking garage.

"Maybe. But it's good cover for your nickname, Ariel."

"I really wish you wouldn't do that."

"Why? It's cute. You can pick a nickname for me if you want."

Little did he know her friends had already taken that liberty. "How about Douchebag? That has a nice ring to it."

"Play nice, Ariel." His voice held a warning tone, but the smile never left his face.

He parked the car and rushed around to open the door for her. He laced their fingers together and led her out onto the street and to the restaurant.

It looked like they were the last to arrive, because when the hostess showed them to their table, it was full of smiling faces. Jade expected there to be two groups at the table: her friends and Drew's friends and family. It seemed, though, that everyone was mingling, talking, and getting to know each other. Several of the faces at the table were familiar even though Jade had never met them.

Aaron Malik, of course, was recognizable as he chatted with a gushing Clare and Stuart. But there were others too.

"Why is Tully Whittaker glaring at me?" Jade whispered to Drew.

"Don't worry about her."

He didn't stay to explain *why* she shouldn't worry about Tully. He moved through the room, greeting people with confidence. It appeared his parents had booked the entire restaurant as all the other tables were empty.

Someone clinked a knife against a glass, and everyone fell silent. Drew appeared instantly at her side and slipped an arm around her waist.

"I'd like to welcome you all to the joyous occasion. To the familiar faces in the room, you'll know how amazing it is that Drew has found a girl that he wants us all to meet, and to those of you I have yet to meet, welcome and I look forward to getting to know you. Now, where is this magical girl who has bewitched my rascal son?"

"Your father doesn't seem to think very highly of you," Jade murmured under her breath as Drew walked her toward the head of the long table where his father was standing.

"I'm shocked." Drew's voice was flat, and Jade was quite sure he was being sarcastic.

"Here she is! It's a pleasure to meet you, Jade," Aaron said, pulling her out of Drew's grasp and twirling her in front of the staring crowd at the table.

She blushed and stared down the row of faces for Clare. She saw her friend and bit her lip. Clare gave her a thumbs-up.

"Enjoy your dinner, everyone," Aaron said loudly. As if on cue, and Jade was sure it was, a parade of waiters appeared carrying plates of food.

The buzz of chatter filled the room, and everyone went back to their conversations.

"Jade, it's lovely to meet you," said a woman with a warm voice.

Jade looked to her right and saw a middle-aged woman with a slightly familiar face. She wasn't sure if the familiarity came from having seen her in magazines or the fact that her son looked so much like her.

"Mrs. Malik, it's nice to meet you too."

"Oh, none of that. Please call me Laura."

Jade smiled.

"This is a bit more than we'd talked about, Dad," Drew said, taking his seat beside Jade.

He patted her knee under the table.

"Well, my playboy son brings home a girl for the first time; I'm going to make a fuss. You must really be something special, my dear," Aaron said, ending his statement with a pointed look at Jade.

"Aaron, please. This is a special night for Drew. Let's not make it awkward for him," Laura said.

Aaron laughed. "If Jade hasn't read about Drew's many women in the tabloids, I'd be very surprised. I'm not telling you anything you don't already know, am I?"

"Err…" Jade didn't know what to say. "Drew has been nothing but a gentleman to me."

Drew gave her an appreciative smile, and Aaron looked genuinely shocked.

"A gentleman, hey? Well, I'm impressed, son. You might have picked up something from the old man after all." He let out a strong belly laugh.

"I've always known you were a gentleman, Drew," Laura said, frowning at her husband.

"Thanks, Mom." Drew appeared thoroughly embarrassed.

Clare came up to Jade's side and hugged her from behind.

"So, you're Dream Guy, huh?" she said.

"Ah, you're the best friend." Drew smiled and shook her hand. "It's nice to meet you. And I usually get my friends to call me Drew. I save *Dream Guy* for formal occasions."

Clare smirked. "Okay. I like you. My name's Clare. I hope I didn't interrupt anything?"

"No, we were just talking about what a gentleman our son is," Laura said.

"I'll say. A little *too much* of a gentleman if you ask me," Clare said, winking at Jade.

"What do you mean by that?" Aaron asked, looking interested.

"Nothing. She means nothing. Clare, I think Stuart is trying to get your attention," Jade said.

That was a bold-faced lie. Stuart was quite happily devouring a bowl of pasta and wasn't looking in their direction at all, but it was enough to get Clare to go back to her seat.

"Fill me in later?" Drew asked, leaning over to whisper in Jade's ear.

She nodded and started to eat.

"Can I get you anything else to drink?" a waitress asked.

"I'll have a gin and tonic," Jade said.

"Vodka on the rocks," Drew said but, after a stern look from his father, changed his order. "Actually, make mine a Coke." He frowned and shoveled food into his mouth.

Jade squeezed his hand under the table and offered him a smile.

Drew's parents were friendly, even if Aaron was a bit boisterous. Jade didn't really know how to take him, but she supposed when you were always the center of attention, you got used to playing that role. Laura was warm and chatty, and she seemed extremely excited to meet Jade.

"Drew spends a lot of his time with girls like Tully. She's a lovely girl, but her vision of reality is so skewed. I'm thrilled that he's getting serious with someone who works for a living and pays her own way." Laura beamed at her.

Jade glanced over at Tully and found the blonde glaring at her again. She didn't know what to make of it. She hadn't had a chance to even speak with Tully yet. Perhaps she was also used to being the center of attention and didn't like that everyone was talking about a nobody like Jade.

"Drew!" Tully squealed, right on cue. She'd been knocking back the cocktails all night and was beginning to look quite disheveled.

"Yes, Tully?" He sounded polite, but Jade could see that his eyes were tight.

"Come and sit by me for a while. I've barely seen you all night."

"Not right now." He turned to Jade and smiled. "Are you ready for your surprise?"

"You mean you're about to jump out of a cake wearing a dress?" she asked, smiling back.

"You wish," Drew said, smirking.

It was surprising how comfortable she was with Drew and his family. They'd all made her feel so welcome. As Drew stood up and dug around in his suit pocket, Laura gave her a curious look, and Jade just shrugged her shoulders, unsure what was happening.

Drew tapped his fork against his water glass. All the table chatter stopped, and heads turned in his direction.

"Thanks for coming, everyone. I hope you've all enjoyed the food. Apologies to those of you I haven't had a chance to speak with one on one, but I'll try to mingle a bit more after the food is gone." There was a round of chuckling from the table. "As you all know, we're here to bring two families together. For my family and friends to meet Jade, and for Jade's friends to meet me. It's wonderful for both of us to see so many people we care about in one room."

He looked down at Jade, who nodded in agreement. She hadn't realized Drew was such a good public speaker, but it was undeniable. Everyone around the room was hanging on every word that left his mouth.

"But I've misled you all about the purpose of tonight."

People shifted in their chairs, and there was a murmur of confusion. Aaron began to stand up, but Laura placed her hand on his arm, calming him.

"The reason we're all here is *more* than what I've let on." Drew turned to Jade and pushed his chair back out of the way.

He dropped to one knee and fished into his jacket pocket.

"Oh my God!" Clare gasped from the other end of the table.

Jade wished she could look around to see if everyone else was as shocked as she was, but she couldn't look away from Drew.

"Jade, I know we've only known each other a few weeks, but they've been the best few weeks of my life. It might seem rushed to other people, but I believe that you *know* when you find the person you're supposed to spend the rest of your life with, and for me, that's you. I'm falling in love with you more every day, and I would be honored if you would be my wife."

Jade's pulse thundered in her ears. The logical part of her brain told her to calm down. His words weren't the truth. He was playing a part, reading a script. This was all part of their contract. He didn't actually mean the words he was saying.

"Will you marry me, Jade?"

Gasps rung out around the room, and Jade was sure one of them had been from her. When Drew had said he had a surprise, she never would have guessed *this*. She'd thought when the time was right, they'd just start telling people they were engaged. She hadn't expected a public proposal.

"Yes…y-yes, I w-will," she stuttered.

He slipped a ring onto her finger and then stood, pulling her up into his arms and pressing his mouth to hers. She was aware of cheering and clapping, but she was lost in the kiss. This wasn't like the practice kisses they'd had. This one *felt* real, even though she knew it wasn't.

"You should see your face," Drew laughed softly into her ear.

"That wasn't fair. You should have warned me."

"And miss this priceless expression? No way."

The moment was broken by the sound of a scraping chair and a glass being knocked over.

"Fuck this!" Tully slurred.

Drew's cousin shrieked as Tully's martini spilled into her lap. Tully staggered between the tables, bumping into chairs, and then disappeared out onto the street.

"Don't let one jealous girl spoil your night," Laura said as they sat down.

Drew gave her a cheesy grin and squeezed Jade's hand. "Don't worry, Mom. Nothing can ruin tonight."

The ring felt hot on Jade's finger, and it was heavier than she'd expected. She held her hand out, admiring the way the large diamond sparkled in the light.

"It looks like several carats," Laura said.

"I wouldn't know," Jade admitted, staring in awe at the ring.

"Don't worry. You'll get used to pretty things. Drew can be very generous, so I'm sure this won't be the last bauble you get during your marriage."

CHAPTER TEN

Paparazzi

"Oh my God! Turn on TMZ right now!" Clare screamed into Jade's ear through her cell phone.

Jade grabbed her remote control and flicked the stations until she saw a familiar face on the screen—hers.

"What the hell?"

She turned the volume up and sat down on the floor, feeling like she could listen better if her brain wasn't concentrating on standing up.

"...*playboy Drew Malik, son of Aaron Malik, has asked a mystery girl to marry him. We got the scoop from Drew's longtime friend and on-again-off-again girlfriend, Tully Whittaker.*"

The image changed to Tully, drunk and slurring, wearing the same dress she'd worn to dinner the night before. Tully looked into the camera and gave what she probably thought was a sexy smile.

"It won't last," she said confidently. "The girl—I can't even remember her name—isn't his type at all. Trust me. This engagement isn't even worth talking about."

Drew's face, looking drunk and trying to hide from a camera, appeared on the screen as the reporter's voice came over the top.

"*Does Tully know Drew well enough to think this is going to fizzle before it even starts, or should we be expecting celebrity wedding bells?*"

"Can you believe this? You're practically famous!" Clare squealed.

"They don't know it's *me*," Jade reasoned. "Thanks for letting me know, Clare. I'll call you later."

She hung up the phone and dialed Drew.

"Hey, Ariel," he said.

"Have you seen the news?" she asked, not bothering with a greeting.

"No. I've been at school training the kids. I only just got home. What's going on? Is it the end of the world?"

"It might be the end of my normal world. We've been found out."

"That didn't take long," Drew said, chuckling.

"You think it's funny? Tully was just on TMZ telling the world that I'm not your type and that our wedding will never go ahead."

Drew sighed. "Don't worry about it. Half the things you see about me in the tabloids aren't true. You'll get used to it. Just try to ignore anything you hear. You and I know the truth, and that's all that matters."

Jade felt the panic in her chest lessen, and she began to see the humor in the situation. "The funny thing is, though, that Tully was right. I'm not your type, and our marriage isn't what you would normally want."

"I never said you weren't my type."

"Oh, so, you're highly attracted to women who have no direct career path, can't pay their electricity bills, and often eat leftovers?"

"I'm getting hot just thinking about it."

"You loser."

They both laughed. It was a shame they'd met under the circumstances they had, because they actually got along very well.

Jade did as Drew asked and put the media out of her mind. No one knew who she was so her life wouldn't be affected for a while yet. She'd just be more aware the next time she and Drew met up for a date to watch out for photographers.

She didn't have to wait long, though. Drew seemed eager to increase their dates and asked her out for dinner the following night.

She peeked out her window and saw him pull up on the street. His car looked so out of place next to all the rusty cars that barely ran. It was nice for her to get to see him when he didn't know she was watching. He had a bounce in his step as he walked up the driveway. He glanced at her window, and she quickly ducked behind the curtain, hoping he hadn't seen her watching.

She'd gone with a more casual approach tonight. He'd said he wanted them to have some fun together, so he was taking her to Six Flags. Jeans and a sweater were perfect attire for that.

She pulled her front door open and saw Drew standing with his hand raised, ready to knock.

"Good timing," he said, smiling.

"I might've seen you coming."

"I have a feeling I'm going to have to keep an eye on you. You're sneaky." He leaned in and gave her a quick kiss.

She was caught off guard, not because she didn't want to kiss him, but because they were in private.

"Can I ask you something, Drew?"

"Of course."

"Why did you just kiss me?"

"It was a hello kiss. Is that okay?"

"I guess I'm just feeling like the lines are blurred. I was under the impression that we only had to be intimate when in public."

Drew leaned away from her, his eyes pained. "Can we talk inside?"

"Sure." She stepped back into the apartment as he entered and then closed the door.

They sat on the couch, and Drew reached for her hand. She let him hold it and waited for him to start talking.

"I like you, Jade. I feel close to you in a way that I've never felt with another girl. For me, it's always been about sex. I've never been in love, and if I'm being honest, I haven't been looking for it."

Jade felt her body tense up.

"Calm down," he said, smiling. "I'm not saying I'm in love you with you. Just that I care about you. I haven't had that with a girl before. I feel comfortable with you, and I enjoy touching you. It feels nice to just hold your hand or to kiss you. I'm sorry if it makes you uncomfortable."

Jade opened her mouth to speak, but Drew continued to talk.

"When we met, we both signed an agreement to marry for money. And I'm still on board for that. I've just come to believe that maybe that's not *all* we have to be. If feelings naturally develop between us, would that be so bad?"

"It could get very messy."

"In what way?" His thumb was stroking the back of her hand in a hypnotizing rhythm.

She pulled her hand from his. She needed to think clearly, and she couldn't do that while he was touching her.

"We're contractually bound to break up in a year. If we let feelings develop, real feelings, we could end up getting hurt. This was a business agreement in the beginning, and I think it's best if we keep it that way."

"If that's what you want." Drew stood and walked to the door. "Should we go?"

The car ride out to Six Flags was tense. Jade didn't know what to say, and Drew wasn't offering any topics of conversation either. Apart from the music on the radio, they remained silent for the entire drive.

"Time to put our relationship act on. I'm sorry, but I am going to have to touch you while we're in the park." Drew's voice was harder than she'd ever heard it.

"I know. That's fine."

He frowned at her and then parked the car, turned it off, and got out, slamming the door more forcefully than was necessary. When he opened her door, his face was completely different. He wore a warm smile and took her hand, squeezing it as he pulled her from the low seats.

They walked to the ticket gates, his arm firmly planted around her waist. He paid for them both to get in, and then they were submerged in a colorful swirl of chaos. The smell of hotdogs and popcorn was overwhelming, and the terrified screams of people on the roller coasters filled the air.

"Which ride would you like to go on first, Ariel?" Drew asked.

Jade looked up at the roller coasters, huge iron snakes curling through the sky. A conflicting mix of excitement and fear pulsed through her. She loved rollercoasters. "Any. I don't mind."

A group of teenage girls caught her attention. They were clustered near a trash can whispering and pointing in their direction.

"What's their problem?" she asked.

Drew looked over and waved at the girls. A round of hysterical giggles broke out, and they ran away.

"That happens sometimes. They recognized me." He shrugged his shoulders as if it were no big deal.

"Does that happen often?" Jade scanned the passing faces and saw recognition on about half of them. One lady even had her cell phone out and was unashamedly taking photos of Drew.

"Just ignore them. It only happens when I go to a high profile place like this. If I'm just walking down the street, it's less common."

"Wait…Did you bring me here as a publicity stunt?"

Drew's smile dropped, and he cricked his neck, politely asking her to follow him. Jade trailed him to a less populated area where people weren't as likely to overhear their conversation.

"That wasn't my main motivation, but I knew it was possible."

"You should have warned me. I would've put on more makeup." She put her hands on her hips.

"Please don't raise your voice." He looked over his shoulder to make sure people weren't staring. "I'm sorry if I did the wrong thing. I thought it would be good for us to get this out in the open. The press knows about us now, so hiding is only going to make them go on a manhunt. If we give them opportunities to photograph us, they'll lose interest."

"You still should have warned me, Drew."

"Hey, it's not as if I called Entertainment Tonight and asked them to come down and spy on us. There was a chance I would be recognized, but I take that chance every time I leave the house."

Jade let out a long breath, letting her anger fade. "Right. Sorry. I'm just not used to being stared at."

"You're photographed hundreds of times a day by strangers."

"That's different," Jade said, laughing. "They aren't photographing *me*; they're photographing Ariel."

"Well, you're my Ariel."

She rolled her eyes. "Fine. Let's just get this over with."

"Hey, try and have fun, okay? I chose Six Flags because I wanted us to enjoy our date."

"All right. Let's flush our bodies with adrenalin and ignore everyone else."

"That's my girl." He grinned and led her back out into the crowd.

His words echoed in her mind as they lined up for the Apocalypse. Was she really his girl? As much as she'd put up the hard front of not wanting to mix emotions into their contract, she couldn't deny that, in her heart, she *wanted* to be his girl.

That thought was terrifying because it would only end in hurt. He didn't want to change his lifestyle. This act was purely to get his inheritance. Once he had his money, she'd be worthless to him and he'd walk away. She had to keep reminding herself of that and not get attached.

The roller coaster was terrifying. She'd been on the rides at Disneyland dozens of times, and she thought she was good on roller coasters. Nothing had prepared her for exactly how fast the Apocalypse was, though.

Her hair whipped around her face as she was twisted and turned like she was in a clothes dryer. The sky was dark, and all she could see was the swirl of lights from the park below. At some point, Drew's hand grabbed hers, and she let him hold it for the remainder of the ride.

"That was incredible," Drew yelled as their cart came to a halt and their restraints were released.

"My heart is pumping so hard!" Jade yelled back. It seemed that both of them had gone temporarily hard of hearing from the excitement.

And then they were blinded by flashes of light. Jade thought she must have burst a blood vessel in her eye on the ride until she heard the yelling.

"Drew! Is that your girl?"

"Drew! Over here!"

"Drew, do you have a comment for TMZ?"

Drew looked just as stunned as Jade felt for about three seconds, and then he smiled and stepped forward.

"Evening, everyone. Is it too much to ask to have a night out with my girl?"

"We just want to get a look at you guys," a woman with frizzy blond hair yelled.

Drew turned to face Jade and mouthed the word, "Sorry."

"It's okay. Better to get this over with, I guess," Jade said.

She stepped forward and gave a little wave. Flashes went off, blinding her again. This was much more invasive than at work.

Usually it was just one camera at a time, or if she was in the parade, the cameras didn't flash in her face.

"What's your name, gorgeous?" the guy from TMZ called loudly.

"Jade," she said.

"Speak up, sweetheart!" TMZ yelled, holding out a voice recorder.

"Jade," she said louder.

Some of the reporters scribbled in notebooks, and others continued to snap pictures. Beyond the barricade of reporters, a group of parkgoers stood around watching, most taking pictures as well.

This was not something Jade had been prepared for. She'd known Drew was semi-famous, but she'd always thought his father would be the media magnet.

"Give us a kiss?"

Drew looked at Jade, and she gave him a little nod. He turned to the crowd and addressed them with a stern voice.

"Okay, guys, we're happy to pose for a few pictures, but after that, we'd appreciate if you'd leave us in peace to enjoy the park. Let's help each other out. Deal?"

Several of the reporters nodded their agreement.

"Let's give them something good so they'll leave us alone, okay?" he said to Jade.

"All right." Truthfully, she was terrified.

Drew wrapped her in an embrace and pulled her against his body, leaning in for a kiss. She was quite passive in her response, but not unhelpful. She just allowed him to kiss her how he felt was best for the photos.

Through her closed eyes, she could still make out the camera flashes, and several of the photographers wolf whistled as they pulled apart. It seemed they weren't appeased, though.

"Show us the ring!" the frizzy blonde yelled.

Drew grabbed Jade's hand and held it up, the diamond sparkling as flashes bombarded the faceted surface of the rock.

"Okay, folks. We've played the caged monkeys for long enough. Thanks for your interest, but it's time to let us go back to our date."

"Congratulations, Drew!"

"Drew! What do you think of the comments that Tully made about Jade?"

Drew gave a well-practiced smile. "Honestly, I haven't spoken to Tully for a few days, and I haven't heard anything she's said. I'm not concerned."

The photographers started to disperse, and Jade was pleased to see that most of them were respectful. One or two lingered, following them from ride to ride, but on the whole, they were able to enjoy their date in peace.

And they had a good time. Spending time with Drew was easy. He was fun loving, and Jade enjoyed talking with him. They went on every ride in the park, a couple more than once, and only left when the park shut down for the night.

Drew drove her home slowly, not in any rush to say good night. When they finally pulled up at her apartment block, the car was full of tension, as if they'd been on a real date.

"I feel like I should kiss you good night," Drew admitted, naming the awkwardness.

He rested his hands on the steering wheel and left the car idling.

Jade had the urge to invite him inside again, but she knew that wouldn't end well. Her heart was getting too involved as it was, and she had to keep her guard up. She took a preemptive strike.

"Thanks for a fun night, Drew. I had a good time."

He smiled and turned to face her. Jade unbuckled her seat belt and opened the car door, letting him know that a kiss was not in the cards.

"Would you like me to walk you to your door?" he asked.

"That's not necessary."

"Well, as my mother so proudly professed the other night, I'm a gentleman."

He climbed out of the car and met Jade at the sidewalk. They walked to the building, both with their hands swinging at their sides. Jade felt as if her hand was tingling, fighting to reach out for his, but she put it in the pocket of her jeans instead.

She waited at the building's door, but Drew made no turn to leave. He must have meant he wanted to walk her to her apartment. Jade unlocked the door, and they walked up the stairs together. With each step, the tension built. It was as if the conversation they'd had before they went to the park had been forgotten. She could tell that Drew was going to kiss her.

"We'll have to schedule another date soon. Keep the momentum going," she said, jingling her keys nervously in her hand as they climbed to the second level.

"How about breakfast?"

"I can't. I'm working tomorrow."

"Oh, okay. Well, I'll call you tomorrow." He sounded disappointed.

They reached Jade's door, and she turned her back on him, fumbling to put her keys in the lock. Drew had other ideas. His hands sat on her waist and twisted her so her back was against the door.

"Ariel, I had a great time with you tonight." His voice was husky as his eyes darted between hers and her lips.

"Me...me too."

He hummed his approval and pushed his body flush against hers.

"Don't you think *this* feels like a good end to the night?" His hips nudged against hers, making her suck in a breath.

"Drew..."

He didn't let her finish her sentence. His mouth was on hers, moving hungrily. He tasted like midnight and popcorn. It would be so easy for her to succumb to him, to invite him inside and lose herself in him. She wanted it. But he wasn't hers to have. At least, not in the way she wanted.

She mustered all her resolve and pushed on his chest, trying to get him to break away. He resisted for a second, but then he conceded to her wishes and stepped back.

"You're really firm on the rules, aren't you? There's no room for fun."

"I'm sorry. It just has to stay professional."

He nodded his head and took another step away from her.

"Your wish is my command. But, if you change your mind, I'm up for a little fun with you."

"That's not going to happen, Drew. I'm sorry."

"Stop apologizing. You're not doing anything wrong. It's isn't a crime to not be attracted to me."

She felt terrible. She hadn't meant to hurt his feelings. "This isn't anything about attraction."

"So, you think I'm sexy." He grinned and gave her a wink. "I knew it."

She smiled. Playful Drew was back.

CHAPTER ELEVEN

Lies and Tiaras

Drew got home feeling hot and bothered. That Ariel was just too sexy for her own good. And the hard-to-get act was driving him crazy. He'd never desired anyone so much in his entire life. The fact that he couldn't have her just made him want her all the more.

He pulled in his driveway and turned off the car. As he walked up to the front door, his mind on Jade's green eyes, he saw a person hiding in the bushes.

"Who's there?"

"It's me." Tully stepped out, looking disheveled.

"Tulls, what are you doing here?"

"I just wanted to see you. Can I come in?"

He looked up at his parents' bedroom window. The light was off.

"All right, but be quiet. Don't wake the parents."

He led her up to his bedroom, guiding her as she wobbled on the stairs. Drew wasn't surprised to see she was drunk—again.

He closed the bedroom door as quietly as he could and turned to see Tully lying on his bed, her already short skirt riding up her thighs. She didn't appear to be doing anything to hide her panties.

"What are you doing here?" he whispered.

"I just wanted to see you. We haven't hung out in ages."

"I've been busy."

"So I've seen. With a redhead."

"My fiancée," he reminded her.

"Come now, Drew. We both know that's not going to last."

"That's none of your concern, Tulls."

"You're not in love with her. I can tell."

"Just drop it. I'm getting married. Nothing you say is going to change that."

She wiggled her body and spread her legs wide, giving him a full view between her thighs.

"Fine. But is there something I can *do?*"

Drew let out a long breath. His cock jumped in his pants at the sight before him. He was a guy, and seeing a girl splayed in his bed had an obvious effect on him. But his heart wasn't craving the blonde. Drew was about to tell Tully, not too kindly, to get out of his house, but what was the point?

Ariel had made it very clear she wasn't interested in him. There was no way he'd be able to stay celibate for a year, and she'd agreed they could have one-night stands. Hell, for all he knew, she had a fuck buddy of her own. The idea upset him more than it should have.

So, instead of kicking Tully out of his bed, he went to her. As he lay over her and removed her clothing, he didn't see her blond hair; he saw red. As he thrust inside her, he didn't see blue eyes looking up at him; he saw green. And when he released, in a shudder of pleasure, he breathed Jade's name into the night.

Drew awoke late in a tangle of limbs. His phone was ringing, and he threw Tully's arm off his chest so he could lean off the bed and dig through his pocket.

"Hello?"

"Hey. I just thought I'd call you on my break to see how you are."

"Ariel!" He glanced at Tully to make sure she was still sleeping and then ducked into his bathroom. "How are you?"

"I feel bad. I'm sorry about how I handled last night. I just wanted to make sure that we're okay."

Drew ran his hand over his face and scratched through his hair.

"We're great. No harm done. I pushed the boundaries. It's my fault if things are awkward."

"Good. I mean…no awkwardness on my part." It sounded like she was smiling, and he pictured her pretty face in his mind. "Your mother called me earlier this morning. Did she tell you?"

"No. I haven't seen her yet. What did she want?"

"She invited me over for dinner tonight to talk about the wedding. I said I could come. That's all right with you, isn't it?"

"Yeah, sure. Sounds good."

"Great. I'll be over after work, then."

"Hey, Ariel, bring your shell bra."

She hung up on him, and he laughed, heading back to his bedroom. His stomach plummeted when he saw Tully still in his bed, and he groaned.

"Hey, Tulls. Rise and shine, time to go."

"What?" She rolled over and pulled a pillow over her head.

"Up!" Drew grabbed the blanket and yanked it off the bed, leaving a naked Tully curled up on the mattress.

She threw the pillow off and smiled at him seductively. "If you're going to expose me, you might as well enjoy the view."

She held her arms out, inviting him into her embrace. Drew considered it for a moment, but Jade's voice was still ringing in his head, and touching Tully was the last thing he wanted to do.

"I've got a busy day. You should go home," he said, trying to keep his voice flat so she took the hint.

She frowned. "I'll come by later tonight, then. We can pick up where we left off."

"No. Jade's coming over tonight to spend some time with my parents. You're not welcome, Tully."

"Jade? But last night—"

"Last night nothing. I'm *engaged*. That hasn't changed."

Drew felt like a dog. Technically he hadn't cheated on Jade. He was still a single guy, but he had to pretend that he'd just cheated.

Tully gathered her clothes and started getting dressed with a sour expression.

"What happened last night is our secret, Tulls. You can't say a word."

"And if I do?" she spat.

"Our friendship will be over."

"If I did tell, your engagement would be over, and I wouldn't have any competition."

Drew panicked. She was calling his bluff.

"Look, you know me well enough to know that I've never been a one-woman guy. There might, on occasion, be times when I'll want some female attention from someone other than Jade. If you want that to be you, you'll keep your mouth shut."

Drew hated himself. Not only was he condoning cheating, something he'd never done—it was one of the reasons he didn't have relationships. He couldn't cheat if he wasn't committed to anyone—but he was lying to a friend he'd had for years. The sick feeling in his stomach grew worse.

"So, you want me to be your dirty little mistress?" Tully pouted her lips.

"Something like that."

Drew reasoned this was probably the only way to keep Tully's mouth shut, and the possibility of sex when he needed it was alluring.

"Will you call me later?" she asked as she put her dress back on.

"Of course, Tulls. We're friends. I'll probably see you soon."

That seemed to appease her. She kissed his cheek, and he heard the click-clack of her heels as she made her way down the staircase. When the front door closed, he let out a breath of relief.

He hated that he'd used Tully. It was obvious she cared about him. In truth, he'd thought about dating Tully at one point, but there was something about them that just didn't match up. She was fun to hang out with and a real party girl, but that wasn't what he would look for in a partner.

Tully didn't stay on his mind for long, though. Drew had a busy day ahead of him at the school, coaching the kids.

As he packed up the basketballs and locked up the equipment after practice, he had a thought and got his cell phone out.

I'm in your neighborhood. Want a ride to dinner?

He sent the message and waited for Jade to reply. He sat on the bleachers and looked up into the sky. The sun was setting, and the clouds were cantaloupe orange and pink smudges against the hazy smog. His phone beeped.

Sure, thanks. I just got home. Come on over.

Drew locked up the court and drove the few blocks to her house. He didn't have to stop the car, however, because she was standing on the sidewalk waiting. She smiled and waved as he drove up.

"Hey," she said, climbing into the car and leaning over to give him a one-armed hug.

"Hey yourself. How was work?"

"Oh, you know. Smile for the photos and continuously get told how pretty I am."

"Well, in that shell bra, who can blame people for being stunned by your beauty?"

"You know I don't wear the shell bra. You've seen me at work."

"So, you're always in that huge dress? That's not very sexy."

Jade punched his arm. "It's not meant to be sexy, you horndog. I spend my day with children."

"Still, I'm sure the dads that are with their children would appreciate a little skin."

"You're welcome to submit your disappointment to the comments section on the web site."

"I might just do that."

He pulled into the driveway of his parents' house and turned off the engine. Jade reached to open her door, but he put his hand on her arm to stop her.

"Can we have a chat for minute?" he asked.

"Sure." She chewed her lip as she waited for him to speak. Drew realized that was her nervous twitch.

"So, I don't know if you'll care, but I want to be honest with you."

"Okay."

He braced his hands on the steering wheel, building courage to say what he needed to say. "I had sex last night," he blurted out.

Jade didn't say anything. He searched her face, looking for some kind of reaction but couldn't see any response at all. She was completely still.

"I know we talked about that when we made this agreement, and we both said that one-night stands were acceptable. I'm not dating anyone; it was just sex. I just feel like I should tell you."

"Thanks?" she said, sounding like she was asking a question.

"Should I have kept it a secret?"

"No. No, really, thank you for telling me."

"Are you okay with it?"

"I guess so. I mean, it's weird that you just had sex with someone else, and now we're going into your parents' house to plan our wedding. But this is a weird situation."

"If you're not okay with it, just say so, and I won't do it again." Drew was surprised as the words left his mouth. Was he really promising to not have sex for a whole year just to please this woman who was still basically a stranger to him?

"I'm okay with it. We're not really a couple."

Her words said one thing, but when he tried to hold her hand as they walked into the house, she pulled away. He hoped she was just processing the information and not actually hurt.

"You're an amazing cook, Laura," Jade said, resisting the urge to lick her plate.

Drew had been trying to catch her eye across the table all through dinner, but Jade couldn't bring herself to look at him. She'd meant what she'd said in the car; Drew was free to do what he wanted. He owed her nothing, but it still stung.

She risked a glance at him while he was passing his plate to his mother, and she couldn't help but imagine him kissing someone else just a few hours before. She shook her head. Thoughts like that weren't going to do her any good.

She was the kind of person who always tried to be positive and see the good in people and situations. She was going to look at this as a blessing. Despite her constant reminders that Drew wasn't hers, she'd allowed herself to begin to develop feelings for him. This was the perfect reminder to keep her feelings in check.

Drew obviously wasn't developing any romantic feelings, so she wouldn't allow herself to either.

"What's your favorite color, Jade?"

"Excuse me?" she said, looking up at Laura.

"So we can build a color scheme."

"Oh. Blue, I guess."

Laura frowned. "Blue *might* work. Drew's eyes would certainly pop with a blue tie. I'm just not sure if blue is happy enough, though. How would you feel about yellow? Or orange?"

"Orange?" Jade asked, trying to hide her disgust. She hated orange.

"Mom, if Jade likes blue, then we'll make it work."

"It's okay, Drew. Your mother has exquisite taste. I'm happy to hear her advice," Jade said, still not looking at him.

"No. Drew's right. I think we can make blue work. Have you two decided on a date?" Laura leaned forward in her seat, her eyes alight with curiosity.

"In the summer. August sometime, around Dad's schedule."

"*This* summer?" his mother asked, sounding shocked.

Jade kept her mouth shut. This was a topic for Drew to sort out with his mother.

"Yes, Mom. We don't want to wait a whole year to start our lives together, and we want good weather."

"Drew, we live in southern California. Unless you marry in the dead of winter, you're pretty much guaranteed good weather," his mother scolded. "Is there a reason you want to marry so fast? August is only five weeks away."

"No reason other than being in love." Drew reached across the table to take Jade's hand.

She let him, reaching out to make the physical connection.

"I don't mean to be rude, and I mean no disrespect to you, Jade, but I have to ask...Is there a baby on the way?"

Jade felt a blush rise up her cheeks. Drew dropped her hand and turned on his mother, his eyes flashing with something that concerned her.

"Of course not! We're not stupid, Mom. Is it so hard to believe that we're in love?"

Jade was worried. He seemed *too* defensive. She worried Laura would pick up on the fact that his inheritance was in the mix and call them on it. She didn't think she could lie to Laura's face if she was asked directly about the inheritance.

"I'm sorry, honey. As I said, I had to ask. And, considering your history, I hope you can understand why I'm shocked you want to rush so quickly into a commitment." She turned to Jade. "You must be an exceptional woman, is all I can say."

Jade tried to give a natural smile, but she felt like trash. Laura was so nice, and she obviously loved her son and wanted him to be happy. It wasn't right that she was investing herself in this fake relationship.

"...roses are always classic, or maybe lilies. What do you think, Jade?"

Jade snapped her head up, looking at Laura with a blank expression.

"Laura, I'll be honest, I don't know a lot about these things, and I especially don't know what's involved with planning a wedding that will be in the eye of the media. I'm happy to take direction from you."

"You know, with the short time frame and your openness to ideas, I'm thinking we should hire a planner. Would that suit you?"

"That's fine with me." Jade honestly didn't feel like planning her dream wedding when it wasn't for real.

"Well, then, I'll phone around and see who's available on short notice. Leave it to me, kids."

Laura got up and walked out of the room, presumably to call around for a wedding planner. Drew looked at Jade with wary eyes.

"You okay?" he asked.

She let out a long breath and leaned back in her chair. "I'm fine. Just a bit overwhelmed with all the wedding stuff."

"Don't worry about it. My mom will take care of it. All you'll have to do is show up on the day." He gave her a dazzling smile.

She smiled back, but it was forced, and his eyes narrowed. He knew something was up.

"Come out to the island with me? I'd love to show you my favorite place in the house."

"All right," Jade said.

She stood and waited for Drew to indicate which way she should walk. He came up behind her and put his hand in the small of her back, guiding her through the halls. The house was grand. That was the only word Jade could think of to describe it.

If she were to picture a movie star's home in her mind, this would be pretty close to her imagination. A grand staircase, marble pillars, iconic artwork on the walls. Drew moved through the rooms, ignoring the beauty around him. Jade supposed that when you lived somewhere and saw the beauty every day, you didn't appreciate it.

They stepped out a set of double doors and onto a wooden decking. Jade gasped. When Drew had said he was taking her to "the island," she wasn't really sure what he'd meant, but he hadn't been speaking in code. There was an island in the middle of a large swimming pool.

"It's really an island," she gasped, staring in amazement.

"Of course. My father loves Fiji and wanted to create a little piece of it here."

The pool looked like a donut, with a wooden bridge leading from the deck over the water to the island. On the island was a palm tree and several chairs.

Drew sat down and pulled Jade into his lap. She struggled.

"My mom might see us out the window. We need to look loved up."

She conceded and settled into his embrace, looking up at the stars.

"Are you all right? You were so playful on the drive over, and since I told you what I did last night, you've been distant."

"I'm sorry, Drew." She spun in his lap so she was straddling him and they could speak face to face. "You haven't done anything wrong. I just wasn't expecting it."

"But we're okay, right?"

"Yes, we're okay."

He pulled her down and kissed her, wrapping his arms around her waist and pulling her against him. Jade was startled but melted into him, allowing the kiss.

"Was your mom watching?" she asked when they pulled away. She glanced over her shoulder toward the house but couldn't see anybody.

"Yeah."

Jade raised her eyebrow, but he gave her an innocent smile, and she let it drop.

"I could get used to this," she said.

"What?"

"Living on a tropical island."

"Really? Coming from Florida, I thought you might be sick of the sand and the sun."

"The water is what I love. My dream holiday would be to go to the Great Barrier Reef."

"My father went there a few years ago. He loved Australia."

"I'll get there one day."

"You can go wherever you want when you get your payment."

"You're right." Jade perked up.

Her life was going to be so different after this was all over. She had to keep reminding herself *why* she was getting involved with Drew. It didn't matter if he was having sex with someone else. He wasn't hers to be jealous over. She was here for the money and for no other reason.

"I think Australia will be my first destination."

CHAPTER TWELVE

Reality Bites

Jade groaned. She reached for her phone as it vibrated on the nightstand.

"Hello?" she asked, her voice hoarse from sleep.

"Jade? Are you with Drew?"

"What? Who is this?" She sat up and rubbed her eyes, trying to place the voice. The last thing she needed was for a reporter to have her private number.

"It's Laura Malik. Are you with him?"

"No, Laura. I'm at home."

"Shit."

"Is everything all right?" The panic in Laura's voice finally registered, and Jade was wide awake. "Has something happened?"

"I don't know. He called me just a moment ago, extremely drunk. His words were so slurred I couldn't understand anything he said, and then the line just went dead. Do you have any idea where he could be?"

Jade wracked her brain. The truth was, unless they had an arranged date, she and Drew didn't talk about their plans. She had no idea what he did at night or where he would be.

"Do you have phone numbers for any of his friends?" Jade asked, trying to be helpful.

"Yes. I tried you first because I hoped you'd be with him. But I can try Tully."

Jealousy bubbled in Jade's stomach, making her feel nauseous. She looked at the clock and saw it was close to three in the morning. More than likely he was at a club.

"Oh, Aaron has Tully on the phone right now," Laura informed her.

Jade waited, hoping for good news. She could hear Aaron talking in the background but couldn't make out what he was saying.

Laura came back on the line. "He's at The Key Club on Sunset. Tully said he's drunk. Aaron's going to pick him up. I'm so sorry to wake you, dear."

Jade chewed her lip. She knew she wasn't really Drew's fiancée, but she still cared about him and wanted to make sure he was okay.

"Do you think it would be okay if I came over to see him?" she asked.

Laura let out a soft sigh. "I think that's a good idea. He'll be angry that he's been brought home like a child. Seeing you will hopefully make him happy."

"Okay, I'll be there soon."

She dressed quickly in jeans and a T-shirt and ran out onto the street. Times like this was when she needed a working car. She'd make sure to take hers to the mechanic in the morning. The power bill payment would have to be delayed a little. She waved down a taxi and gave him the Beverly Hills address.

Her leg bounced the whole way to Drew's house, and she was surprised her fingers weren't bloody stumps from the ferociousness with which she'd attacked her nails. Aaron's car had just pulled up in front of them, and she jumped out of the taxi.

"Thanks for coming, Jade. I'll take care of the cab," Aaron said, getting out of the driver's seat.

He went to pay the driver, and the driveway grew dark as the taxi drove away.

"Drew?" she whispered, leaning through the car's window.

"Ariel?" he asked, his sour expression turning to curious. "What are you doing here?"

"Come on, son. Time to come inside," Aaron said, opening the car door and trying to help Drew to his feet.

"Fuck off."

"Drew!" Jade scolded.

"I don't need your fucking help. I'm not a child." He pushed his father's hands away and got out of the car.

He swayed and staggered all the way to the front door but couldn't manage to open it. His fingers kept slipping off the handle.

"I'm sorry he was so rude," Jade said.

Aaron gave her a dark look. "He's always like this when I bring him home."

Jade frowned. Aaron opened the door and let Drew inside. They both entered, and Jade wondered if she should just go home.

"Come on, Ariel," Drew called from inside.

She walked up to the door and saw he'd collapsed on the day bed in the foyer. Laura came running down the stairs in her nightgown and fussed over her son.

"Drew, we were so worried."

"I'm fine, Mom."

"You're not fine," Aaron said sternly. "This is the last time, Andrew. Do you know the risk I take for you every time I head into Hollywood in the middle of the night? What if I'd been photographed?"

"Because that's what's important, Dad, right? Your career?" He then vomited on the floor.

Jade pressed herself against the wall, trying to stay out of the way. "Would you like me to clean that up?" she offered, unable to picture the regal Laura Malik on her knees mopping up vomit.

"It's fine, Jade. Our housekeeper will take care of it. Perhaps you could help him to bed?" Laura asked.

"Yes," Drew said with a wonky grin. "Join me in bed."

He stood on shaky legs, and Jade ran over, letting him put his weight on her shoulders. She slowly walked him up the stairs to his bedroom.

"Would you like to have a shower?" she asked once the door was closed.

"Only if you join me." He gave her that lazy grin again, and she blushed.

"Probably not a great idea."

"Then just lie with me in bed." He collapsed onto the mattress and fell to sleep right away.

Jade thought about sleeping on the floor, or finding a guest bedroom to sleep in, but what if Laura came to check on Drew? She would find it strange if they didn't share a bed.

So, she slipped her jeans off, kept her shirt on, and climbed under the sheets.

Drew rolled closer and draped his arm over her stomach, holding her close. She fell asleep to the sound of Drew's soft snores and the smell of cigarettes and vomit.

Drew stirred. His head spun a little, but he was more concerned with the warm body next to him. All he could remember from the night before was that the band at the club was fantastic and he'd had fun. It looked like he'd had more fun than he remembered. It wasn't the first time he'd woken with a mysterious girl in his bed.

He brushed the red hair back and started when he saw it was Jade. He didn't remember seeing her at the club, but he couldn't hide the fact he was happy it was her. The attraction he'd felt for Jade had really messed with his heart. Knowing they'd taken their relationship to a physical level would make their deal easier. He wouldn't have to worry about hiding one-night stands from the media.

He reached out and stroked her cheek, making sure she was real, and her eyes slowly opened.

"This is a new development," Drew said, smiling down at her. "I'll be honest that I don't remember a lot of what happened last night, but waking with you in my bed was a lovely surprise."

He leaned down and kissed her. She froze for a second but then kissed him back. With her encouragement, his body shifted and slid over the top of her, pushing her into the mattress.

"Drew," she mumbled into his mouth. "Stop."

He pulled back. "We didn't?"

Jade shook her head, and his heart plummeted. He closed his eyes and tried as hard as he could to remember what'd happened the night before. He had no memory of seeing Jade at all. Tully had been with him, as well as some of her friends. He remembered making out with one of them in the bathroom.

"Why are you here, then?" he asked.

"You were drunk. Your mom called me to see if I knew where you were, and I wanted to make sure you got home safely."

"Oh." His body rolled to the side. She was only there because his meddling mother couldn't keep her mouth shut. It wasn't that she wanted to be there with him.

"Is that okay?" she asked.

He rolled to the other side of the bed and stood up, swaying slightly on his unsteady legs. "I'm going to take a shower."

He left her alone in the bed. When he came back, she was gone.

Drew opened the door and smiled at Jade. He reached for her, pulling her by the waist into his arms and pressed a kiss to her mouth.

"You're very happy to see me," she said.

"Well, I missed you. After you disappeared from my bed the other day, I was worried you'd run."

"I wouldn't do that."

"You ignored my calls." He raised an eyebrow, daring her to deny it.

"I just needed some time to think about things. You scared me the other night. I've never seen you act like that before."

"It's nothing to worry about. I can handle myself," he assured her. "So, we're good?"

"We're great."

He grinned and gave her a pointed look, hoping she'd pick up that she had to play the loving fiancée right off the bat. The buffer of a little time together before they saw anyone else was a luxury they didn't have today. His mother and the wedding planner were waiting for them just down the hall.

"I've missed kissing you," he said loudly so his voice would carry into the house.

"I can tell." She giggled. To Drew's surprise, she grabbed his shirt and pulled him to her, initiating a long kiss. "Is that better?"

"Much." Drew laughed and laced his left hand through her right, guiding her to the den.

"Ah, here they are. Cassandra, I'd like you to meet my son, Drew, and his lovely bride-to-be, Jade."

A scary-looking woman with tightly curled gray hair and a face that had so much Botox it was a wonder she could blink stared back at them. She looked down her nose at the couple and folded her arms over her large chest. Drew thought he'd seen the woman on one of those plastic-surgery-gone-wrong exposés on TV.

"You're a *new* couple," she said with distaste.

"Yes," Laura said. "The relationship is quite new, but it's clear how perfect they are together. My husband and I are very happy for Drew that he's found someone he cares about."

"Hmm," Cassandra hummed, obviously not impressed.

Drew put his arm around Jade's shoulder, hoping to show they were a solid couple, which was actually a little ironic.

"We've already had a few talks, and the palate is going to be centered around blues," Laura said.

"Jade, come and talk with me," Cassandra said, holding her hand out and ignoring Laura's comment.

Jade looked up at Drew, and he released her, but he leaned down and pecked a kiss to her cheek for show.

"All right, Cassandra," Jade said.

The wedding planner stiffened and pursed her lips.

"Cass-ahhhn-dra, not Cass-an-dra," she said curtly.

"Oh, sorry." Jade looked over her shoulder at Drew and cringed. He shrugged to show he couldn't tell the difference in pronunciation. Jade followed her out of the room, and Laura walked over and took her son's hand.

"It's happening, Drew. You're getting married."

She glowed at him, and Drew felt like dirt. For the first time since he'd agreed to go ahead with the fake marriage, he thought about how it was affecting his family.

"I'm just going to see if I can help Jade out," he said, giving his mom a quick hug and heading to his father's study.

He knocked on the door and stuck his head inside. Jade sat on the love seat, her back rigid and her eyes wide as Cassandra paced in front of her, waving her arms to emphasize a point that he'd missed out on hearing.

"Yes, Andrew? Do you need something?" Cassandra asked, turning with a click of her heels and frowning at him.

Jade gave him a pleading look with her eyes.

"I thought my opinion might be of some use in the planning," he said, stepping into the room.

Jade's shoulders relaxed, and she gave him a smile.

"Not necessary. Jade and I have everything under control." Cassandra tapped her long-nailed fingers on the keyboard of her laptop while she spoke.

"I don't mind sitting in. After all, it's my wedding too." He walked across the room and took a seat next to Jade.

She reached over and grabbed his hand, giving it a tight squeeze. Cassandra let out a loud breath and stopped typing.

"Really, Andrew, you'll just be in the way. I'm sure you have more important things to do. Leave this business to us. I won't keep your girl from you for much longer."

"Oh…okay," Drew said, shrugging his shoulders and giving Jade an apologetic look. He hoped it screamed that he'd tried to help her.

He closed the door behind him just as Cassandra asked Jade if she wanted doves or butterflies released after the ceremony. Drew's eyes went wide, and he decided that perhaps it was better that he wasn't helping out.

He figured they would be quite a while so he went out to the backyard to shoot some hoops. He didn't like the fact that several of the kids were better than him. Not that he thought he was the best player out there, but he didn't feel right being the coach if his students had more skills than he did.

He was twenty-three for thirty and sweating profusely when Cassandra appeared at the back door with her hands on her hips.

"Andrew, could you join us inside, please?"

"All right." He jumped and threw a final ball, pumping his fist as it swished through the net without hitting the backboard.

He grabbed a towel from the outside cupboard where his mother kept the pool towels and wiped the sweat from his face and hair. He slung it over his shoulder and headed into the house.

Jade sat in the formal lounge room with her ankles crossed and her hands folded neatly in her lap. He smiled at her, but she gave her head a tiny shake. Obviously they were supposed to stay quiet. He sat next to her and ignored the narrowed eyes of his mother, hoping that he wasn't sweating on her suede couch.

"Jade has given permission for me to plan most of the details myself as she doesn't appear to have any ideas of her own," Cassandra said, looking down her nose at Jade, who shrank back into the cushions.

Drew thought about bringing up the fact that he'd offered his ideas and had been sent away, but he didn't want to take on Cassandra, and he didn't want to embarrass his mother.

"Because of this responsibility, I will require meetings with you on a regular basis to check in on details," she said, looking at Jade.

"Oh, that's not necessary. I trust your judgment, and if you would like clarification on anything, I know Laura has impeccable taste," Jade said.

"If you prefer." Cassandra looked over at Laura, who nodded her head in agreement.

"Very well. Laura and I shall flush out the details, and I'm sure she will fill you in on everything as the decisions are made. In the meantime, I *will* need both bride and groom to be at scheduled fittings, rehearsals, and press appointments. Plus, Jade will need media training."

"Press appointments?" Jade asked, her voice higher than normal.

"Of course," Cassandra said as if it were the most natural thing in the world. "Aaron Malik's son is getting married. Andrew will be the main focus of the attention, but they'll be curious about you too, Jade. I'm surprised they haven't approached you already."

"We've had a few paps following us around," Drew said.

Cassandra nodded her head knowingly.

"I'll schedule some interviews with the media, and hopefully that will help to quell their curiosity. Now, Jade, we only have a few weeks, and it's going to be *impossible* to get your dress made by then, so we can't waste any time. You're going to come with me today, right now in fact, for a fitting." She handed them each a printed timetable. Drew's appointments were highlighted in blue and Jade's in pink. "As you can see, Andrew, you aren't needed today so I'll see you tomorrow for your tuxedo fitting. Jade, follow me please."

"Bye," Jade said, sounding like a child who'd been sent to her room.

Jade tried to think of something that would be worse than her current situation, but nothing seemed that bad.

"Maybe being submerged in a tub of live insects," she pondered softly to herself. "No, this is still worse." She let out a long sigh and stared at the full-length mirror.

"Ouch!" she said.

"Sorry," the seamstress said from under her skirt. "These pesky pins keep slipping. I'll be more careful."

"I like this off-the-shoulder look," Cassandra said, chewing the end of her pen and looking the dress up and down.

It was much fancier than anything Jade would have picked on her own, but she had to admit as she looked in the mirror that it was a beautiful gown. The ivory silk practically glowed as it cascaded over her hips to where the seamstress was hemming the train.

"Fire!" Jade blurted out, causing the seamstress to jump up and Cassandra to spin around, looking wildly around her. "Oh, sorry. There's not a fire."

"Why did you say that?" Cassandra asked, taking a deep breath and laying her hand over her heart.

"Sorry. I was thinking of something else."

Jade decided that being burned alive was worse than this. She stood still for the three hours it took to pin and cut the dress to her measurements and kept reminding herself that at least she wasn't on fire.

"Wanna play some ball?" Sam asked.

Drew sighed and moved the phone from his left ear to his right. "I'm a bit basketballed out."

"What? You love shooting hoops!"

"Yeah, but now I have to do it every day. The fun's kind of been taken out of it."

"A drink then?"

Drew smiled. "That will never lose its fun. I'll be over in ten minutes."

Drew drove the few blocks to Sam's place and let himself into the large house. Sam's trust fund had matured when he was eighteen. The one thing his parents had insisted on was that his first purchase was a house so that even if he wasted the rest of his money, he'd always have somewhere to live.

"I'm out back!" Sam called.

Drew went to the fridge and grabbed a beer on his way out to the pool. Sam was lying on a deck chair wearing sunglasses and a pair of shorts, a beer bottle balanced on his abs.

Drew cracked the top off his own beer and settled down in the deck chair next to Sam.

"'Sup?" he asked.

Sam rolled onto his side and pulled his sunglasses up. "So, how goes the fake wedding plans?"

Drew spat beer down his shirt front. "What?" He pulled his shirt off and dropped it onto the ground.

"Oh come on, Drew. I'm not stupid. You might act all high and mighty that our plan was a joke, but look at you now. A few weeks later, and you're magically engaged. Who is she? She's the blowjob girl, right?"

Drew closed his eyes and settled into the chair, tipping his face up to the sun. He was trying his best to look casual while he thought his way out of this. He couldn't let Sam know he was right. The ego on his friend was ridiculous, and Drew would never live it down.

"It was a coincidence."

"Fuck off!" Sam laughed. "You truly expect me to believe you threw out all those letters and then miraculously met a girl who wanted to marry you instantly? Oh, and that you got a personality transplant and actually *wanted* to get married?"

"It's the truth."

"So, you're in love. You're head over heels. You never want to see another woman naked for as long as you live."

Drew laughed. "I'm still a guy, Sam. I'll always want to see naked girls."

"Nice avoidance, my friend. Come on. I thought we were friends. I'm not going to tell anyone. It was *my* plan all along, remember?"

Drew sighed and drained his beer. "Fine. Jade is the hater girl."

Sam's jaw dropped open, and he hooted with joy. "I knew it! How did you make the *hater* agree to marry you?"

"With my charming wit."

"Phew. You are *good*, my man."

Sam got up, put his empty bottle on the ground, and did a back flip into the pool. When he came up, he shook his hair like a dog, splattering Drew with water.

"You can't tell *anyone*. I'm serious, Sam."

"My lips are sealed. But, seeing as you're not in love with her... that means I can have a crack, right?"

"She's going to be my wife!"

"Legally maybe, but not *really*. And anyway, she's smoking hot. If you're not going to enjoy her, someone should."

Drew glared at his friend. He was going to have to keep Sam away from his Ariel.

"Now, before the wedding, it's going to be important for you to learn how to deal with the media. I've seen clips of you and Drew out together, and your performance was...well, it was pitiful."

"Gee, thanks," Jade said, sighing.

Cassandra smirked. "I'm not paid to be kind, dear."

Jade shifted in her chair. She knew this was inevitable. If she was going to be part of the Malik family for the next year, she'd have to face interviews, and the paparazzi would only get more intense, especially with the wedding coming up.

"Okay, educate me," she said.

Cassandra smiled and gave an approving nod.

"First lesson—posing for photos."

"We can skip that. I have my photo taken for a living," Jade said proudly.

Cassandra set her lips in a thin line. "Posing for a photo you want taken and ones you are being hounded for are two very different things. Just go with me for a few minutes."

Jade spent four hours (Cassandra's version of a few minutes) smiling while showing teeth, smiling without showing teeth, learning how to give a polite I'm-not-happy-you're-taking-my-picture-but-I'm-not-going-to-be-rude face, and some full body stances specifically for the paparazzi.

"You have an excellent figure, so I won't bother teaching you about hiding wide hips or a round tummy. Any way you stand, you look good, so just focus on looking comfortable. Don't ever look directly into a camera lens. Even if you're posing for a specific camera, always look slightly to the side."

"Why?"

Cassandra's advice went against everything she'd been taught for photos at work. When she was Princess Ariel, she always smiled directly into the lens.

"The pros get paid more if they get eye contact. Why do you think they're always screaming at celebrities to look at them? Just don't do it. They are going to make your life hell, so don't do them any favors."

"Got it."

A knock sounded, and Jade wanted to kiss whoever was on the other side of the door. Drew stuck his head in.

"Andrew, how lovely to see you," Cassandra said, her arms held wide in welcome.

"I thought it might be time for a break," he hinted. "Have you stopped for lunch yet?"

"Is it lunch time already?" Cassandra asked, shocked.

"It's almost two," Drew told her. He winked at Jade when she flashed him a grateful smile.

"All right, we'll call it a day on lesson one. You did well, Jade. Tomorrow we'll work on lesson two. Interviews."

She strode out of the room and turned in the direction of the kitchen.

"How was lesson one?" Drew asked, leaning against the doorframe and looking much too handsome for his own good.

Jade gave her best I'm-not-happy-you're-taking-my-picture-but-I'm-not-going-to-be-rude face.

"Very nice," he said, chuckling. "I'm impressed. It took me months to get the I-hate-your-guts-but-have-to-smile face down pat. You wouldn't believe how many pictures there are of teenage me scowling at photographers."

"I think I've seen a few of them."

Drew rolled his eyes. "Of course you have."

"I might have Googled you after we met." She blushed a little.

Drew laughed. "I'm not surprised. I would have done the same thing in your shoes. You hungry?"

"Starving."

He led her out of the study, and they walked down the hall, hand in hand.

"I'm coming!" Jade yelled as she ran from her bedroom to the front door. Someone had been knocking incessantly to wake her up.

She pulled the door open to see Clare, Pam, and several of the girls from work, all dressed up to go out. Jade was very aware of the fact she was in her PJs with her hair in a bird's nest and a face mask on.

"Surprise!" her friends yelled in unison.

"What are you guys doing here?"

Clare grinned. "Well, I know you said you didn't want a bachelorette party…but come on, girl. We weren't going to let you get away with that. You're getting *married!* We have to celebrate!"

"We're so getting our drunk on tonight." Pam cheered.

"Is that even proper English?" Jade asked over her shoulder as Clare dragged her to her bedroom.

"There's no room for grammar lessons on our wild girls' night," Pam yelled after her.

"Why are you ready for bed?" Clare asked.

"I'm not *ready* for bed; I was *in* bed. It's almost midnight."

Clare pulled Jade's closet doors open and started sorting through the clothes while the girls from work, Cinderella and Belle—Lisa and Jen, got to work washing the mask off Jade's face. With a team of women working around her, Jade was primped into looking like a supermodel in less than an hour. The girls piled into a taxi and headed to Hollywood.

Jade had endured four dress fittings, six media lessons, and done a TV interview with Drew, all in preparation for her big day. She felt she deserved a good night's sleep, but it didn't look like her friends agreed.

Jade had never been in a strip club before.

"Why are we looking at naked women?" Jade asked once they were inside the smoke-filled room. It was dark, and she could barely see her friends. The only light came from the well-lit stage, where two girls were currently writhing around a pole.

"Because this is where the men hang out," Pam said, as if it was the most obvious thing in the world.

"That's true," Jade said. "But we're all taken. We're not trying to pick up men."

Clare and Pam looked at each other, and then they all burst out laughing.

"Maybe we'll just go to the bar across the street and have some drinks?" Lisa suggested.

They all agreed and made their way to the bar. It was packed, and the music was so loud, they could barely speak to each other, so they left there too.

"Where are we going to go? We have to do something fun for your bachelorette party!" Pam said with a pout.

"Really, I meant it when I said I didn't want a big fuss. Let's just get some food and go home."

"Wait, that club looks cool!" Clare said, pointing further up the street where there was a long line of people waiting outside a black building with blue lighting.

Jade made her way toward the end of the line, but Clare and Pam dragged her to the front.

"End of the line, ladies," the bouncer said.

"Do we have to? My friend here—" Clare pushed Jade forward "—is getting married in two days, and we're trying to give her a last night of freedom."

The bouncer looked the girls up and down and then gestured for them to go inside. Several people in the line yelled out about favoritism.

"Hey! When you look as good as these girls, I'll let you in too," Jade heard the bouncer say before the door to the club closed. Then all she heard was the pumping music.

"We're going to dance," Lisa said, pulling Jen after her.

"I'll get us some drinks," Pam called above the music and then weaved her way through the crowd.

"I need a bathroom." Clare disappeared as well, and Jade stood, alone, wishing she was at home in bed.

"Jade!"

Jade spun around, looking for who had called her name, but she couldn't see anyone she knew. Perhaps she'd imagined it.

"Jade!"

She tried to ignore it this time, sure that someone standing near her had the same name. She didn't want to be the girl that answered a call that wasn't actually for her.

"I thought that was you. Is Drew with you?"

Jade looked over her shoulder and took a second to realize that Tully Whittaker was standing there, smiling.

"Oh, Tully, hello. We didn't really get introduced properly at the dinner."

To be honest, Jade was shocked that Tully recognized her at all. Or that she'd approached. Tully hadn't been happy about the engagement and had made that fact well known to the media.

"So, is Drew here?" Tully looked around the crowd.

"No, he's in Vegas with his friends. Bachelor party."

"Oh, right." She looked disappointed. "The wedding's this weekend, isn't it?"

As if she didn't know. Drew said that Tully has asked him repeatedly if the wedding was still going ahead.

"Yes. Will you be there?"

"You don't know your own guest list? Jesus. If I was getting married, I'd be all over every single detail."

"I'm pretty relaxed about it, actually. Laura hired Cassandra to plan for us."

"How's everything going with you and Drew? All happy and smiles?"

"Yeah, we're great." Jade could have sworn she saw a look pass over Tully's face when she said they were fine. And it wasn't jealousy, which she would have expected. It was a smug, knowing look.

Jade felt a vibrating in her pocket and pulled out her phone. Drew's name flashed on the screen.

"Speak of the devil," she said to Tully and then answered the call. "Hey, Drew, how's Vegas?"

"I didn't wake you, did I?" There was a lot of noise in the background, and he sounded like he was yelling.

"No, I'm actually out in Hollywood with my friends. They threw me an impromptu bachelorette party."

He laughed. "Are you having fun?"

"I don't know if fun is the right word. I'll catch you up when you get home."

"Cool, cool. I'm at Aria, and it's going off."

"You sound drunk," Jade said.

"What?" he yelled. Cheering went up in the background.

Jade laughed, really hamming it up for Tully. She needed to be convincing that she was in love with Drew.

"I miss you. Please be safe tonight. I don't want to hear about you waking up in the Mexican desert or anything."

"I can't promise *anything*," Drew said, also laughing. "Hey, Ariel, I miss you too."

He hung up, but before she pulled the phone from her ear, she looked at Tully, smiling, and said, "I love you, too."

The blonde's eyes narrowed for a second, but she recovered quickly.

"How sweet. I could just eat you two up."

"Drew is very romantic," Jade agreed.

"You're Tully Whittaker!" Clare yelled in Tully's face.

"No shit, Sherlock." Tully flicked her hair over her shoulder.

Jade opened her mouth, about to tell Tully off for being rude, but she didn't get a chance. A flash of light went off in their faces. All three girls turned, stunned, to see several camera lenses pointed at them. Jade automatically turned away, but Tully pulled her into a hug and posed as the flashes continued.

"I just have to go to the bathroom," Jade said, grabbing Clare's hand, leaving Tully to the reporters.

In the crowd, they bumped into Pam, who was trying to carry three very full glasses without spilling anything.

"We're going," Jade said.

"But I got us Long Island iced teas!" Pam protested.

Jade dragged her friends out onto the street and started walking down the block, eager to get away from the cameras. Jen and Lisa were still inside, so she pulled out her phone and texted Lisa to let them know they'd left. Jen texted back a second later saying they were having fun and wanted to stay. They'd meet up later in the night. Jade sighed. She'd been having such a nice sleep before all of this craziness had happened.

"Can we *please* go home now?" she begged.

"We could," Clare reasoned. "Or we could have an In-N-Out Burger."

"Oh, you devil! Now I'm craving animal-style fries." Jade glared at her friend.

"Let's go!"

The three girls headed to the In-N-Out Burger on Sunset Boulevard, and Jade forgot all about Tully and the photos taken in the club.

CHAPTER THIRTEEN

The Words

"Would you mind sitting still, darling?" asked Jared, the hair stylist. He wore more eyeliner than Jade had ever seen on any other human being, and his spiky hair was blue at the roots, fading to mauve and then silver on the tips. Despite the strange first impression, he really pulled off the look.

"Sorry," Jade muttered, digging for her ringing phone. "Hello?" she said into the device, settling back into the chair so Jared could curl her hair.

"Operation Parent Pickup was a success," Clare said. "You're on speaker."

"Hello, munchkin!" Jade's mom, Lea, said in an echoing voice.

"Hi, Mom. I'm so glad you guys made it safely. Hi, Dad."

"Your friend drives way too fast," her dad, Greg, said.

Jade giggled. "Clare, please don't give my parents a heart attack. I'd like them alive for the ceremony."

"I'm doing the speed limit!" Clare protested. "Just because people drive slow in Florida, it isn't my fault."

"Are you excited, Jadey? Only a few hours until you'll be married!" Lea's voice was so excited that Jade felt like dirt. Her parents would be so disappointed next year when she told them she was getting a divorce.

"Yeah, I can't believe it."

"I'm dropping your folks at their hotel, and then I'm coming to you, okay?" Clare asked.

"See you soon, Clare. Mom, Dad, I can't wait to see you guys."

"We'll be at the church," Greg promised.

"Dad, we're not getting married in a church, remember? I told you guys it'll be at the country club."

Her dad started grumbling about Hollywood people and their blasphemous ways, and with a laugh, Jade hung up the phone.

Having her parents around was a good feeling. She hadn't seen them since she'd moved out to California, and she really missed them. Now that she was going to have some money in her bank account, she promised herself she'd try to visit them more often.

"You're done. Off to makeup with you, princess. Pamela, get your perky little ass in my chair," Jared said playfully.

Jade looked at herself in the mirror and smiled. Her hair was pinned, ready for the veil to be fitted, and fell in waves down her back. Pam sat down in the chair she'd just vacated, and Jared got to work on her blond tresses.

Jade went into the next room of the salon and saw an Asian woman wearing a white coat.

"Hi, I'm Jade."

"Please have a seat. Are you the bride?"

"I am."

Jade took a seat, and the woman put a cape around her neck.

"What color are your flowers?" she asked.

"White and red. I'm sorry. I didn't get your name…"

"Victoria. Would you like red lips to match your flowers?"

"I don't know. I've always felt that red lips with red hair was a bit much. Maybe neutral lips and bigger eyes?"

"Of course."

Unlike Jared, who'd chatted the whole way through doing her hair, Victoria was silent as she worked. She wore a puff on her little finger that dusted against Jade's cheek and presumably stopped her makeup from getting smudged.

"Smoky eyes or just eyelashes and liner?"

"Whatever is more bride-like," Jade said.

She felt like the worst bride ever. She was sure every other woman who'd gotten married in the history of the world had studied for weeks about exactly which color blush they wanted and had done several makeup rehearsals. But, knowing this wedding wasn't real, she just couldn't put her heart into it.

The door opened, and Clare's head popped around the corner.

"Just letting you know I'm here. I'll go get my hair done. You look gorgeous, by the way!"

"Thanks for getting my parents. Did they look well?"

Clare rolled her eyes. "Your dad grumbled the whole time about the weather. Apparently the sun in California isn't as nice as the sun in Florida. He's also pretty hurt that you're not getting married in a church."

Jade sighed. "Yeah, I know. I tried to explain it to him over the phone, but I'll talk to him again after the ceremony."

"I need you to stop moving your lips, please," Victoria said, holding a lipstick brush.

"Sorry." Jade gave Clare a look, and Clare giggled, closing the door.

Victoria really was just all business. No joyous wedding giggles and chatting for her.

Jade's phone beeped, but she didn't dare reach for it. Instead, she hoped it wasn't something important and tried to keep as still as possible. Her reflection in the mirror was changing. Her skin looked smooth, as if it glowed from the inside. Her lips were glossed without being showy, and her eyes looked large and catlike. She'd expected to look just like she did at work, but she didn't. She wore a lot of makeup to become Ariel, but this wasn't makeup for photos, this was makeup to look beautiful, and it made a difference.

As she stared at her reflection, she actually felt more like a princess than when she was dressed as one walking around Disneyland's parks.

"All right. Are you happy?" Victoria asked, stepping back and chewing on the end of her powder brush.

"It looks lovely. Thank you."

Jade went back to the room her friends were in and saw that Pam's hair was finished and Clare was in the hot seat, flirting shamelessly with Jared.

"Do I need to remind you that you're a newlywed, Clare?" Jade joked.

Jared laughed. "Don't worry, honey, I am *so* not interested."

"Hey!" Clare said. "I'm not flirting."

"You are," Jared laughed. "And I'm sorry, but you're not my type."

Jade put her hand over her mouth to stop the outburst of laughter she felt bubbling up inside her and then cringed, hoping she hadn't smudged her lipstick.

"I might be interested in your husband, though." He gave Clare a wink, and she giggled.

"You look gorgeous, Jade," Pam said. "All that's left to do is put the dress on and walk down the aisle."

"Yep, I guess that's all." Jade tried to put some enthusiasm into her voice but couldn't. She had no idea how Drew was feeling about all this. They hadn't spoken to each other since his drunken call during her bachelorette party. He'd gotten back from Las Vegas the night before, but of course her friends wouldn't let them talk, saying it was bad luck or some nonsense.

Jade wanted to tell them that the marriage was doomed anyway, but she couldn't. Remembering she had a text message, she looked at her phone. It was from Drew.

> *Hey, future-Mrs.-me, how's the prep going?*
> *You having fun with the girls?*

She smiled and typed her response, that she just wanted the day to be over. She hated lying to her friends and family, and this was going to be the biggest lie she'd ever told in her life. As much as it upset her father, Jade was thankful the wedding wasn't going to be in a church. If she had to lie to her friends and family, at least she wasn't doing it in a place of worship.

"Is that Drew?" Clare asked.

Jared sprayed hairspray all around her in a circle, and she coughed. "Maybe."

"Pammy, grab her phone. No communicating with Dream Guy!"

Pam held her hand out with a stern look on her face. Jade hit send before passing the phone to Pam.

"What if my parents or Cassandra call?" she asked.

"We'll screen your calls. Everyone but Drew gets through."

Jade rolled her eyes but accepted the terms. She knew her friends were just excited that she was finally getting married. After the bachelorette party, they'd confided in her that just before she told them about Drew, they were thinking of making her an online dating profile because she, in their words, *seriously needed to get loved up.*

Not that marrying Drew was going to help Jade with that, but they had good intentions.

The door opened again, and Cassandra came in. "The boys are on schedule. How are you girls going?" she asked, forgoing a greeting.

"I'm done," Jade said, relieved that she wouldn't get yelled at.

Cassandra had called her every day over the past few weeks, berating her for not having things finished, not making decisions, and not being on time. She was glad she'd finally done something right.

"The bridesmaids have no makeup," she said, not praising Jade at all.

"I'm on my way right now," Pam said, and she ran out of the room.

"I was late because I had to pick up Jade's parents from the airport," Clare said.

It was actually quite amusing how everyone spoke in short, clipped sentences to Cassandra, as if using superfluous words would annoy her. In truth, they probably would.

"Well, we can at least take some casual shots for Twitter. Getting ready, behind-the-scenes type shots. The media will love that." Cassandra pulled out her cell phone and pointed it at Jade.

The flash went off, and Jade blinked. "Hey, I wasn't ready."

"Even better. Have you been using the wedding hashtag?" Cassandra asked as she typed into her phone.

"You have a wedding *hashtag?*" Jared asked, looking impressed.

"Yeah, um, I don't really tweet that much," Jade admitted.

Cassandra frowned.

"But I can send one right now! Oh, wait, Pam has my phone."

"Use mine." Clare handed her phone over, and Jade opened the Twitter app, logging into her account.

She quickly typed out a message and hit send.

@JadePratt89 Prepping for my wedding to @TheRealMalikJr. T minus 2hrs & counting. #DrewAndJade #wedding

Cassandra's phone pinged, and she nodded her approval. "Very nice, Jade. Try and keep it up throughout the day. We want this hashtag to trend. Drew has already sent several tweets this morning."

"Sounds like Drew is the teacher's pet," Jared said, winking at Jade.

She wasn't sure why her wedding was such a media event. Sure, Aaron was famous, but Drew wasn't really. Yes, he smiled for paparazzi when he was out clubbing, but he wasn't an actor himself. She guessed people were just seduced by his lifestyle.

"Clare, you're all done. Off to makeup with you," Jared said, patting her ass as she stood up.

"Jade, we'll go and get your dress sorted out and then get some professional photos done," Cassandra said. "The photographer should be here in about fifteen minutes. Our bridesmaids can come join us when their makeup is finished."

Jade followed Cassandra into the dressing room of the salon and saw her finished dress hanging on the wall. She hadn't actually seen it completed. Cassandra had been furious with her when she'd missed the final fitting, but she couldn't get away from work on time because the other girl who played Ariel had called in sick, causing Jade to have to ride the afternoon parade.

"I just pray to heaven that it fits," Cassandra said, fussing over the skirts as Jade stepped into the dress.

Cassandra fastened the back and fluffed the train.

"Thank the Lord. It would have been a disaster if you'd put on any weight in the past two weeks."

Jade wanted to thank her for her trust, but she held her tongue. Instead, she twirled around and watched the material swish in the mirror.

"I want to wear this every day," she declared, looking over her shoulder at the way the dip in the back of the dress made her waist look small and her hips look curved.

"With how much you paid for it, you might want to," Cassandra said with a laugh.

"Drew's parents paid for the wedding. I actually have no idea how much anything cost."

Cassandra pursed her lips and then leaned in close to Jade's ear. "This dress was twelve thousand," she whispered.

Jade gasped. "That can't be right."

"It is, my dear. I sent Laura the invoice."

"But that's ludicrous! I could buy a car for that money…and I'm only supposed to wear this *once?*"

Cassandra laughed and wrapped her arm around Jade's shoulder, looking at them both in the mirror. "You'll get used to this extravagant lifestyle. Andrew grew up with it, and he's used to living with certain luxuries. You'll adapt. I give it a year before you won't even think twice about spending a thousand dollars on a pair of shoes."

Jade pulled up her skirts and looked at the white heels. "These were a thousand dollars?"

Cassandra laughed again and patted Jade's shoulder. "You look lovely, dear. The vision of a bride. Shall we send out one last tweet before we get in the car?"

"All right."

Jade posed, waiting for another photo, but Cassandra typed something quickly and sent it off, explaining that they didn't want to show the final look as they could sell the photos to a magazine. There was a lot Jade had to learn about living in the public eye.

The door opened, and Pam and Clare came in, both all made up, carrying their ice blue dresses.

"Hurry up, girls. We're ready to leave."

Pam and Clare both stripped down and got into their gowns. Jade thought they looked lovely. Cassandra clicked photos of the three of them and texted them to Jade's phone for her own private memories, but gave strict instructions that they weren't to be sent out on social media.

There was a stretch limousine waiting for them outside, and they climbed in. It wasn't far to the country club, which was why Cassandra had chosen that salon. A crowd of people waited outside the gates, and flashes burned through the windows as they proceeded up the driveway.

"So much for not having pictures," Jade muttered.

"Don't worry. This glass is mirrored. All they got were pictures of themselves," Cassandra informed them, tapping on the window to her left.

A man with thick gray hair and a mustache waited by the door, and Jade squealed. It had been too long since she'd seen her father.

The car pulled up, and when the driver opened the door, Jade pushed past Pam, climbing over her and hiking her skirts up.

She ran across the paved driveway and tackle-hugged her father.

"Daddy!" she squealed. "It's so good to see you." He smelled like peppermint and mothballs, just as she remembered. She breathed him in deeply.

"Well, look at my baby girl," he said, looking her up and down. "You're all grown up."

"I've been grown up for a while now, Dad."

"Twenty-four is still a baby!" he insisted.

"Yes, yes, lovely family reunion and all that, but we're on a schedule here," Cassandra said, pushing Jade and Greg toward the doors.

"Is Mom inside?" Jade asked her father, ignoring Cassandra's words but still walking toward the building.

"Yes, she went in early to get us good seats."

Jade laughed. "You both have reserved seating in the front row. She doesn't have to save your seat."

"We just wanted to be sure, sweetheart."

"I love you, Dad."

"Love you, munchkin."

"I thought I was a big girl now?" she teased as they stepped inside and heard the chatter from the waiting guests.

"You'll always be my munchkin, even when you have munchkins of your own."

He kissed her cheek and threaded his arm through hers, turning toward the large double doors where they were about to enter.

Jade froze for a second. Babies? Her father was talking about her having babies? Well, of course he was, she scolded herself. She was getting *married*. It was only natural that he would be thinking about her starting a family. She chewed her lip, anxious that she was going to hurt her family with what she was doing.

Maybe this fake marriage idea was going to be a disaster, but there she was in a dress that cost a year's rent, with a crowd full of people waiting. She couldn't back out now.

Cassandra tut-tutted and shook her head. "Don't ruin your lipstick." She pulled a small tube out of her pocket and ran it over

Jade's lips. "All right, it's a slow march. Remember the rehearsal. One-together-two-together. Please don't rush down the aisle. Pam, you're up first. Big smile."

She pulled a two-way radio out of her pocket and mumbled, "We're ready out here," into the static. Immediately, the music in the next room changed to the wedding march.

Pam glanced over her shoulder and winked before stepping into the room. A few seconds later, Cassandra waved Clare forward, and she too disappeared into the room. Jade and her father stepped forward. Through the doors, she could make out the backs of people's heads as they watched the bridesmaids walk up the aisle.

The music swelled, and Greg stepped forward into the doorway.

"You are the perfect bride," Cassandra said and patted Jade's ass as she walked past.

Everyone stood, and there were several hushed whispers as she walked down the aisle, her arm linked with her father's. The room was lit with candles and smelled like a garden. There were flowers everywhere: large vases by the altar, bunches at the end of each row of seats, and even garlands tastefully wrapped around the chandeliers. Everyone smiled at her. She glanced at her dad out of the corner of her eye and saw the pride on his face, the high set of his shoulders. When she was a little girl, she would climb into his lap and talk to him about her wedding. She wanted flowers and a beautiful gown and her father to walk her down the aisle. Greg would laugh and hug his daughter tightly, promising to be there on her happy day with bells on.

The strange pattern on his tie suddenly formed an image, and she sucked in a breath. The gold lines she's thought were a random swirled pattern were actually rows of bells set against the black satin background. He'd kept his promise.

Suddenly, it wasn't a fake wedding anymore. Joy overwhelmed her. She looked to the end of the aisle and saw Drew, his smile glowing at her. He looked like a real groom, with love in his eyes and nervous anticipation. Or at least Jade thought he did. She felt like she was truly walking to her destiny.

As they neared the front of the hall, the faces in the congregation became familiar. Her friends from work were on one side and several celebrities on the other. She thought she saw envy on the faces of some of the women on Drew's side, but she wasn't concerned with them, because when she looked to her left, her mother was smiling with teary eyes.

Jade gave a small wave and blew her mom a kiss, causing Lea to break down into actual sobs. They reached the front, and Jade looked up at Drew. He looked at her in such an emotional way, and in her heart, it all felt very real. She was about to *marry* the man in front of her.

"Who gives this woman to this man?" the celebrant said, breaking Jade and Drew's eye contact.

"I do," Greg said in a loud, ringing voice.

"Thank you," Drew said, shaking Greg's hand.

Greg kissed his daughter's cheek and placed her hand in Drew's. The couple stepped forward, and Drew squeezed her hand.

"We're really doing this," he whispered.

"Looks like it."

"Family and friends, we have all come together today to celebrate the love of Andrew Aaron Malik and Jade Emma Pratt."

Jade blacked out during the ceremony. She couldn't remember vowing to commit her life to Drew, even though she had. She came back to reality when she heard Drew say his vows.

"I, Andrew Aaron Malik, take you, Jade Emma Pratt, to be my lawfully wedded wife. I vow to love and cherish you for as long as we both shall live."

Jade swallowed thickly as he placed the ring on her finger.

His voice rang out strong and proud when he broke from the plan and said, loud enough for everyone to hear, "I love you, Jade."

"By the power vested in me by the state of California, I now pronounce you husband and wife. You may kiss your bride," the celebrant said.

Drew pulled her flush against him and kissed her. Cheers and applause broke out throughout the hall. They broke off the kiss, and he grabbed her, swinging her around in a circle. It was like a dream. Drew led her by the hand back down the aisle, and she was passed from hug to hug. Some of the arms around her belonged to familiar people and some to strangers. The only hug she paid attention to was the one from her mother.

"I'm so proud of you, Jadey. You look beautiful."

"I love you, Mom," she called as she was pulled into another embrace.

Cassandra appeared by her side and pulled both her and Drew through the throng of happy people. "We have professional photos to do."

Drew slipped his arm around her waist, and they followed Cassandra back out to the limo. The rest of the bridal party piled into the car, and they took off before anyone started taking pictures.

Jade looked out the window to see Aaron and Laura standing outside, posing for the photographers that had shown up. As the limo zoomed away, Jade realized how used to that life they were. She felt she'd never get used to it, and luckily, she'd only have to put up with it for a few months.

Drew kept her pulled close to his side as he chatted with his best man, Sam.

Jade watched him. He was so at ease, happy even. His arm remained tightly around her, stroking the bare skin of her shoulder as if it was normal to be touching her.

"You're married!" Clare squealed.

Drew's grin spread bigger, and he looked at Jade.

"Yeah," she said.

Drew laughed. "I think you're a bit stunned."

"Maybe a little," she admitted.

The car stopped, and they all got out. They were at the beach. Jade couldn't tell which one, but there wasn't a person in sight, so either it was the private beach of one of Aaron's friends, or they'd arranged security to keep the area clear. Jade wasn't surprised, after hearing how much her dress and shoes had cost.

"I want to start with just Drew and Jade, and we'll do the group shots in a few minutes," the photographer said.

The newly married couple followed him out onto the sand, Jade struggling in her high heels.

"Take the shoes off. I'll carry them if you like," Drew offered.

"Thanks." She pulled them off, and he hooked his fingers into the heels, swinging them in one hand with her fingers laced in the other. They gave each other a small smile, and a flash went off in their face.

"That was great. Moments like those are exactly what we want to capture," the photographer said.

They posed in several positions: Drew on his knees looking up at her, carrying Jade in the honeymoon hold with her skirts blowing behind them in the breeze, her holding her skirts up and his pants rolled up to his knees as they ran through the shallow water. All the cliché shots that Jade could imagine, they did.

Their friends joined them, and they posed as a group, some formal and some playful. There were close-ups of their ringed fingers and then solo shots of everyone.

"We're losing the light, so we'll wrap up soon. We might just get a few silhouettes of our couple in the sunset."

When all the pictures were taken, they drove back to the country club. The large hall they'd been married in had been completely transformed in the two hours they'd been gone. Small round tables filled the space now, with a large dance floor set up in front of a stage. Fairy lights and candles had been added too, and there was no overhead lighting, just the twinkle from the small lights, causing the whole room to glow.

Classical music played, and several people were slow dancing. As Jade and Drew moved through the room, people realized they'd arrived, and a hush fell over the room, followed by a loud round of applause.

Aaron appeared on the stage and welcomed all the guests, wishing everyone a good night and welcoming Jade into the family. Jade's father then appeared and gushed about how proud he was of his daughter and how he and his wife looked forward to getting to know Drew.

The smell of food filled the room as several waiters appeared with large silver trays and began putting plates on the tables. There was a rush of people moving to sit down, and Drew and Jade made their way to the bridal table near the stage. The photographer from the beach wandered around, snapping candid pictures of people enjoying the reception.

After the meal, Sam got up on the stage and gave his best man speech.

"Drew and I grew up together. He never had trouble finding girls, but he did have trouble finding one that lasted longer than a weekend."

Everyone around the room laughed and nodded their heads. Drew's reputation was well known.

"But when he met Jade, everything changed. Drew changed. We thought he was joking when he told us he was getting married. We all know this was a short engagement. Drew and Jade have only known each other a few months, but one thing about Drew, when he knows something, when he really believes in it, he jumps. Well, he's practically flung himself off a cliff today, but he's smiling. And who better to catch him from falling than that beautiful woman sitting by his side."

Jade blushed.

"To Drew and Jade!"

Everyone clinked glasses and echoed his wish. Clare stepped up beside him and practically pushed Sam out of the way to get to the microphone. A laugh rippled through the room.

"I haven't known Jade since childhood. She only moved out to Los Angeles a few years ago, but I've grown to love her, and I can't blame Drew for falling so hard so quickly, because I did the same thing. Jade is caring and loving, and Drew is in for a lifetime of that love. He's a lucky bastard. Take a look at them right now..."

All heads in the room turned to face them, and Jade wanted to duck under Drew's arm and hide from all the stares.

"Just look at them and what do you see? Love. I recently got married myself, and I love my husband very much, but I can tell you that it's hard. It takes work, and it takes patience. But these two, they make it look easy."

Suddenly, music swelled. Different music than was playing earlier. This wasn't classical. It had a definite beat, and a male voice started singing. Jade giggled, because it was "Love Is Easy" by McFly. She loved that song.

Just as she was starting to enjoy it, chairs started scraping, and people rushed past her. She recognized every single person that filled the dance floor and started dancing in sync. They were her work friends from Disneyland. They swayed and twirled in perfect sync, rushing between the tables in an obviously organized flash mob.

Then, in complete shock to Jade, Drew stood and started singing along with the song. Her mouth fell open as she watched him move in time with the dancers. He'd known this was going to happen. He'd learned the dance and spent time with her friends behind her back! She had no idea when he'd had time, but she couldn't help but burst into laughter.

He sang the words with such conviction that for a second, one tiny perfect moment, she allowed herself to believe that this wedding was real, and when Drew sang about love being easy with her, he really meant it. As the music faded and the dancers cheered themselves for their effort, Drew swept across the room and pulled Jade to her feet, dipping her over his knee and kissing her in true Hollywood fashion.

The stunned expressions of the audience turned into a huge round of applause.

"You should have seen your face," Drew laughed when they sat down.

"I can't believe you did that!"

"I wanted to do something special for you. Clare approached me, and it sounded like fun, so I went along with it. Plus, it makes this whole thing look all the more real for the guests."

And BANG! Just like that, the fantasy was shattered. He'd done it for the lie, not for her. She tried her best to keep smiling until she felt like she couldn't bear to keep her face frozen in the fake grin for another second. She excused herself to sit with her parents.

She spent the rest of the night with them, talking about their life back home, how her cat was doing, and how happy all her parents' friends were that she'd found love. Apparently, Lea had been bragging to everyone that her daughter was marrying a movie star.

"Drew's not actually an actor, mom," Jade said.

"He's close enough. There are genuine movie stars in this room!"

Jade looked around. It was true. It was so surreal to see people like Aaron Malik and Tully Whittaker mingling with her friends from work. After the cake was cut, the bouquet thrown, and the garter flung, there wasn't any way for Jade to hide from Drew any longer. She'd posed with him at the cake but made a beeline back to her parents, saying she wanted to spend as much time with them as possible. But now they had to leave or they'd miss their flight. She was about to be alone with Drew in the car to the airport, and she didn't think she'd be able to hide from him there. Perhaps she could say she was exhausted and pretend to sleep.

They waved good-bye to their guests and settled into the back of the limo. Drew reached to pull her close, but she sat on the opposite side of the car, facing him. There was no one to show off for now.

Drew frowned and watched her for several minutes, trying to make eye contact.

"You all right?" he asked.

"Just tired. It's been a long day."

He hmm'd, as if he didn't believe her.

"Aren't you curious about where we're going for our honeymoon?" he asked.

"I'm sure it'll be fine. It doesn't really matter. It's all for show, right?"

"Right…but that doesn't mean we can't have a good time together. Think of it as a holiday, if that makes you more comfortable."

Jade shrugged and slumped down in the seat.

"When can I change out of this dress?" she asked.

"Whenever you like. There are clothes in that bag." He pointed to an overnight bag on the seat next to her. "But I think you look absolutely stunning. No need to rush."

Jade looked at him for a moment and then dug around in the bag, pulling out some jeans and a T-shirt.

She undid her seat belt and turned around. "Can you please undo this?"

His fingers moved quickly, and the material slackened around her body, gaping open.

"Thanks," she said. "Can you close your eyes?"

Drew obeyed her request and closed his eyes. As quickly as she could, Jade removed the dress and pulled on the more casual clothes.

"Okay, I'm decent. Thanks for thinking to bring these." Her voice was dull, lacking any of the joy she'd felt just an hour before.

Drew looked at her and then down at himself. "Well, I feel a bit silly now, dressed like this."

Jade smirked. He might have done the dancing for the act, but she couldn't stay upset. She'd come into this agreement with her eyes open. No point in being mad at him for only living up to their contract. "I think you look very handsome."

Drew ran a hand through his hair and gave her a profile view of his face. She giggled.

"All right, Fabio, tell me where this honeymoon location is."

"Look in the bag."

Jade dug around in the bag that her jeans had been in, handing Drew his own casual clothes, and found the itinerary for their flights along with their passports. Drew had really been prepared.

She flipped through the papers from a travel agent in Beverly Hills until she found the flight details. Los Angeles to Honolulu.

"Oh, we're going to Hawaii? That's fantastic."

"Keep reading." Drew looked smug, as if he was waiting for a pretty drastic reaction from her.

Jade turned the page over and saw that Honolulu was just a stopover. There was another flight from Honolulu to Cairns, Australia.

Drew got the response he was waiting for. Jade flung the seat belt off and threw herself across the car, crushing him in a hug as she settled beside him.

"Oh my God! We're going to Cairns? Are you freaking serious?" she screamed.

Drew's smile glowed at her response.

"I thought you might like that."

"*Might like that?*" Jade gasped. "Drew, I'm speechless. You're amazing!"

She hugged him again and stared at the paper, her hands shaking as she read the words again. She was going to swim on the Great Barrier Reef.

CHAPTER FOURTEEN

Passion

As well as paying for the wedding, Drew's parents had booked them first class tickets for their flight, and despite it being a twenty-hour ordeal, Jade never complained once. As soon as the plane landed and they were able to switch on their electronic devices, Drew was tapping frantically on his phone.

"Yes!" he hissed, so as not to alert anyone else.

"What?"

"My inheritance is in my account. I was hoping they'd transfer the money quickly. We can really enjoy the trip now."

Jade laid her head back in the seat and looked out the window as the plane taxied on the runway. Cairns actually looked a lot like Hawaii. Palm trees, blue skies, and green mountains surrounded them.

"Check your bank account," Drew said. "I arranged with my lawyer for your first payment to be put in as soon as my money came through. I want to make sure it's arrived."

"Thank you, Drew. I feel like I owe you something."

She pulled her phone out and logged into her bank's app. Sure enough, a large deposit had arrived while they'd been in the air. Jade had never seen that many zeros in her entire life.

"No. Thank *you*, Jade. I wouldn't have anything if you hadn't agreed to this. Let's have the best time we can here, okay?"

"Deal."

They disembarked and collected their luggage. Walking outside was a shock for Drew, who wasn't used to humidity, but it was similar to Florida weather, so Jade felt at home.

They took a taxi to a beach called Palm Cove, and Jade practically hung her head out the open window like a dog the whole way. She loved the smells and the sounds of this place. It felt so relaxed but, at the same time, had such a vibrant energy.

The hotel was grand and right on its own private stretch of the beach. There was a strip of shops and restaurants just outside the hotel, and the concierge told them a shuttle would pick them up the following morning and take them to the Reef Fleet Terminal, where they could catch a boat out to one of the islands. He recommended Green Island as a great place for snorkeling.

The hotel room was lovely. There was a huge bed next to floor-to-ceiling glass doors that opened out onto a balcony which overlooked the beach. Jade only stayed in the room long enough to dump her suitcase, take a quick shower, and get changed. She then headed out to walk the beach and spend some of her newfound cash in the stores. Drew, who hadn't been able to sleep on the plane, lay down for a nap.

Jade came back to the hotel laden with shopping bags and saw Drew was still asleep. She didn't want to wake him, so she went to a café she'd seen a block up the strip for a quick dinner and a sunset walk along the beach, and then had an early night.

She awoke the following morning and saw that Drew was sitting up, typing on his laptop.

"Morning," she said, hating her groggy morning voice.

He looked down at her and smiled. "I've just organized for the construction crews to start work on the house. By the time we get home, they should be almost finished. We can move in pretty soon after we get back."

"That's great."

"Now that I've got the money to pay them, things will move quickly. Speaking of which, you better move your butt, or we'll miss the shuttle."

"Oh, right!" Jade jumped up and had the quickest shower of her life, excited about going out to the reef.

She dressed in a bikini with denim cut-offs and a loose T-shirt over the top. When she left the bathroom, Drew tossed her a bottle of sunscreen. "You'll want that. Apparently the sun here burns worse than at home."

"Thanks." She dumped the bottle in her beach bag along with her towel, sunglasses, and a bottle of water.

The ride into the city was longer than she remembered coming from the airport, but the sights were so pretty that she didn't care. Drew's phone kept beeping with emails flooding in, and he was glued to his device the whole way.

The Reef Fleet Terminal was bustling. It was a melting pot of cultures and people of all ages, everyone wanting to see the reef. Drew booked them on a boat to Green Island that had the added benefit of a submarine tour.

Jade stood outside on the boat, watching the waves churn from the turbines as they headed out into open water. Cairns disappeared, and she walked to the front of the boat, breathing in the salty air and watching for dolphins.

Drew watched the wind blowing Jade's hair as they walked down the long jetty that led to the island. The boat ride had been less than an hour, but he was glad they were back on solid ground. Any longer and he might have become sick. He'd never been good with boats.

Jade's skin already looked golden from the sun, and along with her radiant smile, she was practically glowing. She had her snorkel and flippers under one arm and was pointing out things with the other.

"Look, Drew, there's the reef!"

Drew couldn't really see anything. Where she was pointing just looked like a brown smudge under the waves, but he trusted that she knew what she was talking about. They walked along the beach awhile and then put on their flippers and masks, wading out into the water.

"You ready?" he asked.

Jade already had the snorkel in her mouth, so she nodded her head and gave him a thumbs-up. They swam out to where others were already snorkeling and dove under the water. That brown smudge

Drew had seen was actually a vibrant rainbow of colors. Corals in every hue imaginable were home to a diverse variety of fish. Drew didn't know what any of them were, but it was pretty. He followed along after Jade, letting her lead the way.

One of the items Jade had bought the day before while he'd slept was a waterproof case for her digital camera. Drew watched as she pressed the camera against her mask and snapped dozens of pictures. She turned the camera on him, and he blew a bunch of bubbles, hoping to make a funny picture.

She swam over to him, put her arm around his shoulder, and pointed the camera at them both, taking an underwater selfie. She waved and swam away to take a picture of a turtle.

Even though they couldn't speak with the snorkels in, Drew could tell Jade was enjoying herself. It warmed his heart to know he'd had a part in putting that smile on her face. He'd never felt that before with a girl, and it felt good.

He motioned that he was going to go back to the beach. His stomach wasn't faring too well in the buoyant water, and he wanted to sit on solid ground for a while. He emerged from the water and pushed the mask off his face, breathing in deeply.

"That was amazing!" Jade said from behind him.

Drew turned to see her coming out of the water. Her bikini fit her body perfectly, hugging her hips and accenting her curves. He watched a few drops of water as they cascaded down her taut stomach.

"You didn't have to leave. I'm happy to wait here for you."

"Nah. Don't get me wrong, I *loved* it, but I'm happy to explore the island with you for a while. I might snorkel again before we go back."

Drew held out his hand, and she took it as they walked up the beach. The island was quite small, a tall forest of palm trees with a small resort in the center and a ring of beach all the way around. They followed the beach, walking the perimeter of the forest until they came across an old fallen tree. It wasn't a palm tree, so Drew couldn't imagine that it was from the island. He wondered if it had washed ashore.

However it had gotten there, it had been there a long time. The wood was white from salt and age and as smooth as stone. Jade climbed up and swung her leg over the log, looking out at the blue horizon.

"This really is paradise," she said. "It's the most beautiful place in the whole world."

Drew followed her gaze. The water was crystal clear, sparkling under the sunlight. The sky was the bluest he'd ever seen, with small patches of fluffy white clouds. The breeze smelled like salt and flowers, and Jade looked glorious with the wind in her hair and the sun on her face.

He crawled up onto the tree as well and sat beside her. "I'm very happy to be here with you, Jade."

She leaned into him and laid her head on his shoulder. He was glad she finally seemed comfortable with physical contact, even in private. They sat there together for a long time, sometimes in silence, sometimes talking, but the whole time happy and content.

When they finally boarded the boat to go back to Cairns, Drew leaned over and kissed her cheek. He'd wanted to kiss her properly on the log on the far side of the island but hadn't wanted to make their time together awkward. This seemed like a safe option. He just didn't want the experience to go by without showing her how much he enjoyed being there with her.

"Let's send out a tweet," Jade said. "Cassandra would want us to do that."

"All right."

He pulled out his phone and opened Twitter. He typed a tweet and showed it to Jade for her approval.

@TheRealMalikJr: Having a great time with @JadePratt89 on our honeymoon. #DrewAndJade #honeymoon #barrierreef

"Should we add a photo?" she asked.

"Sure."

They leaned together and took a selfie, and Drew added it to the tweet before sending it off.

"Did our hashtag trend?" Jade asked, leaning over to look at the screen.

"I have no idea."

He touched their tag and waited while the tweets loaded. They read through a few of them.

I can't wait to see the wedding pictures! I've been in love with @TheRealMalikJr for years! #DrewAndJade

**Congratulations to Drew. So happy he found
his soul mate. #DrewAndJade**

**I fkd @TheRealMalikJr a year ago in a club bthrm.
Jade is in for a wild honeymoon! #DrewAndJade
#hotsex #hunglikeahorse**

Jade snorted out loud. "Hung like a horse?"

"I guess I impressed 'at party girl nineteen eighty-nine' with my skills."

Jade snorted again and placed her hand on his arm. He tensed briefly at the contact and scolded himself. When had *he* ever been nervous around girls?

There were hundreds more tweets, all offering their congratulations. They scrolled through, laughing at some and replying to any that interested them. When they arrived back at port in Cairns, they put the phone away and caught a taxi back to their hotel.

"You must be starving. You barely ate anything today and slept through dinner last night," Jade said after her shower.

"I am, actually. Would you like to have dinner with me, Ariel?"

It seemed a bit silly to him to ask his *wife* to have dinner, but their situation was unique, and it wasn't his right to assume she'd want to spend time with him.

"I'd love to. There's a restaurant just outside the hotel. When I walked past it last night, the food smelled amazing."

"Let's go."

They both decided to have the buffet and enjoyed the best seafood they'd ever had. Jade also indulged in a few cocktails, and Drew sampled several of the local beers as they ate.

While Drew asked the waiter for the check, Jade drained the last of her sixth cocktail. The room swam around her in a haze of color and sound. Drew's face was mingled in there somewhere, the only familiar thing in this foreign place.

"I had the best day of my entire life today," she said, hearing her own voice as it slurred the words.

"I'm glad. I love seeing you smile."

She spread her mouth wide in a large, toothy grin. He reached across the table and stroked her hand, fingering her wedding ring. It was still hard for her to believe she was married. But she was, and she was going to make the most of having a man at her disposal.

"There's a bar next door. Do you feel like dancing?" she asked.

"Sure."

Drew paid the bill, and they walked toward the loud music coming from next door. The bar had low lighting, and Jade stumbled, tripping over the leg of a stool.

"Sorry," she said to the person she'd bumped.

"Are you okay?" Drew asked, slipping his arm around her waist to keep her standing.

"Yeah. Stupid stool jumped out at me. *Bastard.*"

Drew chuckled. "I like drunk Jade. She's fun."

"Jade isn't drunk!"

The music pumped, and Jade's body moved without her control as she grabbed Drew and dragged him onto the dance floor. She was impressed with his moves. He could certainly hold his own. She watched his hips move, his body sway, and couldn't stop her thoughts from wandering to how his body would feel moving against hers.

With a steadying breath, she stepped closer, grinding against his leg. His eyes went wide, but he seemed happy to play along. He grabbed her and held her close, moving against her. Jade's heart pounded in her chest. She didn't know if it was from the dancing, the alcohol, or being so close to Drew, but she didn't care.

Drew pulled her closer as the music changed and nuzzled his face into her neck.

"You smell amazing," he said.

Jade giggled. She didn't know why she was laughing, just that it seemed funny to have Drew's arms around her. Lights flashed around them, strobe lights from the ceiling mixing with camera flashes. But neither of them noticed, their focus only on each other.

Drew looked into her eyes, and with what must have been a sudden rush of courage, or perhaps stupidity, he kissed her. She didn't even blink an eye. She kissed him back, totally lost in the moment.

His lips felt soft against hers, and he tasted sweet, like the drinks they'd had at dinner. She wanted more drinks. She wanted the happy day to continue, to have Drew's kisses mixed with more drinks and the memories of the reef.

She broke from his mouth, and he leaned toward her, his eyes still closed, searching for her lips.

"Let's have shots!" she said.

Drew's eyes flew open, and he grinned. "All right."

They made their way to the bar and ordered two shots each, downing them quickly and then moving back to the dance floor. Their arms found each other again, melding their bodies back together, and Drew kissed her, not wasting any time.

Jade broke the kiss again, twirling around to the music. "I love this song!"

She noticed how Drew watched her dance and liked his hands sliding over her waist and hips. He kept pulling her back for kisses, but he couldn't keep her still for long. After a while, Jade started to lose her buzz and slowed down.

"Do you want to go back to the room? You're looking tired," Drew said.

She nodded and let him lead her out of the bar. The hotel was only a block away so they were back in their room in only a few minutes.

Jade's head was swimming with a combination of the cocktails she'd drunk and the affection that Drew had been showing her.

"This room is fucking amazing!" Drew said, looking around at the amenities as though he hadn't seen them before. It seemed his buzz was still in full effect.

"I might have a soak. I feel like relaxing in a bubble bath."

"Mind if I join you?"

Jade breathed heavily. It wasn't that she was out of breath; she was just excited. The blood pumped through her body, and she didn't want Drew to stop the kisses they'd been having. Even though she knew she'd regret it later, she didn't want to say no.

"Okay." Jade's heart rate sped up. She was about to have a bath with Drew.

She dug around in her suitcase for her spare bikini and took it into the bathroom. She quickly changed while the tub filled and poured in some bubble bath.

She wished she could turn the jets on, but the churning water mixed with the bubbles would be a disaster. When the tub was filled, she opened the bathroom door to let Drew know he could come in, and then she stepped into the tub.

The water was hot, and it stung her skin as she sat down. It was nothing like the tepid ocean they'd swum in at the reef. Drew appeared in the bathroom wearing his swimming shorts and a cheeky grin.

"May I?" he asked.

"Please."

As he climbed into the tub, his foot slipped, and he fell into the water, sloshing waves over the edge and onto the floor.

"Are you okay?"

Drew laughed hysterically, clutching the side of the tub as he sat down. "I'm fine."

They both laughed until it became awkward, and then they fell into silence. His thigh was pressed against hers, and Jade felt a tingling where their skin touched. The tension between them was ridiculous. She knew it was a forbidden fruit situation for him. He didn't actually desire *her*. He only saw her as a challenge, something to strive for. She knew all too well the male desire for the chase.

"Damn. I should have ordered some champagne," Drew said.

"It's okay. I think we've both drunk enough for one night."

"But we should celebrate. We're on our honeymoon."

Jade laughed and then froze. His hand had crept along the seat and was gently stroking her leg. She didn't know what to do. It felt so good to have him touching her that she didn't want it to stop. But she knew she should push him away.

Before she could make her decision, Drew slid along the bench seat right up next to her.

"Ariel, I know this isn't a real honeymoon, and we're not married in the traditional sense of the word, but I do care about you. More than I've cared for any other woman."

"I care about you too, Drew."

She rested her hand on top of his on her leg, but didn't push it away. He seemed to take that as encouragement and ran his fingers up her thigh.

"You've made your rules very clear, and I know your boundary."

She laughed. "That wall is crumbling very quickly."

He smiled and stroked his thumb over her cheek with the hand that wasn't planted on her leg. "Is that a good thing?"

"I don't know," she admitted.

Picking up that he stood a chance, Drew moved his body closer, intoxicating her with his closeness.

"You never know what we could be if you never give us a chance, Ariel," he whispered.

His words were enough to throw her inner conflict from chaos into clarity. It wouldn't hurt to try.

She closed the small gap between them, pressing her lips to his. Drew took her lead and ran with it, spreading her lips and seeking out her tongue. They'd never kissed like this before. It had always been for show. Now they were genuinely kissing each other.

Jade nibbled on his bottom lip with her teeth, and he growled, pushing her back into the wall of the tub. His hands explored her body, sliding over the slippery skin of her stomach and up over her ribs.

"I've wanted this for so long," he breathed into her mouth.

"Me too," she admitted, lost in the moment.

His hands continued to travel up, into her hair and resting at the base of her neck. He pulled the ties that held her bikini top in place and looked into her eyes, begging for permission to release the fabric's hold on her flesh.

She gave a tiny nod, and the material fell, floating on the surface of the water, leaving her exposed.

"I knew you'd be beautiful," he said, taking her in.

"Take me to the bedroom," Jade said, throwing caution to the wind.

Drew didn't need to be told twice. He stood and held his hand out, helping Jade out of the tub. He grabbed a towel and dried her slowly, making sure every part of her was shown attention. His lips followed the trail of the towel, kissing her newly-dried skin. Her bikini bottoms were removed as the towel moved over her hips, and she stepped out of them, pushing her nerves away.

Drew quickly rubbed the towel over himself, not taking anywhere near the care he'd shown to her, and then scooped her up into his arms, carrying her to the bedroom. He laid her on the bed gently and crawled up her body.

"You want this, right?" he asked hopefully.

"Yes." The word came out as a soft moan as his hands began exploring her skin.

He pressed his body over hers, pushing her down into the mattress with his weight. She curled her legs up, holding his hips to hers and squirming beneath him.

His tongue trailed down her neck, and he sucked a nipple into his mouth, flicking the tip. Lightning shot through her body, making her jerk beneath him. He smiled around the nub, apparently enjoying her reactions to his touch.

She was desperate for him, and he wasn't moving fast enough for her liking, so she took the initiative. She pushed against him, flipping them over so he was lying on his back. When she untied his shorts and pushed them down to his ankles, his cock sprang to attention and bounced in the air, ready for her.

Drew smiled, watching her as she stroked him, getting him ready.

"You're eager," he said.

She smirked and showed him just how eager she was. Normally, she enjoyed giving blowjobs, but right now wasn't the time for that. She didn't want to drag this out any longer than it already had been. She needed him inside her.

She crawled up the bed, straddling him, until she was in position over his groin. Drew's eyes went wide, obviously surprised that she was fast-forwarding the action.

"You want this?" she asked, swirling her entrance over the tip of his cock.

"Fuck yes."

His hands rested on her hips, and he pulled her down, impaling himself in her. They both cried out and started moving against each other, eager for more friction.

A part of Jade told her to slow down. She didn't want Drew to think of her as a cheap fuck. But she was so desperate for him that she couldn't stop her hips from bucking over him.

"God, Ariel," he gasped, his hands kneading her breasts.

She sped up, rocking her body over his at a furious pace. Without warning, he flipped them over and started pounding into her. She wrapped her legs around him, urging his thrusts on.

"You're so wet," he groaned.

Inside, Jade felt like she was on fire. Every nerve in her body throbbed as Drew moved over her. She'd known he would be good in bed, he had a reputation for exactly that, but she hadn't expected it to be so intense. She felt as if she might explode around him.

"Drew," she gasped.

He chuckled. "I love hearing you say my name."

His lips found hers, and he sucked her tongue into his mouth, stroking it at the same feverish pace as his hips.

"Oh my God, yes!" she cried as her orgasm built.

There was good sex, there was great sex, and then there was Drew's sex. She'd never felt so connected to anyone. She'd never felt like her whole body was melting into a delicious puddle with each thrust of his hips.

"That's it. Come for me, Ariel," he coaxed, speeding his hips and pressing kisses over her cheeks and throat.

Jade gasped for breath and cried out as her body jerked and writhed out of her control. She was soaring, and she never wanted to come down. His thrusting didn't waiver; it kept her flying for longer than she thought was possible. Her muscles convulsed, milking his own release, and he roared in pleasure before falling onto her, breathing heavily.

"God."

"I know," Jade said, giggling.

He groaned as her body convulsed with laughter, milking him further. Slowly, he leaned back and rolled so he was lying on his back, his arm slung loosely over her breasts.

They both lay gasping for several seconds, and then she turned her face to the side to look at him. He was staring at her with wonder in his eyes and a large grin.

"You're amazing, Ariel," he said, reaching up to stroke her face.

"You're pretty good yourself."

"It certainly looked like you enjoyed yourself."

"It was okay," she said, shrugging.

"Only okay? Guess I better improve, huh?" He pulled her toward himself, kissing her deeply. "Round two?"

"Definitely!"

CHAPTER FIFTEEN

The Morning After

Drew woke in a puddle of sunlight, wrapped around someone. Jade felt warm and soft in his arms, and he pulled her in tightly, pressing a kiss into her hair. She stirred, moaning softly and snuggling against him.

"Morning, beautiful."

She jerked in his arms and then stilled. "Uh, morning."

Jade rolled out of his arms and clutched the blanket around her as she sat up.

"What's wrong?"

"Nothing. My head hurts."

Drew relaxed. For a second, he'd feared that she'd regretted their night together.

"Well, you did drink an awful lot last night."

She peered under the covers and groaned. "Did we…?"

"You don't remember?"

She bit her lip and looked at him with worried eyes. Drew's heart fell into his guts. She *did* regret it.

"Were we safe?" she asked, her voice shaking.

"Um…" Drew said. Honestly, he hadn't even thought about protection in the moment, and she hadn't seemed concerned about it either. "I assumed you were on the pill."

"I am," she admitted. "But I left my tablets at home by accident, so I haven't taken it for a few days. Fuck."

"Fuck," he echoed.

She stood awkwardly, pulling the blanket from the bed as she walked to the bathroom, wrapped in a fluffy cocoon.

She closed the door, and Drew flung himself back on the bed. He'd made a real mess of things now. He scrubbed his hands over his face, trying to imagine a way to make things right with Jade.

He hadn't forced anything. He'd checked with her, and she'd wanted it. But where did he stand if it was just the cocktails in her system that wanted it? He was in deep shit, and their contract was in jeopardy.

A whimpering sound was coming from the bathroom, and he got up, walking over to listen at the door. He could clearly hear she was crying. He knocked on the door.

"Ariel, please don't cry. Come out and talk to me."

The sobbing stopped, but she didn't come out. Drew rested his head against the door and took a few deep breaths.

"Please come out," he said softly.

"Why don't you go and have breakfast? I'm just going to have a shower and get ready for the day," she called, her shaking voice making it clear that she was still crying.

"If that's what you want."

He didn't want to make the morning harder for her, so he quickly dressed and went down to have breakfast at the hotel buffet.

He was just finishing his coffee when Jade appeared, looking at him sheepishly.

"Sorry about that. I was just taken off guard. I'm fine," she assured him.

"Would you like to get some food? I can sit with you while you eat."

"No, I'm not hungry. Let's get this day started."

He could see the determination in her eyes and knew she was putting on a brave face.

They'd booked a tour of the Daintree and sat in silence on the bus ride through the rainforest. Drew turned to Jade a few times, wanting to point at something out the window for her to see, but the stern expression on her face stopped him each time.

The tension continued for the rest of the week. When out in public, she was polite and smiled in the photos they took for Twitter, but when they got back to the hotel, she fell silent, and she'd started eating alone. In bed, she lay with her back to him, as far to the edge of the mattress as she could get. Drew lay in bed at night and wished he could reach out to her, but he couldn't.

On their last night in Australia, he fell asleep early. Jade had still been watching TV, so when he awoke in a dark room, he assumed she was asleep. He lay on his back and stared at the ceiling. He needed to make things right. They had to live together for months, and if she wasn't even willing to talk to him, it wasn't going to work.

"Ariel," he said softly.

She didn't wake up. He reached across the bed, but the sheets were cold. He sat up and turned on the lamp. The room was empty.

"Shit!" he said under his breath. He pulled on some jeans and a shirt and went out onto the balcony. She wasn't out there, but he could see a lone shadow sitting on the beach. Her red hair was visible under the full moon.

With a sigh of relief, he grabbed his cell phone and the room key and went to the elevator. He walked through the lobby barefoot and out onto the beach.

"I was worried about you," he said when he got close to her.

She turned and looked over her shoulder. She offered him a small smile which lessened the tight feeling on his heart. That was the first real smile she'd given him in days.

"Sorry. I just wanted to sit on the beach one last time before we go home."

"Do you mind if I join you?"

She shook her head and turned back to the water. He sat down next to her in the sand. The only sound was the crashing of the waves.

"The stars are so pretty here. In LA, you can't really see them all that well. Too much light pollution. Just look how many stars there are!"

Drew lay back on the sand and stared up. The sky was pitch black and dotted with thousands of white spots.

"I wish I knew the constellations for the southern hemisphere," she said wistfully.

"I have an app in my phone that shows the constellations."

"Can I see it?"

He opened the app and handed it to her. She stood and held it up to the sky. Lines joined all the stars, but her hand shook, and the images wouldn't come into focus.

Drew stood and walked up behind her.

"Your hands are shaking too much. Here." He reached around her shoulders and held her still.

The constellations appeared. The scent of her hair was strong as the wind blew up from the ocean. He took a tiny step closer, closing his arms around her. It felt good to be close to her, and he wished she thought so too.

"There's Hercules!" she said, excited, pointing up into the sky.

"Ariel, turn around," he whispered.

Her body tensed, but she did as he asked, the stars forgotten. She chewed her bottom lip, a sign that she was nervous, but he had to say what was on his mind or he'd regret it.

"I know you think we made a mistake the other night, but I don't regret it. We're two adults who care about each other, and we're both single. Well, technically we're married, but you know what I mean. We didn't hurt anybody. If we want to get closer, there's nothing wrong with that."

Her eyes sparkled under the moon, but she didn't say anything. Drew decided he needed to prove his point so he leaned in slowly, moving to kiss her. Just as their lips touched, she pushed him away and wiggled out of his arms.

"Drew, don't. This deal we have is only going to work if we keep it professional. You're right that we're not hurting anyone else, but we might end up hurting ourselves. I really think it's best if we just keep this as a friendship."

Drew followed her as she walked away.

"We didn't plan it, but sometimes fate has a way of bringing people together. We might be going to have a baby. If that's the case, I'll do the right thing by you."

She stopped walking and turned.

"Is *that* what this is about? You trying to do the right thing? Well, don't worry about it, Drew. My period started this morning. You're off the hook. So let's just go back to our deal."

She walked back up the beach toward the hotel, but Drew stayed on the sand. He'd expected to feel relief at her news, but all he felt was disappointment.

"The kitchen's done!" Clare yelled.

"Thanks. Can you help me with the closet?"

Jade wiped the sweat from her brow with the back of her hand and looked at the piles of stacked boxes. She was moving out today and into Drew's house.

They'd been back from Australia for five days, and the construction crew had finished up. Her temporary home was ready to be lived in, and she kept reminding herself it was just the next step in the process, one step closer to having her own life back.

"How have you managed to be away from Drew for *five days?*" Clare asked, appearing in the bedroom.

"It's not that bad. It's actually kind of nice having my own space."

Clare shook her head.

"I saw the pictures in the magazines. You guys were hot and heavy in that bar in Cairns. God only knows what went on when you were actually in private." She giggled and picked up a box, carrying it to the living room.

Jade and Drew had come home to a flurry of media. Apparently they hadn't gone unnoticed during their dance/make-out session in the bar. Several grainy cell phone photos had appeared online. Drew thought it was great, reinforcing their story, but Jade cringed every time she saw them. They were just an ugly reminder of what she couldn't have.

Clare came back into the room. "The moving truck just pulled up outside."

"Great, thanks."

Jade ran outside to greet the driver and watched as the pair of men carried everything she owned out to the truck. She gave them her new address and promised to meet them there.

Back in her now-empty apartment, Jade looked around. She'd hated this place. The reason she'd gotten into this situation in the first place was to get out of this dump, and yet she felt sad as she looked at the empty rooms.

"Come on. I want to ride in your new car," Clare said, turning off the lights as she walked through the apartment.

"You don't have to come with me. I'm going to have a fun night of unpacking ahead of me. I'm sure you'd much rather be with Stuart."

"No way! I want to see this swanky new house with your perfect husband. Plus, I need to organize your closet, or you'll be mismatched."

"All right. Come on, then." With a last look, she left her house key on the kitchen counter and locked the door.

"It's so shiny!" Clare gushed as she climbed into Jade's new car.

One of the first things she'd done when she got home from the honeymoon was buy a new car. She thought that was a sensible purchase, but shopping for it had been anything but. In her mind, she'd imagined herself in a classy sedan, maybe a neutral color so it wouldn't depreciate as fast. But when she'd seen the gleaming rows of brightly colored, two-door coupes, she was lost to the dark side of materialism.

In her driveway sat a midnight blue Nissan 370Z. She looked at it with awe, still unable to believe the sexy beast was *her* car.

They pulled up behind the truck, and Jade held in a groan. Drew had also indulged in a new toy. His black convertible sat in the driveway. She'd hoped he would be out. But she couldn't let Clare know she'd rather he not be there, so she put on her happy face and practically skipped up the drive.

"Honey, I'm home," she called as cheerfully as she could through the door.

Drew appeared with a confused look on his face.

"Honey?" he asked, laughing. He saw Clare, and a knowing look came over his face. "I'm so glad you're finally here. I asked the guys to put your boxes in the formal living room. We can sort it all out later."

"All right."

"Dream Guy, show me around," Clare said, pushing past Jade into the house.

Drew took her arm and gave her a tour while Jade started carrying boxes upstairs to her bedroom.

"No!" Clare said when Jade wheeled the suitcase into her bedroom. "That goes in your room, silly." She grabbed the suitcase and dragged it across the hall into Drew's room.

"Shit," Jade said under her breath. She ran after her friend and glared at Drew on the way past.

"What did I do?" he asked softly.

"Clare, you don't have to do my closet. Really, I can manage. Why don't we have some dinner? Do you feel like Chinese food?"

Clare stared into Drew's large walk-in closet that was filled with his own clothes.

"Drew, you haven't left any room for Jade's things."

He gave Jade a look. "Oh, right. Sorry, Jade. I've never lived with anyone before. I'll move some of my stuff into the spare room." He gave her a hug and pecked a kiss to the tip of her nose. "Forgive me?"

"Aww, you guys are so cute." Clare gazed at them as if she were staring at a basket of puppies.

"Okay, let's order food. I'm starving!" Jade said.

Drew lay in bed, listening to the cicadas chirping outside. There weren't cicadas at his parents' place. His first night in his own house hadn't turned out the way he'd planned. An awkward dinner with his fake wife and her best friend wasn't in the cards when he'd dreamed of having his own place.

His eyes flew open when he heard a door creak and footsteps pad past his door.

He climbed out of bed and went out into the hall. It was empty. A creak on the stairs let him know that he hadn't imagined it. He followed the noise and blinked when a light flooded the stairwell.

"Jade?" he called out.

He walked into the kitchen and saw her drinking a glass of water. She put the cup down on the sink and turned around. "Sorry. I didn't mean to wake you."

She wore a camisole and boxer shorts. It was a warm night, and the cami clung to her body in all the right ways, showing the curve of her breasts and the flat plain of her stomach. Drew forced himself to look at her face, but that was no better. Her hair was tied back, but a few curls had come loose and hung around her face, and her cheeks were flushed from the warm air.

"Drew? Are you sleepwalking?" she asked.

He realized he'd just been standing there staring at her, not saying a word.

"Sorry." He shook his head. "Don't worry about it. I was awake. I couldn't sleep."

"Me either."

"We could sit and chat," he offered.

"I don't think so. I have my last day of work tomorrow so I should at least *try* and go to bed."

"Oh. All right."

He watched as she left the room, and he could hear her bedroom door close. He went back up to his own room and saw that she wasn't trying to sleep at all. Her light was on. She was just avoiding him. He wasn't going to have any of that. He knocked on her door.

"Come in."

He opened the door and saw her sitting on the floor, an open box in front of her, piling books into the bookcase under the window.

"There's something I need to say." He folded his arms across his chest.

"All right."

He walked into the room and sat on the foot of her bed.

"I know you want to keep what we have professional, and that's fine, but we were friends at the beginning of this. I'd hate to think we've lost that. This is your home for the next few months, and I want you to feel comfortable here. You don't have to hide in your room."

"Thank you for saying that, Drew."

"And if you happen to leave your door open when you change, that's okay because I've already seen you naked."

He waited, hoping his joke had its desired effect of making her laugh and it didn't backfire and make things worse.

She threw a book at him and then dove up onto the bed, tackling him. "You jerk!"

She laughed as she play-hit him, and he struggled against her. He rolled so he was pinning her to the bed and held her wrists tightly above her head. Having her beneath him sent flashes of their night together though his memory. He could still see her naked, writhing around him, breathing his name. His breath caught in this throat, and he felt her pulse in her wrists beating quickly.

They looked into each other's eyes, and he wanted to kiss her, badly. Tingles ran up his spine and over his scalp, an odd sensation against the heat of the night.

"This is more like it," he whispered.

She smiled the prettiest smile he'd ever seen. Innocent and playful with a blush rising over her cheeks.

"Friendly enough for you?" she asked.

"Almost." He leaned forward, following his urge to kiss her, but then pulled back.

He saw the flash of panic that filled her eyes. She didn't want him to kiss her, and he wasn't going to force it. He rolled off and lay on his side, watching her reaction. Her chest rose and fell as she let out a sigh. He wasn't sure if she was relieved or disappointed, but what he did know was that *he* was confused.

"Thanks, Drew. I think I can sleep now."

"Yeah, I should get some sleep too."

He lay on her bed a second longer, hoping she'd ask him to sleep there, but she didn't. When the silence started to feel awkward, he leaned over and kissed her forehead.

"Good night, Ariel."

"Good night, Drew."

She climbed under the covers and watched him walk to the door.

"I'll be just across the hall," he said.

She laughed. "I know."

He flicked off her light and pulled the door closed behind him.

Jade grabbed a beer from the cooler and sat down on the sand. Drew and his friends were throwing a football down by the water. She watched them for a while, and when she got bored, she lay back on the hot sand and closed her eyes, allowing her legs to tan.

"Damn, you look good laying there."

Her eyes flew open, and she stared up at Sam's smiling face.

"Er, thanks." She closed her eyes again and hoped he'd go away. She felt the sand under her shift, and she groaned internally. He'd sat down next to her.

"How's married life?" he asked.

"It's great."

"Really? I heard it's not all it's cracked up to be."

Jade sat up and stared at Drew's friend.

"And what's that supposed to mean? Has Drew said something?" Her mind raced as she tried to think of something he could have said. True, she'd been distant since they'd gotten back from Australia, but she didn't think they were fighting. She was just trying to be professional. Unless he was starting the breakdown of their relationship already? She made a mental note to ask him when they got home.

Sam smiled and leaned in close. "I know."

"You know what?"

"I *know*."

"Okay, you're a freak." She laughed, trying to play it off as a joke, but she looked over at Drew, hoping he'd come rescue her from the conversation. But he was oblivious to her discomfort, still throwing the ball.

"Don't play games, Jade. I'm telling you that I know. I was the one who placed the ad in the first place."

Realization suddenly clicked, and Jade understood. Sam had placed the ad in the newspaper that she'd originally written to. He *knew* the marriage was fake. Why hadn't Drew told her that his friends knew?

"Oh." She didn't know what else to say.

"I wish I'd met you first, but the reality is that you're still actually available, aren't you?"

Her stomach clenched, unsure what her reaction should be. "I'm married to your best friend."

Sam laughed. "If you say so."

"You were at the ceremony, Sam."

"Yeah. Yeah. Just keep it in mind that I'm interested. And when Drew sets his eyes on a new girl, which he will before you know it, I'll be waiting."

Sam got up, winked at her, and then ran off to play with his friends. Jade sat in the sand by herself, watching them play until the sun started to set, and they decided to go back to Drew and Jade's house for a BBQ.

"Did you get a nice tan?" Drew asked in the car as they drove home.

"Yeah." She wondered if she should tell Drew about what Sam had said. But the truth was, Sam's words had hit a little too close to home. She was free to see other people, and undoubtedly, another girl would catch Drew's eye soon enough.

When they arrived home, she feigned a headache from the sun and went up to her bedroom while the boys drank beer and cooked meat in the backyard.

Jade put on some soft music and curled up in her armchair with a book she'd been meaning to read for months. The smell of the food was enticing as it drifted up through her open window, but she resisted her grumbling stomach. She didn't want to get caught down there with Sam.

Instead, she closed the window and went back to her book. A knock at her door brought her out of her imagination. It was probably Drew checking if she wanted some food.

"Come in," she called.

Sam's face appeared around the door as it opened.

"Hey, I just wanted to see how you're feeling. We're all going for a swim. Why don't you join us? The cool water will help your headache."

Jade rested the paperback on her lap, her finger acting as a bookmark. "Thanks, but I'm fine up here."

She thought that was the end of it and looked back down at her book, but the door didn't close. Instead, Sam walked across the room and sat on the foot of her bed, facing her.

"In that case, I'd rather stay up here with you."

"Why?"

"You're better company than those idiots."

"Those *idiots* are your friends."

"True. But they're still idiots. Why would any of them want to be downstairs when they could be up here in your lovely company?"

Jade knew it was a line, but she felt a blush rise on her cheeks. She hated herself for falling for his smooth ways.

"You're welcome to a book, if you want to read," Jade offered, knowing that wasn't what Sam meant.

He smiled and leaned forward so their knees were almost touching.

"Why don't you come sit here by me?" he asked, patting the bed.

Jade knew it was a bad idea, but she couldn't think of a reason to say no without sounding like a rude bitch. She put the book down and moved onto the end of the bed.

Sam looked into her eyes, and she had to admit he was attractive. He had a strong jaw with just the right amount of stubble, and his brown eyes were just a shade lighter than his hair, giving him that classic tall, dark, and handsome look.

"Jade, I like you, and before you protest, I know the rules. I know you have a contract with Drew, and I know there are going to be boundaries. I can keep a secret. I can be discreet. But I like do you, and I'd like to get to know you better."

"Sam…"

"Just don't say no without giving me a chance. One kiss is all I ask. If you feel no chemistry, I'll leave you alone and never bring it up again."

She chewed her lip. What could one kiss hurt, really? She knew for a fact that Drew had slept with at least one girl since they'd been together, and her failed attempt with Rick was basically a joke. If the kiss sucked, no harm done. But, what if the kiss was good? Should she pass up the opportunity to be with someone who might actually like her?

"All right. One kiss," she said.

She expected Sam to jump on her right away, but he didn't. He smiled, blushing softly, and he looked at her as if she were a wonder. His reached out a hand and stroked her cheek. His touch was gentle, doting. She'd always been attracted to fair guys. Blond hair, with blue or green eyes, but while staring at Sam, she had to admit there was something comforting about the warmth of Sam's big brown eyes.

She felt like she was melting into them. He leaned forward without breaking eye contact, his lips still curled up in a smile. When he finally moved close enough for her to feel his breath on her skin, she reached for him, twining her fingers into his hair. He crushed his lips to hers and wrapped her in a tight embrace.

He hummed against her mouth, urging her lips apart. She opened to him and breathed in as his tongue met hers. The kiss was nice. Her heart didn't go into overdrive like when Drew kissed her, but it was nice nonetheless. She was about to pull away, needing to take a breath, when Sam pushed forward, rocking her backward onto the mattress. Her back hit the comforter, and he balanced himself over her.

"Hey, Ariel, I brought you a... *What the fuck?*"

Sam rolled away instantly, and Jade sat up, wiping her mouth with the back of her hand. Drew stood in her doorway with a burger on a plastic plate in his hand.

She opened her mouth to explain, but he wasn't looking at her. Drew's gaze was focused squarely on Sam.

"That's my wife!" he roared.

Sam put his hands up in a reassuring gesture. "We both know—"

"No, you don't know *anything*. Get the fuck away from her."

Sam tried to protest, but Drew's hands balled into fists and his eyes flashed. Jade could see he was dangerously angry and jumped in before Sam said something to get himself pummeled.

"Sam, you better go."

He glanced at over his shoulder at her and then back at Drew. "Yeah. Uh, can I call you, Jade?"

"No, you can't call her. Get out!" Drew took a step forward.

Sam took the hint and ducked around him, headed for the stairs. Drew turned, looking at her for the first time since entering the room.

"Drew, look..."

"Don't. We have an agreement. You can fuck whoever you want. Just not my friends, okay? Here." He handed her the burger and left the room.

Jade held the plastic plate with a shaking hand. His voice had been so cold, so detached. She'd never heard him talk to her like that before.

CHAPTER SIXTEEN

Play Acting

A week after the kiss with Sam, Jade was lying in bed, unable to sleep. Drew had been distant all week, leaving rooms when she entered them, avoiding eye contact when they did speak to each other. A creak on the stairs made her sit up. She looked at the clock and saw it was close to midnight. She threw the covers off and crept out into the hallway.

"Drew?" she called.

She heard keys jingle downstairs, and she followed the noise. He stood in the kitchen, dressed to go out in worn jeans and a button-up shirt. He glanced up when she appeared in the doorway.

"Did I wake you up?" he asked.

"No, I was awake. Are you going somewhere?"

He glanced at his phone. "Yeah. There's an after party from a premiere. Some of my friends are going, and I haven't been out for a while."

"Sounds fun." She tapped her hand on her thigh, hoping he'd invite her to come along.

She was sick of their silent breakfasts, their grunts of acknowledgment, and their fake smiles. She missed her friend Drew.

"It'll be okay." He moved toward the door.

Jade panicked. "I could use a drink," she blurted out.

He froze, his back to her. He was silent for several seconds and then spun, an accusing look on his face.

"Wanting an excuse to see Sam again?" he spat.

"What? How would I even know if he was going to be there?" She put her hands on her hips.

"Aren't you two speaking?"

"No. Why would we?"

"Oh come on." He threw his hands up in frustration. "We're all adults. You don't have to be coy."

"I'm telling the truth, Drew. There was never anything going on between me and Sam."

"Yeah, it sure looked like nothing was going on when he was lying on top of you with his tongue in your mouth."

Jade sighed. She didn't want to fight with Drew. But she had to admit that it was better than the cold shoulder he'd given her the past week.

"It was *one* kiss. He's a tricky talker, and he confused me. And you said not to date your friends, so that's the end of it. I *haven't* spoken to him."

"Well, he's going to be there tonight." The hardness in his eyes was gone, but his voice was still full of attitude.

"Then it will give him the opportunity to see that I'm yours."

Drew cocked an eyebrow. He thought for a moment, and Jade held her breath, hoping he'd take the bait. Drew was territorial. She hadn't realized that at the beginning, but she'd guessed that the main reason he'd been upset about Sam kissing her wasn't jealousy, it was pride.

"All right. Put on something sexy and meet me in the car."

Jade smiled and ran up the stairs. Finally, she'd seen a hint of the old Drew.

She grabbed a short dress out of her closet and threw it on the bed along with her sexiest pair of heels. If she was going to be Drew's wife, she'd have to play the part right. There were sure to be photographers there.

She pulled her hair back into a tight ponytail and straightened the ends. She applied more makeup than was comfortable and changed into the dress. After a quick once-over in the mirror and assuring herself that Clare would approve of the look, she ran down the stairs and out to the convertible.

Drew whistled when she climbed into the low seat of the car and smiled.

"You clean up nice," he said.

"Oh, I just threw this together." She shrugged a shoulder and smiled. She literally *had* thrown it together.

Jade was glad she'd tied her hair up because with the car's top down, it would have been a disaster if she'd left it out. She looked up into the sky and frowned. All she could see was gray smog.

"Remember how many stars were in the sky in Australia?" she asked.

Drew smiled and rubbed her bare thigh. "They're up there. We just can't see them."

Jade nodded. His hand was warm on her bare skin. A part of her thought about dragging his fingers up just a little higher under her skirt, but before she could reach for him, he put his hand back on the steering wheel. She let out a breath. She'd almost given in.

A throng of photographers hugged the entrance of a large property, and security pushed them back as Drew drove up to the gate.

"Mr. Malik," one of the guards said, waving him through.

Drew drove to the house and parked in the circular driveway. He climbed out of the car, tossed his keys to the valet, and opened Jade's door. She stood, adjusting her short skirt, and looked up at the mansion. Ivy climbed up the cream bricks by the front door and followed a drainpipe up three levels. The air smelled of smoke and midnight, and the deep thumping base of the music from inside vibrated in her chest.

A group of people huddled by the double front doors in a cloud of smoke. Drew went and shook hands with one of the men. Jade covered her mouth to cough.

"Ah, the newlyweds. We haven't seen you out, Drew. Guess you've been keeping yourself busy with the little woman," the man said. He winked at Jade.

Drew smiled. "Oh, you know what it's like, Richard. We can't keep our hands off each other."

Richard laughed and offered Drew a cigarette. He accepted and took a long drag once it was lit. Jade frowned. She'd never seen Drew smoke before. She coughed again.

"Why are you all crowded out here?" Drew asked the group.

One of the women rolled her eyes and blew a long stream of white smoke into the air. "The owner doesn't let anyone smoke inside because his daughter has asthma or some shit. The girl's not even here."

Drew shrugged and blew a cloud of smoke, which caught in the wind and swirled around Jade.

"Sorry," he said, waving his hand through the cloud to clear it for her.

She gave him a tight smile. He turned back to the group.

"We're going inside," he said to them and stubbed the cigarette out on the ground.

"Sorry about that. I have to make the rounds," he said once they were inside the house.

"I'm not here to cramp your style," she said, grabbing a glass of wine from a serving tray on the side table. She handed it to Drew and grabbed another for herself.

He drained the glass and took a second.

"Come on. Let me introduce you to some people."

For the next hour, Jade was introduced to some of the most influential people in Hollywood. Directors, producers, network executives. They were all on a first-name basis with Drew and all seemed to know a lot about Jade. She shook so many hands that she felt like she needed some moisturizer.

Everyone complimented her dress, or her hair, or just her looks in general. A plastic surgeon even asked her to come into his office so he could photograph her. Apparently, people had been asking for her nose. That blew her mind.

"Wanna get some fresh air?" Drew asked, his hand in the small of her back.

"Sure."

He ushered her out to the pool deck. People were in the water, naked, and others lay on deck chairs. One of the guys in the pool was familiar, and Jade gasped when she realized it was Sam.

"Drew! Jade!" he yelled, waving them over.

Drew purposefully looked in the opposite direction and pulled Jade to the outside bar.

"Four shots of vodka," he said to the bartender.

"Oh, I don't want any," Jade said.

Drew winked. "These are all for me."

She watched as he downed all four shots without even a grimace, and she ran after him when he darted off to the far side of the pool. They leaned against a railing that had an amazing view of the city.

"So, you're just ignoring me? Come on, man."

Jade looked over her shoulder and saw Sam dripping water behind them. He'd put some jeans on, and the waistband was soaked in water that still ran down his bare chest.

"Sam, didn't see you there." Drew didn't bother to turn around.

"Hey, Jade. You look beautiful tonight," Sam said.

Drew tensed and turned around with a fiery expression. Jade put a hand on his chest to quiet him before he made a scene.

"Thanks, Sam," she said. "Drew and I are just looking to have some time alone."

Sam frowned. "Right."

Drew's hand crept around her back and clamped firmly on her hip. Sam's eyes flicked to his hand and then back up to Jade's face.

"Okay, then. Give me a call, I guess." Sam turned and strode into the house, leaving wet footprints in his wake.

"Thanks," Drew said.

He went to remove his hand, but Jade held it in place.

"While we're here, we're a real married couple. These people all need to see us together, right? So, for tonight, all my walls are down. If that's what you want," she said.

Drew tipped his head to the side and took in her expression.

"*All* your walls?"

To answer his question, Jade reached up and kissed him. Drew responded immediately, wrapping her in an embrace. His kiss brought back the flood of emotions she'd felt in Australia. Her head swam with Drew. The smell of him, the feel of him, the taste. It brought her body to life.

"We need to go out in public more often," he murmured against her mouth.

Jade giggled.

Drew pressed a kiss to her forehead and held her against his chest.

"Wanna get out of here?" he whispered.

"You want to go home?"

"Not home. Just not so public. There's about a million bedrooms in this house. One of them has to be free."

"Um…" Jade's heart fell into her stomach. She wanted to go upstairs with Drew more than she wanted air. But she knew it would end badly. Their situation was still the same.

"Don't worry, Ariel. It's all for show. I have a plan."

That piqued her curiosity.

"All right."

They walked through the house, wrapped around each other. Jade felt a little guilty when she saw Sam's sad face watching them walk up the stairs, but her loyalty was to the man whose arms were firmly wrapped around her. She'd signed a contract. But more than that, she *cared* about Drew. She cared about his reputation, and she cared about his feelings.

All the doors on the second floor were closed, so they kept going up to the third floor. Drew walked straight to an open door at the end of the hallway. They went in, and he closed the door and flicked on the light.

Pink walls, pink curtains, and a pink bedspread burned their eyes. They were in the asthma daughter's bedroom.

"Lucky we're not actually going to have sex." Drew laughed. "I don't think I could do it in here."

He picked up a purple unicorn covered in glitter stars and threw it at Jade. She laughed and hugged the toy.

"Thanks for doing that," he said, sitting on the bed and bouncing the mattress. "The kiss was a nice touch. I appreciate it."

Jade sat next to him and held his hand.

"It's okay. I agreed to this too. It's not torture to kiss you, you know."

"Well, that's good to know."

They smiled at each other.

"So, can I hear this plan?"

Drew turned and crossed his legs on the mattress.

"That kiss downstairs was very in character for me at a party. If we hadn't been affectionate, people would've talked. It's expected of me to have sex at these parties."

"Why?"

Drew shrugged. "Just a reputation. I did it to myself. At first it was rebelliousness. I wanted to have fun and fuck the consequences. But when you do something enough times, people just expect it."

Jade chewed her lip.

"What?" he asked.

"Nothing," she said, though realizing her tone implied there really was something.

"Spit it out, Ariel."

"I was just wondering how many girls you've slept with. But I don't think I want to know the answer." She gave a nervous laugh.

Drew smirked. "*Do* you want to know?"

"No. No, I don't." She shook her head firmly, deciding nothing good would come from knowing.

"I don't have any secrets, you know. If you change your mind, let me know."

"You still haven't told me the plan."

"Oh! Right." He leaned forward excitedly. "Well, I thought we could playact."

"Playact sex?"

"Yeah." He smiled.

Jade shook her head. "I don't understand."

"You know...bounce on the bed, scream each other's names. Make people *think* I'm living up to my reputation."

Jade burst out laughing. "Are you serious?"

"Unless you want to put on a real show?" He wiggled his eyebrows.

"Okay, playacting it is. How do we do this?"

Drew jumped up so he was standing on the bed and started jumping.

"Fuck, yeah!" he yelled, louder than was necessary.

Jade giggled, her body shaking from side to side from the mattress party Drew was creating with his feet.

"God, you're so good," he continued.

A shadow moved by the door, and Drew pointed, showing Jade they had an audience.

"Come on, Ariel. Make me sound impressive," he whispered with a wink.

Jade thumped her fist into the wall and groaned as loudly as she could.

"Oh, Drew, you're so big!"

She felt ridiculous and covered her mouth so she wouldn't laugh out loud.

"Mm-mm, that's my girl. You're so bad."

"Uh, yes!" she shrieked. "Yes!"

"Don't get too excited. You'll make me sound like a quick fuck," Drew whispered.

"Or," Jade reasoned as he continued to jump on the bed, "it'll sound like you have *mad* sex skills."

Drew's eyebrows rose. "You're right. Go nuts."

"Fuck me harder, baby. Make me come!" she yelled and punched the wall again.

"Ooh, you're so naughty," Drew said.

He jumped off the bed and slammed against the door, banging his hips into it over and over while Jade tried to control her giggling. They could hear whispers coming from outside the door.

"I'm so close, baby," he said, right into the door.

The shadows outside moved. It was time to bring this home. Jade got ready for the curtain call and ran over to the door so her voice was close to Drew's.

"Oh, fuck, yes. I'm coming so hard on your cock!"

Drew raised his eyebrows and gave her an impressed look. He let out an almighty grunt and then flung himself against the door.

"Oh, babe, that was the best," he groaned.

He reached for Jade and kissed her, hard. His mouth was more exploratory than usual, his lips moving around her mouth, smearing her lipstick. His fingers untied her hair and let it hang free before tousling it.

When they broke apart, he messed his own hair and unbuttoned his shirt, redoing the buttons in the wrong holes. He had lipstick smeared over his mouth and really looked post coital.

Jade pulled her skirt a little higher and let one of the straps fall off her shoulder, adding to their look. Drew looked her over and nodded his head.

"Damn, you look sexy," he said.

She winked at him. "How long do we wait before we can go out?"

Drew listened at the door. "Now should be fine. We've made our impression."

He grabbed her and held her close by his side, kissing her neck as he flung the door open.

"Let's get home," he growled.

A handful of people stood in the hallway with deer-caught-in-the-headlights looks on their faces. The guys all wore dopey, blood-rushed-away-from-their-brains expressions, and the women wouldn't make eye contact with Jade.

"Wow, looks like we had an audience," Drew said, sounding like he was surprised.

Jade blushed even though they hadn't actually done anything, and she absentmindedly tugged the hem of her skirt down.

Drew led her through their audience and down the stairs.

"We totally pulled that off," he said once they were downstairs.

"And it was kinda fun."

"But now I would make a quick exit, having achieved my goal of hooking up."

"Okay, let's go."

They walked through the house, people giving them deliberate looks at their dishevelled state.

"Don't forget to grab a gift bag. Get me one too," Drew said when they passed the door.

A long table stacked high with what looked like shoe boxes was beside the door. Jade picked up two and followed Drew out. The valet brought the car around, and Jade took the keys from Drew's hand.

"You're not driving," she said. "You've drunk too much."

Drew smirked and folded his arms over his chest. "Do I look drunk?"

Jade looked him up and down. It was true; he was a very high-functioning drunk. But his eyes were red, and she'd seen how many drinks he'd downed during the night.

"Yes." She walked around to the driver's side and climbed into the car. "Are you coming?"

Drew laughed and got into the passenger seat. "You're too up-tight," he said, but he wasn't mad.

Jade handed him the shoe boxes and pulled out onto the street. The photographers were gone, and they had a pretty good run of traffic back to Los Feliz. As she drove, Drew looked through the gift bag.

"It's a pretty good haul this time," he said.

"That's an iPad!" Jade said, seeing a thin white box.

"Yeah, looks like the new version that just got released last month."

"And everyone gets one?" she asked.

"Yeah, it's like a party favor."

"But there must have been two hundred people at that party."

Drew pulled out a pair of sunglasses and put them on.

"Wait, there's *more* in there?" she shrieked, looking away from the road.

CHAPTER SEVENTEEN

Limbo

"**A**re you ready to go? Dad will freak if we're late," Drew called up the stairs.

"I'm coming!"

Jade looked in the full-length mirror. The blue dress Laura had helped her pick out was fancier than anything she'd ever worn, except her wedding dress.

"Come on, Ariel! The car is waiting."

"Okay, okay," she grumbled under her breath. Events like these might have been normal for Drew, but she was freaking out.

She ran down the stairs as fast as she could in her heels and straight out the front door, Drew following closely behind. They both climbed into the back of the limousine, and the driver drove them downtown, weaving through the traffic as best he could, while Jade tapped her fingers nervously on her leg.

"Don't worry. Everyone is going to love you," Drew assured her.

She stared out the window in amazement. One moment they were in normal LA traffic, and the next they were in chaos. Police had the streets blocked off in all directions and screaming people lined the sidewalks behind barricades.

Jade had seen things like this on the news but never thought she'd be a part of it. A policeman waved their car over, and the driver stopped, opening the window and holding their VIP pass out for the man to see. He nodded his head and waved them through.

"Are you ready?" Drew asked, taking her hand.

"Not in the slightest."

"Just smile and wave at the fans. Pose for any photos that I stop for. You don't have to say anything. I'll talk to the reporters."

She took a deep breath. "Okay."

The car stopped, and a man outside opened Drew's door. Loud screaming filled the car, and Jade almost backed out. Aaron would understand if she said she had a stomach bug and asked to driver to just take her home. Wouldn't he?

"Here we go," Drew said, and he climbed out of the car.

He gave a quick wave to the screaming fans and held his hand out to help Jade. She stepped out onto the red carpet and lost all her senses. Every part of her was on overload. The screaming was so loud that she didn't actually hear anything. There were so many spotlights, camera flashes, and faces swimming in front of her that she didn't really see any of them.

She plastered a smile on her face and waved her hand at the faceless people in the crowd. She was Drew's shadow, mimicking every step he took. Slowly, as she grew accustomed to the sensory overload, she began to make out her surroundings.

People were screaming for Drew, and more surprisingly, they were screaming her name too.

"Jade, over here!"

She spun, and a flash went off in her face. She blinked and turned back to Drew.

"You doing okay?" he asked.

"I'm good."

Every time another car pulled up, the screaming would grow louder. When Laura and Aaron arrived, the crowd went crazy, and the camera flashes were blinding. Laura made a beeline down the red carpet straight for them and hugged them both.

"You look lovely, dear. Just hold it together a few more minutes, and we'll all go inside," she said to Jade.

They turned and saw Drew and Aaron posing for pictures together. Laura beamed. She obviously loved her men very much.

Huge posters of Aaron's face were hung all around. Jade had never attended a movie premiere before, and she never expected to be a guest on the red carpet at one.

"Can we get a family shot?" one of the photographers yelled.

Aaron waved them over, and Drew pulled her close, hugging her to his side and standing tall next to his parents. For the first time, the magnitude of who Drew really was sunk in. Sure, she'd recognized his face from pictures, seen him interact with the paparazzi, and had a verified Twitter account, but now, standing next to his father on the red carpet with a hundred camera lenses in his face, she understood.

She'd married Drew Malik. How strange that seemed. To the world, he was a party boy and a golden child. To her, he was the annoying housemate who never washed the dishes and snored so loudly she could hear him through two closed doors.

It was a surreal moment.

A man talking into a two-way radio waved them along the carpet. "We have to get you inside for the Q and A, Mr. Malik."

"All right. Sorry, folks," Aaron said, addressing the media. "One more shot and then I've gotta go inside."

The cameras went crazy, all trying to get the best shot of the night. The Maliks gave the screaming crowds one last wave and then moved into the theater. Drew didn't let go of Jade the entire time, keeping either their fingers laced together or a guiding hand on her waist. It felt reassuring to have him there.

They were guided to their seats, and Aaron left them, heading to the front of the stage with the director and the other actors from the movie.

"You did very well," Laura said, leaning around her son.

"Thanks."

Drew squeezed her hand, and even though the lights went down and there was no one to show off for, he didn't let go through the entire movie.

Jade had never watched a movie with a person she knew was actually *in* the film. She'd known Aaron for several months and perceived him to be a jovial and friendly man. Seeing him on screen swearing, smoking, and shooting people was quite a shock. She looked at Drew, who appeared to be engrossed in the film, and then across at Laura, who beamed up at the screen with pride. It was obvious that she only saw her husband and not the murdering bank robber everyone else saw.

When they left the cinema, there was just as much media outside as on the way in, but most of the general public had left, which helped calm Jade's nerves. She was still getting used to being Drew Malik's wife, and being Aaron Malik's daughter-in-law was another terrifying step into the limelight she wasn't prepared for.

"Drew! Can I ask a question? Drew!"

Drew nodded in acknowledgment and held his hand out to Jade. She slipped her fingers into his, and they walked over to the reporter.

"Drew, good to see you."

"Thanks."

"What did you think of the film?"

"It was fantastic. I think it's the best my dad's done in a long time."

"And, Jade, what did you think?"

Jade's eyes bugged, and she chewed her lip. Drew smirked. She'd been lucky on the way into the movie. He'd been able to field all the questions, and no one had addressed her directly. But Drew didn't jump in to save her. If they were going to be married, she was going to have to learn to deal with the media. She tried her best to remember the lessons Cassandra had given her and took a deep breath.

"It was excellent. Aaron was really good. Although I'll be more careful at family dinners now and make sure to check him for concealed weapons."

The reporter laughed. Out of the corner of her eye, Jade saw Drew smile, and he squeezed her hand.

"So tell me, what's married life like? Is he sleeping in the doghouse yet?"

Jade laughed and snuggled into Drew's side. "It's great. I'm very lucky. This guy is a keeper."

She leaned her head up, and Drew took the cue, leaning down to give her a quick kiss. The reporter looked like Christmas had come early.

"Come on, there must be one little secret you can tell us about him," he pushed.

Jade thought for a moment, looking up at Drew's face. Drew froze, his eyes wary.

"Well, he…"

"Drew, can you join me for a moment?" his mother called from further down the carpet, cutting Jade off.

He looked over his shoulder and nodded.

"Join me when you're done here, okay?" he asked Jade.

"All right."

He kissed her cheek and walked over to his mother.

Jade turned back to the reporter.

"So, you were saying?"

"Oh right," Jade said. "He snores."

The reporter laughed. "Awesome. While I have you, Jade, do you have a response to the statement Tully Whittaker made about your marriage? Did you really agree to that arrangement?"

"What arrangement?"

Jade hadn't heard anything about Tully in weeks. She hadn't even seen her since bumping into her in the bar at her bachelorette party. She'd been at the wedding, but Jade had barely seen her except for glimpses in the crowd.

The reporter pulled a magazine out of his satchel and handed it to her. She flicked through the pages until she saw a picture of her and Tully. It was from the bachelorette party, when the paparazzi had cornered them in the bar. Jade scanned the article. It said that the two had become close friends, bonding over their shared love of Drew, and had agreed to an arrangement where Tully and Drew got to spend one night together a week.

Jade read the words, and her mouth dropped open. She wanted to ask Drew if he'd seen this and kept it a secret from her, but when she looked over her shoulder, he was deep in conversation with a group of people.

"Can I keep this?" she asked the reporter.

"Sure. Is it true?"

Jade snapped the pages shut. "No, it's not true." She stomped over to Drew with the magazine tucked under her arm. He smiled when she approached and introduced her as his wife to everyone he'd been speaking with.

Jade played the dutiful daughter-in-law for the rest of the night as they all had dinner together, but she kept as quiet as she could, only speaking when spoken to. It didn't go unnoticed by Drew, who questioned her as soon as they got into the limousine to go home.

"What's up with you?" he asked.

"Nothing." She slumped down in the seat, the seat belt cutting into her neck.

He reached over and stroked her cheek, pulling her chin up to look at him. "Something's up."

Jade sighed. "Are you fucking Tully?"

Drew's hand dropped. "Where did that come from?"

She handed him the magazine, open at the article about her, and waited for him to read.

"This is just tabloid trash. Something you have to learn being in the public eye is that things will get reported about you, and most of it's not true."

"Most of it? So is *this* true?"

"No. Have you seen Tully around once a week? I've actually barely seen her since I met you."

"If you want to sleep with her, you can. You're free to do whatever you want."

"Jade, don't sulk. There's nothing going on."

"All I'm saying is that it would be fine if there *was* something going on."

"Okay, I get it," he snapped.

They turned away from each other, each staring out opposite windows until they got home, and then they went into their own bedrooms without saying another word.

Drew stewed on her words as he changed out of his suit. She'd been so adamant that she didn't care if he fucked Tully. It was almost as if she *wanted* him to.

The sound of her shower let him know that she was occupied, so he snuck out of the house. He drove into Hollywood and went to his favorite bar. He ordered a drink and continued to think. Perhaps she wanted him to start seeing Tully because she was seeing someone and felt guilty about it. Maybe she'd lied and was seeing Sam behind his back.

That thought upset him more than he liked, and he drained his drink. He thought about the last sex he'd had, with Jade in Australia. Three months was the longest he'd been abstinent since he lost his virginity. Well, if she wanted him to do it, then he would.

He called Tully, and she agreed to meet him at the bar. She was at another bar just a few blocks over so it didn't take her long to arrive. She sauntered in, smugness all over her face.

"I knew you'd get bored of her eventually. I didn't expect it to be so fast," she said, sitting down next to him.

"You don't know what you're talking about, Tully."

"I know you called me here."

He didn't have anything to say to that. He already regretted calling her. She wasn't the woman he wanted to be with. But he didn't send her away.

CHAPTER EIGHTEEN

Good-Bye

Jade opened her eyes to the sound of thudding. After living in her apartment for a few years, she'd grown used to the usual sounds of traffic and sirens during the night, but this was a new noise, something unfamiliar.

She crept out of bed, hissing as her feet hit the cold wooden floorboards. The sound was coming from across the hall. Carefully she opened her door and peered out into the hallway. It was dark except for a sliver of golden light coming from under Drew's bedroom door. The thudding was louder now, and it was accompanied by a new noise—a woman moaning.

"Yes. Fuck me harder," the woman groaned, clearly audible through the closed door.

The thudding sound, which Jade assumed was the headboard smacking against the wall, sped up. Jade felt bile rise in her throat. Drew was having sex while she was in the house.

She didn't know what to do. She stood, barefoot, in the hallway for several minutes, torturing herself with the symphony going on in his bedroom. Each thud of the bed was like a hammer hitting a nail into her heart. And yet she couldn't move away. Her feet were rooted to the ground as her tears fell onto the floorboards.

When the house finally went silent and she heard Drew's husky voice murmur, "You know how to let yourself out, right?" she slipped back into her room.

She went to the window and waited, staring through the darkness until a woman appeared from the front door and danced down driveway to hail a cab, her blond hair glittering like gold under the street lights. Tully Fucking Whittaker. Drew had lied to her.

Jade lay back in her bed but couldn't sleep. She kept her eyes open because every time she closed them, she saw Drew's flushed face. She wished she didn't know what his sex face looked like. She stared at the ceiling until the orange light of dawn lit up her room. She showered and headed downstairs, grateful that the pain in her chest had dulled to a hollow numbness. The newspaper was waiting on the front stoop as it always was, and she scanned the headlines while she waited for the coffee to brew.

Going about her normal morning routine was a challenge. Her thoughts kept darting back to the night before. Drew didn't owe her anything. In fact, she'd *told* him she wasn't interested. At the beginning of their arrangement, they'd both agreed that one-night stands were acceptable. She'd told him that again in Australia, and again last night. She had no reason to be mad at him. And yet her heart ached.

After she'd had two cups of coffee, her stomach rumbled, and she decided to go for a walk to get some breakfast. There was a small café around the corner that made the most amazing cream cheese muffins. Her aching heart felt like she deserved a treat.

Jade ate her muffin as she wandered aimlessly through the streets. As much as she wanted to avoid thinking about what she'd heard the night before, it was the only thing on her mind. It wasn't as if she was in love with Drew. In fact, she'd worked very hard at *not* falling in love with him. She'd just hoped that he would have more respect for her than to bring a girl into her home. She'd let his promise that nothing was happening comfort her. She should have known better.

She eventually found herself back at Drew's house. She looked up at the door, and despite the fact she'd lived there for over three months, it suddenly felt alien to her.

The brass knocker shaped like a fleur de lis glinted in the sunlight, but she couldn't bring herself to reach forward and open the door. She felt like she needed a little time before she faced Drew. She was about to turn and walk down the street to find something to do, anything that could occupy another hour of her time, when the door opened.

"Oh, there you are," Drew said, looking relieved. "I couldn't find you anywhere, and your room was empty."

"I just went to get a muffin." Jade was surprised at how steady her voice was.

Inside, her stomach rolled and her heart clenched in a vice. So much for that comforting numbness. She'd been so stupid. Seeing him now, with his messy bed hair and his I'm-happy-to-see-you smile was all too much for her. She loved him. She couldn't lie to herself any longer. She fucking loved him.

He glanced down at her empty hands and frowned. "You didn't bring me one?"

"No, sorry."

She pushed past him into the house and made an escape attempt for the staircase. Maybe if she locked herself in her bedroom for the rest of the day, she could sort through her feelings and work out how to move forward. The only thing she could think of was to get away from him, but she knew that was just the hurt and panic talking. When she calmed down, she was sure that she could be more rational.

"Hey, what's up with you?" he called, following her to the stairs.

"Nothing."

"Jade." He grabbed her arm and spun her to face him. "Seriously, what's up?"

The metal of his wedding ring burned against her arm. She jerked free of his grasp, and he gave her a stunned look.

"I just want to go to my room, okay?"

She turned to go back up the stairs, but he raced ahead of her and blocked her path. He folded his arms across his chest and stared her down, moving from side to side to block her attempts to get past him.

"Get out of my way," she seethed.

"I will as soon as you tell me what the hell's wrong with you this morning."

"You want to know what's wrong?" There was anger in her voice, a lot of anger. She'd been trying her best to keep her emotions under control until she'd gotten to her room, but his pushing had made them explode. "I don't appreciate being woken up at two in the fucking morning by Tully screaming."

His eyes went wide, and he leaned back a bit, dropping his arms to his sides. She took advantage of his stunned silence and physically pushed him to the side of the staircase so she could get past. She heard him scrambling up the stairs behind her, and when she reached the landing, he caught up and held her arm tightly.

"I'm sorry if we woke you up, but I get the feeling that a little lost sleep isn't really why you're upset."

"Of course it's why I'm upset."

"Is it really? Or are you upset about *why* you were woken?"

Jade sputtered, not able to form words. She hated that her emotions were obviously so plain on her face that Drew could see straight through her.

"Because," he said, not waiting for her to answer, "you've made your feelings about me perfectly clear. All we have is a business arrangement. You've told me that over and over again."

"I know that," she snapped.

"So, which is it, then? This seems like a bit of an overreaction to just losing an hour of sleep."

His eyes were boring into hers, looking for some meaning that she didn't want him to discover. She couldn't tell him that it hadn't just been an hour of sleep, that she hadn't been able to close her eyes without imagining the visual to go along with the audio she'd heard. She couldn't tell him that she felt sick to her stomach just looking at his face because she knew he'd been kissing someone else just a few hours ago, or that the sexy bed hair he was sporting was the effect of another woman running her fingers through it.

No, she couldn't tell him any of that. Instead, she turned and ran back down the stairs, heading for the front door.

"Jade!" he cried in frustration, catching her just has she put her hand on the door knob.

He turned her to face him, and he was closer than she'd been expecting. His face was only inches from hers, and she hated that he smelled so good, like coffee and cinnamon. He pulled her out of the entryway and into the formal living room. They never used the room, and it added to her feeling of alienation in her own home.

"Sit," he commanded.

She sat and folded her arms over her chest, looking determinedly at the ground. He sat next to her, annoyance radiating off him, but there was something else as well...Concern, perhaps?

"Jade, please. What's wrong?" His voice was softer than it had been on the staircase, and when she looked at his face, his eyes were big and full of worry.

"Nothing. I'm sorry. I'm just tired and—"

"Don't give me that bullshit. You're upset, and I want to know *why*. I'm your husband, damn it, and I deserve to know."

"Oh," she laughed. "You're my *husband?* Is that why there was another woman in your bed last night?"

"I knew it!" he said, shooting to his feet and beginning to pace in front of the sofa where she was still seated. "You've never shown any interest in having a physical relationship with me since...well, since the honeymoon."

"I know," she said miserably, feeling like a hypocrite.

"So, do you?"

"What?"

"Do you have a physical interest in me? You have to know that if I thought having *you* was an option, then Tully wouldn't have been here."

"I...I don't know."

He glared at her, frustration and lust pouring out of his features. Suddenly he was on his knees in front of her, breathing heavily.

"Is it an option?"

"Drew, don't." She leaned back in the chair, away from him.

"Is it an option?" he asked again with a bit more force.

"Is what an option?" she whispered, trying to buy herself some time.

He let out a low growl and pressed himself against her. "You. Me. Together. Is it an option?"

Jade bit her lip. A part of her wanted to scream that of course it was. That it had been an option since their first meeting in the café. But even as she thought how to compose the words, the sound of Tully begging him to fuck her harder echoed in her ears.

Drew didn't wait for an answer. He leaned forward and claimed her lips. She resisted at first, leaning back into the couch until she had nowhere else to go. He moved with her, pinning her below him, and too easily, they were horizontal.

"Tell me to stop," he breathed into her mouth.

She hummed wordlessly, but she couldn't bring herself to push him away.

"Tell me you don't want this," he tried again.

She opened her eyes, and they stared at each other for a long moment. His burned with an intensity that helped melt away some of her hesitation. How much pain would it cause her to go along with this? She knew he didn't love her, that he was just fulfilling a physical need. She knew she would be discarded just as Tully and every other girl on his very long list of conquests had been. How would she face him for the next few months until they were free of each other?

"We shouldn't."

He stopped his advance, his head falling onto her shoulder, and he took a few deep breaths. After a moment, he stood up. Cool air made her shiver when his body moved away.

"I really don't understand you, Ariel. Are you jealous? Because that would mean that someone else had something you wanted for yourself, but when that thing is given to you freely, you turn it down. You turn *me* down."

"You're so conceited," she spat, sitting up and smoothing her hair that had been smooshed into the cushions.

"Excuse me?"

"You are! You think that every woman should want you just because you're rich. And, yes, I've helped that perception along by marrying you for payment, but that doesn't mean I belong to you or that I'm at your beck and call."

"I've *never* treated you that way," he protested. "I *care* about you, Jade. I've tried to show it to you but you always push me away. I just don't understand what it is you want."

"What do *you* want?" she yelled, turning the question back on him.

"I want *you!*" he yelled back.

She stared at him, trying to work out if he was telling the truth. Something changed inside her, a decision being made, a guard being released.

"If you want me, then take me," she whispered.

It came out as a dare, a dare that Drew appeared very willing to accept.

He practically launched himself at her, crushing himself against her. She was only wearing a summer dress, and his body heat was welcoming as it melted through the thin cotton.

It felt so good to have him pressed against her. His touch was urgent, holding her against him.

"I want you, Jade." His voice was barely audible as he murmured against her throat.

She wanted him too, and she wished she could tell him, but with every touch of his hand, she thought of him touching Tully. Every kiss to her throat was a reminder that he'd kissed someone else just hours ago.

When she'd built up enough strength to push him away, she did, shoving him hard in the chest and running up the stairs.

"Jade?" he called after her.

"Just leave me alone, Drew. I mean it."

She slammed her bedroom door and frantically started throwing her clothes into a suitcase. All she could think about was getting away from this house, away from Drew. She didn't care about the money. He could keep his second payment. She didn't want anything from him.

He knocked on the door repeatedly. "What the hell just happened?"

"Leave me alone."

She heard him swear loudly, and then his own bedroom door slammed. Once she had the suitcase full of clothes, she chanced opening the door. She could just make out the sound of the TV on his bedroom so she snuck as quietly as she could down the stairs.

In the kitchen, she wrote Drew a note on a scrap of paper and left it by the coffee maker, knowing he'd find it there.

Drew,

I'm sorry. I can't do this anymore. I shouldn't have agreed to do this in the first place. Thank you for showing me the reef. I'll never forget it. Do what you need to do with the contract. I'll sign the divorce papers whenever you want me to. Keep the final payment. I don't deserve it. I wish you all the best.

Jade

There was so much more she wanted to say, but she just couldn't. She heard movement upstairs and panicked, grabbing her handbag and running out of the house with her suitcase. She'd come back for the rest of her things when she knew he wouldn't be home.

She backed her car out of the driveway and refused to look in the rearview mirror as she drove away. She had to put Drew and that life out of her mind. She was moving forward with the life she should've had. She couldn't help that she'd bought the car, and in all honesty, she needed it.

But any money that she hadn't spent, after she'd set up a new apartment, she'd send back to him. She didn't want to owe him anything.

She drove to Clare and Stuart's house. She didn't know where else to go. She knocked on the door, suitcase resting against her leg, and waited. Clare opened the door and smiled, then gave the suitcase a confused look.

"What's wrong?" she asked.

Jade burst into tears. Clare pulled her inside and sat her down on the couch.

"What did that bastard do? He cheated, didn't he? I knew he would, you know. Once a playboy, always a playboy. So much for being a Dream Guy. More like *Nightmare* Guy! I'm going to kill him!"

Jade didn't have to speak. Clare knew she just needed a friend. They watched cartoons because that was the only thing that didn't make Jade cry harder, and ate ice cream straight out of the container.

Jade slept on the couch that night. Well, she lay on the couch while sleep evaded her. She wondered if Drew had noticed the note she'd left, or if he even cared. It probably made his life easier not to have to sneak Tully in and out of the house in the middle of the night.

Torturing herself, she pulled out her phone. Clare had refused to let her look at it all night, but she was curious to see if he'd even bothered to call her. He had. There were six missed calls, all from Drew, and a voice message.

She called her voice mail and listened.

"Where are you? Why aren't you answering your phone? You're scaring me, Ariel. I have no idea what happened earlier, and then I went to talk to you and your room was empty. You didn't even say good-bye. Call me back. I'm worried."

She wished she hadn't listened to the message. Against her will, she called him back. She didn't want to talk to him, but she also hated the thought of him worrying. He had sounded frantic.

"Ariel, thank God!" he said, relief evident in his voice.

"You can stop calling. I'm fine."

"Where are you? When are you coming back so we can talk about this?"

"I'm not coming back, Drew. Didn't you get my note?"

"Note? No. You left a note?"

"It's by the coffee maker."

She heard him walking and then the rustling of paper. She sighed. She'd thought the coffee maker was the most obvious place to look. Again, she didn't know him as well as she thought she did. She probably should have left it on the bar.

"That's it? That's all you were going to say to me?" His voice was angry now.

"I'm sorry to back out of the contract. I mean it; you can keep the money."

"I don't care about the fucking money. Please, just come home."

"I'm not coming back." She tried to be as firm as she could while not raising her voice. She didn't want to wake her hosts.

Drew let out a long breath. "Ariel—"

"That's not my fucking name! My name is *Jade*. I'm not a mermaid princess, and you're not my prince charming, no matter what the media calls us. This was a huge mistake from the get-go. There's no fairy-tale ending for us."

"I love you, Jade. I've felt that way for a long time, but I haven't said anything because you've been so adamant that we were only friends. Today I saw a glimpse that maybe your feelings are stronger than that, so I'm telling you how I feel. I love you, and I want you to be here with me."

Jade laughed. She didn't know why—his words weren't funny—but the irony was unbelievable.

"I've heard you say that before, Drew. You're a great actor. You vowed to the whole world that you were in love with me, and still you had no problem sleeping with someone else. Those words don't *mean* anything from you."

She hung up the phone and lay staring at the ceiling until sunlight flooded the room.

Drew threw his phone against the wall. No woman had ever infuriated him so much. Yet he wasn't angry. He was devastated. He'd grown used to having her around. And even though he hadn't been able to be with her the way he wished he could, she'd still been there. He'd seen her smile every morning, heard her singing to herself as she cooked dinner for them at night.

And most of all, for several hours a week, he could pretend that she really was his. He could hold her hand, kiss her and claim her as his own. Those few hours made all the other times, watching and longing for her, worth it.

And now she was gone, really gone. Many women had passed through his life, and he hadn't missed any of them when they'd left, not even Tully. Jade was different. He was sure he loved her; there was no doubt in his mind.

It had hurt when she'd said his words were meaningless to her. But he understood. They'd both played their roles so well, how was she to know when he was playing it up for the cameras and when it was real? But if she wanted more than words, if she wanted actions, he'd give them to her.

CHAPTER NINETEEN

The Wake-Up Call

Jade put the empty ice cream container on the coffee table in front of her. It'd been a week, and she felt no better about leaving Drew. She flicked through channels on the TV and stopped when his face appeared on the screen. She turned the volume up and leaned forward.

"Drew, you're alone tonight. Where's your beautiful wife?"

Drew's eyes were red, and Jade knew that he was either drunk or hung over. She wasn't surprised.

"She couldn't make it tonight," he said, his words slightly slurred. So, still drunk it was.

"Is there any truth to the reports that you've been fighting? Witnesses have said they haven't seen her at your home for several days."

His eyes flashed as if he were about to yell at the reporter, but he reined himself in.

"She's not been feeling well and has been in bed for the past few days."

He turned and walked away. The reporter faced the camera and held the microphone up to his mouth. "You heard it here; Drew's marriage is intact. It's good to hear that he wasn't another Hollywood statistic so early in his marriage. Oh! Here comes Tamara Farrell, let's get her attention. Tamara!"

Jade turned the TV off. Another Hollywood statistic. Jade hadn't thought of herself like that, but she supposed it was true.

"I'm home!" Clare called, and the front door slammed.

Jade turned the TV back on and tried to look interested in an infomercial of a new vacuum cleaner.

"Enjoy your ice cream?" Clare asked, picking up the discarded container.

"Oh, sorry. I was about to get that."

"Here, I thought you might like something to read." She handed Jade some magazines. "You know, I'm sure you could get your job back. It wasn't like you got fired. You only stopped so you could go to school…which you haven't done. Everyone says how much they miss you. Want me to ask tomorrow?"

"Yeah, I guess. I can't sit around here forever."

Jade still had Drew's money in her account. She wanted to give it back, she knew that morally she should, but once she did that, it was really over, and she wasn't quite ready for the finality of that. It might be good to have an income to help her get a new apartment.

"No, you can't. Look, I was thinking that you and I might have a girl's night tonight. What do you think? We'll go out and do something girly, just you and me. Or we can invite Pam too, if you like."

"Sounds fun."

"Why do you look like it wouldn't be fun at all?"

"No, sorry, we should go out. I'm over it. Let's have some fun."

"Let's not get ahead of ourselves. You're not over it. How could you be? You've just broken up from a marriage. But we can start to take the first step to being over it. And that involves tequila and loud music."

"It's a date."

"Stop calling me!"

Drew hung up the phone and threw it across the room. It rang again right away, Tully's name flashing on the screen. He grabbed the phone up off the floor and answered it.

"Fuck off, Tully. I'm serious."

"Just wait. Don't hang up. Answer one question for me, okay?"

He waited, not bothering to verbally agree.

"Okay, you need to grow up and stop being a fucking baby—"

Drew hung up the phone again. He didn't have time for her shit. The whiskey bottle on the counter greeted him as he entered the kitchen, and he took a swig, not even bothering with a glass.

He could hear his phone ringing again, but he ignored it. Tully had ruined his life; he didn't need to hear her bitching at him about it too.

He stumbled through the house and collapsed on the couch in the formal lounge. He'd hoped this room would be a solace from memories of Jade, seeing as she'd rarely entered it, but it had been the last place he'd seen her before she'd left. They'd almost made love on the very couch he was lying on.

He groaned and tipped the bottle over his face, getting some in his mouth but more over the cushions. And then he must have passed out because the next thing he knew, he was being jerked awake by a loud banging.

It was dark in the house now, and he turned lights on as he moved to the front door.

"I'm coming!" he yelled as the banging continued.

He pulled the door open and then tried to close it again right away. Tully pushed her way past before he could lock her outside.

"I don't want you to be here!" he said.

Every night, he hoped Jade would come home. Maybe tonight would be the night, he'd tell himself. It was the only way he could keep himself from driving all over Los Angeles searching for her. What would she think if she showed up and Tully was there? No, she had to go.

Drew grabbed her arm and tried to maneuver her back toward the door, but she shook herself free.

"I won't stay. Just listen for two minutes, for fuck's sake. Geez, you're a mess!"

"Is that what you came to say?" He turned and walked back to the couch. His whiskey bottle lay on the ground, much of the amber liquid pooled on the floor. There was still enough left in the bottle for a good swig, though, and he drained it dry.

Tully followed him into the formal lounge and stood shaking her head at him.

"Drew, you can't blame me for your marriage breaking down. Yes, we were cheating and you got caught, but you know what? *You* made the decision to cheat. I didn't chain you up and force you. You invited me here. Take some responsibility and stop being a victim. And for God's sake, stop drinking. You think Jade's going to want to come back to you in this state? You can barely even stand up. I bet you want to lick that spilled liquor off the floor, don't you?"

"Fuck you," was all Drew could say. He hated that she was right.

"You did. And that's why you're in this mess. If you want Jade back—and don't try to pretend you don't, I know you well enough to know this isn't one of your usual benders—then you need to clean yourself up and be the kind of guy she'll want to come home to."

"Get out, Tully."

He slumped down on the couch and closed his eyes, trying to block Tully's words from his mind. He didn't know how long she stayed, but when he opened his eyes again, she was gone.

It infuriated him that she was right. But she was. He was a mess. If Jade saw him like this, she'd run for the hills and never look back.

He went back into the kitchen and got his phone, then called Jade for the millionth time. Just like every other time, he got her voice mail.

"Ariel, I don't know if you're listening to these messages. I hope you are. I want you to know that I'm sorry. I'm so sorry. I'm going to make this right. Please just give me the time to make this right. I'm going to rehab. Please give me a call so we can talk."

The thought of going to rehab hadn't even occurred to him until the words were leaving his mouth. Once it was said, though, he knew it was what he had to do, so he made another call.

"Drew! Good to hear from you, son. How is everything?"

"Hey, Dad. I'm not so good." There was silence on the other end of the phone, so Drew kept talking. "Jade left. She's been gone a week, and she won't answer my calls. I'm a mess. I was hoping you could talk to your agent and find a good rehab. I want to grow up and be the man that Jade needs."

Drew had never spoken so honestly with his father before. But he needed the help, and he would take the shame that came with raw honesty.

Aaron let out a long breath. "I'm proud of you, Drew. I'll get you some details. Why don't you come stay at the house with your mother and me tonight?"

Drew hesitated. He wanted to be home in case Jade came over, but the chances of that were remote. It would be good to have his parents looking out for him.

"Thanks, Dad."

"I'll come pick you up."

Jade wasn't sure what brought her back to her old neighborhood. The only thing she could put it down to was that she missed the simple life she'd had when she lived there. Her face hadn't been plastered on the cover of tabloid magazines, photographers didn't chase her down the streets, and Drew was just some guy she'd vaguely heard of.

Everything was so different now. She kicked a pebble along the sidewalk as she walked past the school. The sounds of boys yelling came from inside, but it didn't sound like a fight, it was cheering.

She thought about stopping to see what was going on, but it was nearly dusk and she wanted to get home before it was dark, so she turned to head back to her car. Back to her crazy new life.

"Hey, miss!"

Jade heard the greeting but assumed it must have been for someone else. She didn't know anyone who lived on this street.

"Miss!"

The voice was closer. Thundering footsteps approached her from behind. She spun and prepared to defend herself, expecting her bag to be snatched. A young man raced toward her. He looked to be in his mid-teens and wore his black hair in a ponytail. He slowed as he approached her with a huge smile. She couldn't feel any threat coming from him, so she relaxed.

"Are you talking to me?" she asked.

"You're Drew's girl, right?" the boy asked, breathing heavily from running after her.

"Uh..." Jade didn't really feel like getting into her complex love life with a stranger on the street.

"I knew it was you. Craig said you weren't, but I recognized your hair."

"Is there something I can do for you?" she asked, expecting the boy to say he had a message for her from Drew. Apparently he was getting kids to do his dirty work for him now.

"Have you seen Drew?"

"Have I...? Haven't you seen him?" His question threw her off.

"He hasn't been coming to practice for a few weeks, and he missed our championship game."

"I'm sorry. He's got some personal things going on right now. I'm sure he would have been there if he could."

The boy shrugged his shoulders. "It's okay. We just *wanted* him to be there because he trained us so well. We won the Regionals."

The boy's face shone with pride as his chest puffed out.

"Congratulations."

"Can you tell Drew when you see him? We just want to say thanks for turning us into a strong team. And tell him we miss him."

"All right."

The boy, whose name she didn't even know, ran back to the school and disappeared inside.

Jade's face flushed with heat. That boy was so sweet and all he wanted was for his coach to watch him win a game. That wasn't too much to ask, and Drew had let his team down.

In a burst of fury, she forgot her promise not to call him and pulled out her phone. She called his number and tapped her foot on the sidewalk as she waited for him to pick up.

His voice mail answered.

"Oh, this is just great! You've been calling me constantly, and then, when I want to talk to you, you don't answer?" she said into the phone. "Well, good, actually. I don't want to talk to you either. All I'm calling to say is that you're an asshole. Those kids you coached won their regional championship game, and you weren't even there to watch them play. I guess you really do only care about yourself, you selfish bastard."

She hung up the phone and felt like throwing it, but knew she'd regret that later. She just wished she could see the look on his face when he listened to her message.

CHAPTER TWENTY

More Than Words

"Have you heard from Drew?" Clare asked.

"Not since I left that nasty message for him." Jade sighed. "I guess he finally got the hint."

"But you're still married to him. Don't you think you should talk?"

"I don't know. What's the point? Can anything he says change the situation?"

Clare chewed her lip. "Well, no."

"Exactly. So, what do you think?" Jade moved through her new apartment, showing Clare how she'd added her personal touches since moving in six weeks earlier. It was a nice place, she thought—lots of light with good air circulation. The furniture was much better quality than what she'd had in her old apartment. She felt she could be happy here.

"I like it. And it's close to me and Stuart, so we can visit all the time."

"I like it too. It suits the new me."

Six weeks, she thought again. That's how long it had been since she'd last heard from Drew. It had served as a time of healing for her, and she was starting to feel like her old self. She'd started work as Princess Ariel again and enjoyed being back at on the job and working with the kids.

Drew's lawyer had send a curt email to acknowledge that they'd received the money she'd sent back, but not one word from Drew himself. She missed him terribly but was relieved that he seemed to have accepted that she needed to move on.

She'd had a long day at work so she grabbed a pizza for dinner and settled in on the couch for a night at home. Unfortunately, there was nothing good on TV, and without realizing it, she found herself watching the entertainment news.

"Drew Malik, son of Academy Award winner Aaron Malik, has been seen out and about for the first time since his four-week stint in rehab. Connor spoke to Drew at last night's Young Hollywood party."

The image cut from the young woman sitting in front of a picture of Drew to a red carpet outside a party with people swarming everywhere. Drew's smiling face came onto the screen, and Jade leaned forward. He looked good.

"How are you feeling?" Connor asked.

"Great. I'm great. It was just time to grow up and make some adult choices in my life."

"Jade's not with you tonight?"

"No."

"I don't think I've ever seen you attend a party without a date. Is this the new you?"

Drew laughed. "It is. There isn't anyone else I'd want to spend my time with. I love my wife."

Connor turned to the camera. "You have it right here, ladies. Drew Malik has grown up. Jade is one lucky lady."

The show cut back to the newsroom, but Jade lost interest. Drew had been to rehab? That was news to her. And it would explain the lack of phone calls over the past few weeks.

"Well, good for him," she said out loud.

She was glad he was making some positive changes in his life. The declaration of love and not taking a date to the party was all for show, though, she was convinced. Technically they were still married, and there'd been no formal announcement that they'd separated.

Until the divorce went through in a few months, he'd probably still be saying things like that.

A little voice in the back of her head reminded her that he'd told her the same things on the phone, and that wasn't for show. She'd told him she didn't believe the words, that she needed more than that…Was this action? Going to rehab? Not dating anyone else even though she'd been absent from his life for weeks? She didn't know. She really needed to know his motives.

She chewed her bottom lip and tapped her phone against her leg as she thought. Maybe she could call him. Maybe that would be okay. She *had* missed him. It didn't mean anything would happen. She'd just say she'd seen the news and was happy that his life was moving in a positive direction. She certainly didn't hate him, and they'd started off as friends, so she could be friendly.

With her mind made up, and before she lost her nerve, she dialed his number.

"Jade?" he asked, surprise in his voice.

"You didn't call me Ariel," she said.

Her face flushed at the sound of his voice. She hadn't realized how much she'd missed him until she heard him speak. Tears welled in her eyes, and she clutched the phone tightly to her ear, trying to be close to him, as if she could hug him though the phone.

"Yeah, well, that's not your fucking name," he said, reminding her of the last words she'd said to him.

"I'm sorry about that. I was emotional and I shouldn't have —"

"No, I was the jerk, Jade. You have no idea how happy I am that you called…Why *did* you call?"

"Oh, right. I just saw you on the news. They said you were in rehab."

"I left you a voice message about it."

"Oh." She hung her head in shame.

"You didn't listen to any of the messages, did you?"

"No," she admitted.

"Jade, can we meet up? There are some things I really want to talk to you about, but I want to say them in person."

"I don't know, Drew. I just wanted to call and say I'm happy your life is going well now. I think seeing you in person might be a mistake."

"I just miss you." His voice sounded so soft and sincere that her resolve melted. She'd missed him too, and she wanted to see him very much.

"All right. Do you want to have dinner?"

"Being in public might be hard right now. We'd need to act all loved up, and I don't think we're in a good place for that. How about you come to the house?"

"Uh, no." She couldn't bring herself to go back there. It felt like home to her after living there for so many months, and she needed to make sure she kept her guard up. She needed to be in control. "Why don't you come to my new place?"

"All right."

She gave him the address, and half an hour later, he knocked on the door. She'd quickly showered and put on fresh makeup, wanting to look nice and hating herself for caring what he thought of her.

She opened the door and invited him in. He looked around the living room, and his brow creased.

"This furniture all looks secondhand."

"It came with the apartment when I rented it," she said.

"Rented? I thought you would have bought something."

Jade paused. "I gave you back the money, Drew."

"You did?" He genuinely looked shocked.

"Yes. I sent it to your lawyer weeks ago. All I have left is the car."

Drew kicked at the edge of the frayed rug. "You didn't have to do that. You earned the money. I'll get it transferred back to you tomorrow."

"Thank you, but I don't want it."

An awkward silence filled the room.

"Okay. Well, that's not what I came here to talk about anyway."

Jade's heart rate sped up. She wasn't ready to hear what he wanted to say.

"Are you hungry?" she blurted out. "I could cook something."

"No. I'm fine."

"Thirsty? I have soda."

Drew smirked. He knew her well enough to know what she was doing.

"Jade, just come and sit with me." He sat on the couch and patted the cushion next to him.

"My name sounds weird coming from your lips. I'm not used to it."

"I thought that's what you wanted."

"I…I don't know what I want."

His hair fell into his eyes as he smiled at her. It had grown longer since she'd last seen him, and she liked how it hung around his face, giving him a sexy, messy look.

"Well, I know exactly what I want. That's what I came to talk to you about."

She let out a sigh. He obviously wasn't going to be distracted.

"I'd like a drink. You sure you don't want one?"

"Jade."

"No, I'm not avoiding. I'll be right back."

She ducked into the kitchen and leaned on the counter, breathing deeply. She whispered to herself to get it together. She wished he didn't look so sexy with his long eyelashes and messy hair.

She poured a glass of diet cola and listened to the bubbles popping as she carried the glass into the living room. Drew was waiting, tapping his hands on his crossed leg.

Jade sat on the couch and took a long sip of her drink.

"Okay," she said, turning the glass in her hands.

"You said you didn't want to hear me say I loved you because you'd heard it before and it was a lie."

She nodded, her leg bouncing from nerves.

"Well, that's true. When we got married, I said I loved you, and I didn't. But you need to know that I genuinely developed real feelings for you. When I called you the night you left and said I loved you, I honestly meant it with my whole heart."

"I believe you."

"Good." He relaxed into the couch. "But it's more than that. You make me want to be a better person, Jade. Before you, I was living a selfish life. I did what I wanted, when I wanted, and expected everyone to cater to me. Suddenly, I was thrust into living like an adult. I had a wife when I'd never even had a girlfriend. I was developing real feelings for a girl who refused to even talk about us being together…Why was that? Has this always been about the money for you? Sometimes I thought you might care about me, but your wall was so strong I couldn't break through it."

"It was never about the money for me," she admitted. "Well, maybe the first week. I originally agreed to the contract because I needed money, but I wouldn't have gone through with it if I didn't like you."

"So, you *do* like me."

She laughed and then bit her lip. She looked up at him through her eyelashes. "Yes. Very much."

"How much? Enough not to call it like?"

"Then what would we call it?"

"Maybe another word that starts with L?" He gave her a sheepish grin. It felt right to be flirty and playful together. It was a role they both played well. And that's where Jade's fear came from... Was this still an act?

No. There was no one to act for in her living room. It was just them.

"Lust?" she asked.

Drew laughed. "That wasn't what I was thinking, but lust certainly works for me." He shifted on the couch so he was a few inches closer to her. "I was thinking about another L word."

She tried her best to think of another word that started with L, but he must have known she was stalling because he said her name with a playful, warning tone.

She giggled. "Yes, Drew. I loved you."

"In the past tense only?" He slid closer on the couch again.

"Does that matter?"

"It does to me."

"You're the only one here," she said, both in response to his statement, but also to remind herself that this was real. He wasn't acting for anyone.

His arms slipped around her, and he held her close to his chest.

"I grew up for you, Jade. I wouldn't have done it for anyone else. You wanted more than the words. You wanted proof of how I feel... Well, there it is. I haven't had a drink for ninety-six days. And if you need more convincing, then here's an action to prove my feelings. No words needed."

He pulled her in and kissed her. It wasn't like any of the other kisses they'd shared. She could feel the difference. Drew wasn't putting on an act, or holding his own feelings in check. He was loving her with his hands on her waist. He was loving her with his lips on hers. He was loving her with every breath he took.

And she believed him.

When they broke apart, he looked at her with a worried expression, and she knew why. He'd played his ace card and was waiting to see if it was enough.

"Present tense," she said.

The grin that spread over his face was luminous. He pulled her in for another kiss and whispered in her ear, "I love you, Ariel."

EPILOGUE

Coming Clean

"*A*re you sure you want to tell your parents tonight?" Jade asked from the passenger seat. Her leg bounced idly, and she gripped the seat when Drew took the corner a little too quickly.

"I think it's better to just get it over and done with, don't you?" He glanced away from the road and frowned at her bouncing leg. "Please don't tell me you're still nervous around my parents."

"Well, they're not exactly going to be happy when we tell them."

Drew rolled his eyes as he pulled up in his parents' driveway.

"Look," he said. "We both know this isn't working the way it is. It's better for everyone if we're just honest about it. Then we can all move on and forget this whole mess ever happened. We need a fresh start without all the baggage."

Jade sighed. "You're right. I just don't want to see the disappointment on their faces."

Drew nodded and got out of the car. During their fake marriage, he'd always made a show of opening her car door. He didn't do that anymore. She followed him inside and looked around the now familiar entryway. If she'd tried to tell herself a year ago that she'd be relaxed in Aaron Malik's home, she'd have committed herself to the nearest psychiatric institution. How things change.

"Drew!" Laura appeared in the doorway and hugged her son. She smiled at Jade over his shoulder.

Jade's stomach churned. She really didn't want to upset Laura, even if it was the right thing to do for her and Drew.

"Come on in, you two. Dinner's on the table." Laura pulled Drew by the hand into the dining room, and Jade followed.

"Hello, Caroline," Drew said, giving the housekeeper a wave as they passed the kitchen.

The smell of roasted meat and freshly baked bread would normally have had Jade salivating, but she was too nervous to eat. She'd been nauseous all day.

"Where's Aaron?" she asked.

Laura gave a dismissive wave of her hand. "He's stuck on set. Something about bad lighting and needing to do reshoots. Hopefully he'll be home before you leave."

Drew shot Jade a questioning look that she interpreted as *Do we still do this?* She gave a small nod. Giving bad news was always best done quickly. Drew frowned.

"Mom, do you mind if Jade and I talk in private for a moment?"

"Of course, dear." Laura disappeared into the kitchen, speaking to Caroline about lumps in the gravy.

"Maybe we should wait." Drew ran his right hand over the scruff on his chin. Jade hated when he didn't shave. Looking disheveled only reminded her of the alcoholic playboy he'd been when they'd first met.

"There's never going to be a good time to tell her we're getting divorced, Drew."

"What?" Laura screeched from the kitchen. She ran into the dining room and stared at them both with wide eyes. "You're getting divorced?"

Drew shot Jade an annoyed look and moved across the room to pull his mother into a hug. "Mom, please just let us explain."

"What did you *do*, Andrew? Are you drinking again?"

"Laura," Jade said, keeping her voice even. "Why don't we go into the living room and sit down? We'll explain everything to you."

Laura shook her head sadly and began to cry as they all went to sit on the sofa.

"Mom, it's not that Jade and I don't love each other—"

"I'm home!" Aaron roared from the front door. "I made it. You haven't started eating, have you?"

"We're in the living room, Dad," Drew called, loud enough to be heard over his mother's cries.

Aaron appeared in the doorway and froze. He looked at the blubbering mess that was his wife and a huge grin spread across his face. "You're having a baby!" He moved quickly through the room and pulled Jade up into a bear hug, swinging her legs off the ground.

Laura wailed even louder and began stuttering. "Th-They're... divor—breaking up..."

Aaron put Jade down and looked at her, confusion clouding his features.

"You're getting divorced?"

"Have a seat, please, Aaron," Jade said.

It took over an hour for Drew and Jade to explain their situation. Aaron kept interrupting with questions, and Laura sniffled and kept wiping her eyes. They started at the beginning, describing how they met, their contract, and the reasons for the fake marriage.

Jade had hoped that knowing that the marriage wasn't real would soften the blow of the divorce, but it appeared to hurt them more.

"So, let me get this straight," Aaron said, cutting them off for what felt like the hundredth time. "You only got married to get around the clause in the will about your trust fund?"

Drew nodded, color rising up his cheeks.

"Unbelievable!" Aaron stood and started pacing the room. "I'd really started to think you'd grown up, Drew. I was proud of the man you'd become, but it was all a lie."

Drew's face crumpled, and Jade felt the need to cut in.

"Aaron, you're right. At first it was just a plot, and I'm ashamed to say that I agreed to marry Drew for the money. I did give most of it back when I realized I couldn't go through with it, but that doesn't change the fact that we did it in the first place. I'm sorry we hurt you."

Laura gave her a small smile, but her tears showed she wasn't all right with their explanation.

Drew appeared to energize at her words. He sat up straighter, and the gleam came back into his eyes.

"So, we're getting divorced," he said, sounding more proud than upset. "The wedding we had was fake. The vows were lies, and the sentiment wasn't there."

"That's not something to brag about, Andrew." Aaron still paced the room.

Drew stood and went to sit next to Jade, taking her hand and holding it in both of his. "We know that, Dad. And despite how it all started, Jade and I began to develop real feelings for each other. We're in love. For real."

Laura coughed and looked at them, her eyes narrowed. "I don't understand."

Jade smiled. *This* was the moment she'd been waiting for all night. She took the wedding ring and engagement rings off her finger and placed them neatly on the coffee table. Both of her in-laws stared at the little pile of jewelry.

What they were about to do was important to both Drew and Jade, and they couldn't have done it without coming clean about what they'd done before.

"We're getting a divorce," Drew said again, "so that we can do it right."

He dropped to his knee and kept a tight hold of Jade's hand.

"Jade," he said, "I utterly adore you."

Both Aaron and Laura fell deathly silent as he pulled a ring box out of his pocket and exposed the brilliant diamond.

"The last time I asked this question, I didn't understand the depth of what love was. I didn't fathom the enormity of what a marriage meant, and I certainly didn't treat you the way a husband should. But I know what love is now. I grasp the idea of committing myself to one person—you—for the rest of my life, and I vow to treat you with tenderness and respect every day. Jade, will you marry me…again?"

She knew it was coming. The whole reason they'd been honest with his parents was so they could get married for real, and yet hearing the words and knowing they were sincere was mesmerizing. Her heart swelled, and tears welled in her eyes as she smiled down at the man she loved.

"Yes," she said simply.

Drew leapt to his feet and pulled her up into his arms, kissing her deeply and smiling against her mouth.

"I'm so confused," Laura said with a laugh. "So, you're *not* getting divorced?"

"We are. But then we'll get married again. The right way," Drew said, hugging Jade to his side.

"With a pre-nup," Aaron added.

Jade looked over at her father-in-law and saw distrust in his eyes. She couldn't blame him. His family had a lot of money, and she'd just blatantly admitted to marrying his son for the sole purpose of getting paid.

"Dad!" Drew said.

"No, Drew, it's fine. I'm happy to sign a pre-nup. We're getting married for love. I don't care about the money."

Aaron appeared appeased. Jade knew that, in time, she'd wind him around her little finger again. He was too good a man not to forgive her.

"Caroline! We need champagne in here. Oh!" Laura looked at her son. "And a glass of sparkling apple juice, please? We're celebrating."

Drew smiled down at his fiancée and rested his hand on her stomach.

"Actually, Mom, just two glasses of champagne. Jade and I are both non-drinkers now."

Aaron smiled, all tension disappearing from his face, and Laura gasped.

"Are you pregnant?" Laura asked, new tears welling in her eyes.

Jade placed her hand over Drew's and nodded.

"That's why we want to make things right," she said proudly. Despite their rough start, or perhaps because of it, Jade knew she and Drew were strong together, willing and wanting to be dedicated to each other and their future. "We're going to be a real family."

ACKNOWLEDGMENTS

So many people have worked hard on this book. First I have to start by thanking the whole team at Omnific Publishing for continuing to believe in me and for allowing me to share my stories with the world. Especially to my hard working editors, Jen, Kasi, and Cindy, who have been so supportive and encouraging.

Thanks to my pre-readers, and friends, Bree and Mikahla, for loving this story when it was just a draft and for brainstorming the ending with me. I also want to thank my mom for believing in me, supporting me and giving me a love of books and reading. I never would have been an author if she hadn't taught me to love words. And to my friend, Josh Campbell, who will always be my image of Drew Malik. Keep an eye on this young new actor, he's going places!

And finally, to the readers…thank you. Honestly, you're the best. Without you, I wouldn't be able to keep writing, and that would make me very, very sad.

ABOUT THE AUTHOR

Joy is a fiery redhead who takes full advantage of the Australian life-style, sunning herself on tropical beaches and flirting with handsome lifeguards. She loves cats, books and chocolate, and of course the male physique. Joy started writing as a teenager and never stopped, although she writes about much more mature topics now. You can often find Joy browsing the shelves of her local bookstore or researching her favorite city, New York, in preparation of fulfilling her lifelong dream to live there one day.

check out these titles from

OMNIFIC PUBLISHING

←······→ Contemporary Romance ←······→

Keeping the Peace by Linda Cunningham
Stitches and Scars by Elizabeth A. Vincent
Pieces of Us by Hannah Downing
The Way That You Play It by BJ Thornton
The Poughkeepsie Brotherhood series: *Poughkeepsie* & *Return to Poughkeepsie*
by Debra Anastasia
Recaptured Dreams and *All-American Girl* and *Until Next Time* by Justine Dell
Once Upon a Second Chance by Marian Vere
The Englishman by Nina Lewis
16 Marsden Place by Rachel Brimble
Sleepers, Awake by Eden Barber
The Runaway Year by Shani Struthers
The Hydraulic series: *Hydraulic Level Five* & *Skygods* by Sarah Latchaw
Fix You by Beck Anderson
Just Once by Julianna Keyes
The WORDS series: *The Weight of Words* & *Better Deeds Than Words* by Georgina Guthrie
The Brit Out of Water series: *Theatricks* & *Jazz Hands* by Eleanor Gwyn-Jones
The Sacrificial Lamb by Elle Fiore
The Plan by Qwen Salsbury
The Kiss Me series: *Kiss Me Goodnight* & *Kiss Me by Moonlight* by Michele Zurlo
Saint Kate of the Cupcake: The Dangers of Lust and Baking by LC Fenton
Exposure by Morgan & Jennifer Locklear
Playing All the Angles by Nicole Lane
Redemption by Kathryn Barrett
The Playboy's Princess by Joy Fulcher

←······→ Young Adult Romance ←······→

The Ember series: *Ember* & *Iridescent* by Carol Oates
Breaking Point by Jess Bowen
Life, Liberty, and Pursuit by Susan Kaye Quinn
The Embrace series: *Embrace* & *Hold Tight* by Cherie Colyer
Destiny's Fire by Trisha Wolfe
The Reaper series: *Reaping Me Softly* & *UnReap My Heart* by Kate Evangelista
The Legendary Saga: *Legendary* by LH Nicole
The Fatal series: *Fatal* by T.A. Brock
The Prometheus Order series: *Byronic* by Sandi Beth Jones
One Smart Cookie by Kym Brunner
Variables of Love by MK Schiller

New Adult Romance

Three Daves by Nicki Elson
Streamline by Jennifer Lane
The Shades series: *Shades of Atlantis* & *Shades of Avalon* by Carol Oates
The Heart series: *Beside Your Heart, Disclosure of the Heart* & *Forever Your Heart*
by Mary Whitney
Romancing the Bookworm by Kate Evangelista
Flirting with Chaos by Kenya Wright
The Vice, Virtue & Video series: *Revealed, Captured* & *Desired* by Bianca Giovanni
Granton University series: *Loving Lies* by Linda Kage

Paranormal Romance

The Light series: *Seers of Light, Whisper of Light* & *Circle of Light* by Jennifer DeLucy
The Hanaford Park series: *Eve of Samhain* & *Pleasures Untold* by Lisa Sanchez
Immortal Awakening by KC Randall
The Seraphim series: *Crushed Seraphim* & *Bittersweet Seraphim* by Debra Anastasia
The Guardian's Wild Child by Feather Stone
Grave Refrain by Sarah M. Glover
The Divinity series: *Divinity* by Patricia Leever
The Blood Vine series: *Blood Vine, Blood Entangled* & *Blood Reunited*
by Amber Belldene
Divine Temptation by Nicki Elson
The Dead Rapture series: *Love in the Time of the Dead* & *Love at the End of Days*
by Tera Shanley

Romantic Suspense

Whirlwind by Robin DeJarnett
The CONduct series: *With Good Behavior, Bad Behavior* & *On Best Behavior*
by Jennifer Lane
Indivisible by Jessica McQuinn
Between the Lies by Alison Oburia
Blind Man's Bargain by Tracy Winegar

Erotic Romance

The Keyhole series: *Becoming sage* (book 1) by Kasi Alexander
The Keyhole series: *Saving sunni* (book 2) by Kasi & Reggie Alexander
The Winemaker's Dinner: *Appetizers* & *Entrée* by Dr. Ivan Rusilko & Everly Drummond
The Winemaker's Dinner: *Dessert* by Dr. Ivan Rusilko
Client N° 5 by Joy Fulcher

Historical Romance

Cat O' Nine Tails by Patricia Leever
Burning Embers by Hannah Fielding
Seven for a Secret by Rumer Haven

Anthologies

A Valentine Anthology including short stories by
Alice Clayton ("With a Double Oven"),
Jennifer DeLucy ("Magnus of Pfelt, Conquering Viking Lord"),
Nicki Elson ("I Don't Do Valentine's Day"),
Jessica McQuinn ("Better Than One Dead Rose and a Monkey Card"),
Victoria Michaels ("Home to Jackson"), and
Alison Oburia ("The Bridge")

Taking Liberties including an introduction by Tiffany Reisz and short stories by
Mina Vaughn ("John Hancock-Blocked"),
Linda Cunningham ("A Boston Marriage"),
Joy Fulcher ("Tea for Two"),
KC Holly ("The British Are Coming!"),
Kimberly Jensen & Scott Stark ("E. Pluribus Threesome"), and
Vivian Rider ("M'Lady's Secret Service")

Singles and Novellas

It's Only Kinky the First Time (A Keyhole series single) by Kasi Alexander
Learning the Ropes (A Keyhole series single) by Kasi & Reggie Alexander
The Winemaker's Dinner: RSVP by Dr. Ivan Rusilko
The Winemaker's Dinner: No Reservations by Everly Drummond
Big Guns by Jessica McQuinn
Concessions by Robin DeJarnett
Starstruck by Lisa Sanchez
New Flame by BJ Thornton
Shackled by Debra Anastasia
Swim Recruit by Jennifer Lane
Sway by Nicki Elson
Full Speed Ahead by Susan Kaye Quinn
The Second Sunrise by Hannah Downing
The Summer Prince by Carol Oates
Whatever it Takes by Sarah M. Glover
Clarity (A *Divinity* prequel single) by Patricia Leever
A Christmas Wish (A *Cocktails & Dreams* single) by Autumn Markus
Late Night with Andres by Debra Anastasia
Poughkeepsie (enhanced iPad app collector's edition) by Debra Anastasia

+—···—▸Sets◂—···—▸

The Heart Series Box Set (*Beside Your Heart, Disclosure of the Heart &
Forever Your Heart*) by Mary Whitney
The CONduct Series Box Set (*With Good Behavior, Bad Behavior &
On Best Behavior*) by Jennifer Lane
The Light Series Box Set (*Seers of Light, Whisper of Light, Circle of Light &
Glimpse of Light*) by Jennifer DeLucy
The Blood Vine Series Box Set (*Blood Vine, Blood Entangled, Blood Reunited &
Blood Eternal* by Amber Belldene)

coming soon from
OMNIFIC PUBLISHING

The Jeweler by Beck Anderson
The Fatal series: *Brutal* (novella 1.5) by T.A. Brock
The Vice, Virtue & Video series: *Devoted* (book 4) by Bianca Giovanni
The Divinity series: *Entity* (book 2) by Patricia Leever
The WORDS series: *The Truest of Words* (book 3) by Georgina Guthrie